THOMASINA

by Paul Gallico

Thomasina

THE CAT WHO THOUGHT SHE WAS GOD

by Paul Gallico

Doubleday & Company, Inc., Garden City, New York

TO VIRGINIA

Library of Congress Catalog Card Number 57-13018
Copyright © 1957 by Paul Gallico
Designed by Diana Klemin
Frontispiece by Gioia Fiammenghi

THOMASINA

1   Mr. Andrew MacDhui, veterinary surgeon, thrust his brick-red, bristling beard through the door of the waiting room adjacent to the surgery and looked with cold, hostile eyes upon the people seated there on the plain pine, yellow chairs with their pets on their laps or at their feet awaiting his attendance.

Willie Bannock, his brisk, wiry man of all work in dispensary, office, and animal hospital had already gossiped a partial list of those present that morning to Mr. MacDhui, including his friend and next-door neighbor the minister, Angus Peddie. Mr. Peddie, of course, would be there with or because of his insufferable little pug dog, whose gastric disturbances were brought on by pampering and the feeding of forbidden sweets. Mr. MacDhui's glance dropped to the narrow lap of the short-legged, round little clergyman, and for a moment his eye was caught up in the unhappy, milky one of the pug, rolled in his direction, filled with the misery of bellyache, and yet expressing a certain hope and longing as well. The animal had come to associate his visits to this place, the smells, and the huge man with the fur on his face with relief.

The veterinary disentangled himself from the hypnotic eye and wished angrily that Peddie would follow his advice on feeding the animal and not be there wasting his time. He noted the rich builder's wife from Glasgow on holiday with her rheumy little Yorkshire terrier, an animal he particularly detested, with its ridiculous velvet bow laced into its silken topknot. There was Mrs. Kinloch over the ears of her Siamese cat, which lay upon her knee, occasionally shaking its head and complaining in a raucous voice, and, too, there was Mr. Dobbie, the grocer, whose long and doleful countenance reflected that of his Scots terrier, who was suffering from the mange and looked as though a visit to the upholsterer would be more practical.

There were a half dozen or so others, including a small boy whom he seemed to have seen somewhere before, and at the head of the line he recognized old, obese Mrs. Laggan, proprietress of the newspaper and tobacco shop, who, with her aged, wheezing, nondescript, black mongrel, Rabbie, his muzzle grayed, his eyes rheumy with age, was a landmark of Inveranoch and seemingly had been so for years.

Mrs. Laggan was a widow and had been for the past twenty-five years of her seventy-odd. For the last fifteen of them her dog Rabbie had been her only companion, and his fat form draped across the doorsill of Mrs. Laggan's shop was as familiar a figure, to natives as well as visitors to the Highland town, as that of the fat widow in her Paisley shawl. Since the doorsill was Rabbie's place, nose between forepaws, eyes rolled upward, clients of the widow Laggan had learned to step over Rabbie when entering and departing. It was said in the High Street that descendants of these clients were already born with this precaution bred into them.

Mr. MacDhui looked his clients over and the clients looked back at him with varying degrees of anxiety, hope, deference, or in some cases a return of the hostility that seemed to be written all over the well-marked features of his face, the high brow, the indignantly flaring red-tufted eyebrows, commanding blue eyes, strong nose, full and sometimes mocking lips, half seen through the bristle of red mustache and beard and the truculent and aggressive chin.

His eyes and, above all, his manner always seemed cold and angry, perhaps because, it was said in Inveranoch, he was on the whole a cold and angry man.

A widower of the stature and flamboyance of Mr. Veterinary Surgeon MacDhui was subject enough for gossip in a Highland town the size of Inveranoch in Argyllshire, where he had been in practice for only a little over eighteen months. By the nature of his profession he was a figure of importance there, since he looked after not only the personal and private pets of the townspeople, but was responsible also for the health of the livestock raised in the outlying farms of the district, the herds of Angus cattle and black-faced sheep, pigs, and fowl. In addition, he was the appointed veterinary of the district for the inspection of meat and milk and sanitary husbandry as well.

The gossips allowed that Andrew MacDhui was an honest, forthright, and fair-dealing man, but, and this was the opinion of the strictly religiously inclined, a queer one to be dealing with God's dumb creatures, since he appeared to have no love for animals, very little for man, and neither the inclination nor time for God. Whether or not he was an out-and-out unbeliever, as many claimed, he certainly never was seen in Mr. Peddie's church, even though the two were known to be good friends. Others claimed that when his wife had died his heart had turned to stone, all but the corner devoted to his love for his seven-year-old child Mary Ruadh, the one who was never seen without that ill-favored, queer-marked ginger cat she called Thomasina.

Mind you, said the tattlers, no one denied that he was a good doctor for the beasties, and efficient. Quick to cure or kill, and a mite too handy with the chloroform rag, was the word that went around. Those who felt kindly toward him held that he was a humane man, not disposed to see a hopelessly sick animal suffer needlessly, while those who disliked him and his high-handed ways called him a hard, cruel man to whom the life of an animal was as nothing, and who was openly contemptuous of people who were sentimentally attached to their pets.

And many of those who did not encounter him professionally were inclined to the belief that there must be some good in the man else he would not have had the friendship and esteem of Mr. Angus Peddie, pastor and guide of the Presbyterian flock of Inveranoch. It was said that the minister, who had known MacDhui in their student days, had been largely instrumental in persuading his friend, upon the death of his wife Anne, to purchase the practice of Inveranoch's retiring vet and move thither, leaving behind him the unhappy memories that had bedeviled him in Glasgow.

Several of the inhabitants of Inveranoch remembered Mr. MacDhui's late father John, himself a Glasgow veterinary, a dour, tyrannical old man with a strong religious bent, who, holding the purse strings, had compelled his son to follow in his footsteps. The story was that Andrew MacDhui had wished to study to become a surgeon in his youth but in the end had been compelled for financial reasons to yield to his father's wishes and likewise become a veterinary.

One of these inhabitants had once paid a visit to the gloomy old house in Dunear Street in Glasgow where for a time father and son practiced together until the old man died, and had nothing good to say about it, except that it was not much to wonder at that Mr. MacDhui had turned out as he had.

Mr. Peddie had known MacDhui's father as a psalm-singing old hypocrite in whose home God served merely as an auxiliary policeman. Whatever seemed healthy or fun, old John MacDhui's God was against, and Andrew MacDhui had grown up first hating Him and then denying Him. . . . The tragedy of the loss of his wife Anne, when his daughter, Mary Ruadh, was only three, had confirmed him in his bitterness.

His scrutiny completed, MacDhui now pointed his beard at

old, fat Mrs. Laggan and jerked with his head in the direction of his office. She gave a little bleat of fright, picked Rabbie up out of her lap, and arose painfully, holding him in her arms, where he lay on his back, forepaws bent limply, watery eyes revolving. He resembled an overstuffed black and gray porker and he wheezed at every breath like a catarrhal old man snoring.

Mr. Angus Peddie pulled in his feet to let her by and gave her a warm, cherubic smile of encouragement, for he was the very opposite of the figure that a dour Scots churchman is supposed to resemble. He was short, inclined to stoutness, sweet-natured, and extraordinarily vital. He had a round, dimpled face and mischievous eyes and smile, which, however, could instantly express the deepest sympathy, penetrating understanding, and concern.

Peddie's pug dog, who, as well as suffering from chronic indigestion, staggered under the name of Fin de Siècle, an indication of the kind of humor one might be expected to encounter in the large Peddie family, lay likewise wheezing in the minister's lap. Peddie lifted him into a sitting position so that he could better see Mrs. Laggan and her sick dog go by. He said, "That's Mrs. Laggan's Rabbie, Fin. The poor wee thing isn't feeling well just now." The rolling eyes of the two dogs met for a moment in melancholy exchange.

Mrs. Laggan followed Mr. MacDhui into the examining room of the surgery and deposited Rabbie on his back upon the long, white-enameled examining table, where he remained, his forepaws still limp and his breath coming in difficult gasps.

The veterinarian lifted the lip of the animal, glanced at its teeth, pulled down its eyelids, and placed one hand for a moment upon its heaving belly. "How old is this dog?" he asked.

Mrs. Laggan, traditionally dressed as became a respectable widow, in rusty black with a Paisley shawl over her shoulders, seemed to shrink inside her clothes. "Fifteen years and a bit," she replied. "Well, fourteen, since he's been grown from the wee pup he was the day I got him," she added, as though by quickly subtracting a year from his age she might lure fate into permitting him to remain a year longer. Fifteen was very old for a dog. With fourteen there was always hope they might live to be fifteen, like Mrs. Campbell's old sheep dog, which was actually going on sixteen.

The veterinarian nodded, glanced perfunctorily at the dog again, and said, "He ought to be put out of his misery. You can see how bad his asthma is. He can hardly breathe." He picked the dog up and set him on his feet on the floor, where he promptly collapsed onto his belly with his chin flat on the floor and his eyes turned up adoringly to the person of Mrs. Laggan. "Or walk," concluded MacDhui.

The widow had many chins. Fear set them all to quivering. "Put him away? Put the puir beastie to death? But whatever should I do then when he's all I've got in this world? We've been together for fifteen years now, and me a lonely widow for twenty-five. What would I do without Rabbie?"

"Get another dog," MacDhui replied. "It shouldn't be difficult. The village is full of them."

"Och, how can ye speak so? It would no' be Rabbie. Can ye not be giving him a wee bit o' medicine to tide him over until he gets well? He's been a very healthy dog."

Animals, reflected Mr. MacDhui, were never a problem; it was the sentimentality of their owners that created all the difficulties. "The dog must die soon," he said. "He is very old and very ill. Anyone with half an eye can see that his life has become a burden to him and that he is suffering. If I gave him some medicine, you would be back here within a fortnight. It might prolong his life for a month, at the most six months. I am a busy man," he concluded, but then added more gently, "It would be kinder to make an end to him."

The quivering of her chins now had spread to her small mouth, as Mrs. Laggan looked fearfully into the day that would be without Rabbie; no one to talk to, no one to whose breathing she would hearken whilest she had her evening cup of tea, or lay in bed at night. She said what came into her head, but not what was bursting her heart. "The coostomers who come to my shop will miss Rabbie sore if he's no' there for them to be stepping over." But she was meaning, "I'm an old woman. I have not many days left myself. I am lonely. The dog has been my companion and my comfort for so long. He and I know one another's ways so well."

"Yes, yes, Mrs. Laggan, no doubt. But you must make up your mind, for I have other patients waiting."

Mrs. Laggan looked uneasily to the big, vital man with the red mustache and beard. "I suppose I should no' be selfish if puir Rabbie is suffering. . . ."

Mr. MacDhui did not reply, but sat waiting.

Life without Rabbie—the once cold nose pressed against her hand, the edge of pink tongue that protruded when he was contemplative, his great sigh of contentment when he was fed full—but above all his presence; Rabbie always within sight, sound, or touch. Old dogs must die; old people must die. She was minded to plead for the bit of medicine, for another month, a week, a day more with Rabbie, but she was rushed and nervous and fearful. And so she said, "Ye would be very gentle with him——"

MacDhui sighed with impatient relief. "He will not feel a thing, I assure you." He arose. "I think you are doing what is right, Mrs. Laggan."

"Very well then. Make away with him. What will it be I'll be owing you?"

The veterinarian had a moment's pang brought on by the sight of the trembling lips and chins and cursed himself for it. "There will be no charge," he said curtly.

The widow Laggan regained sudden control of her face and her dignity, though her eyes were wet. "I'll be paying for your services——"

"Two shillings then——"

She paid out of a small black purse, setting the florin onto his desk with a snap that caused Rabbie to prick up his graying ears for a moment. Without another glance at her oldest and dearest friend, Mrs. Laggan made for the door. She held herself as proudly and erectly as she could, for she would not be a fat old woman dissolving into grief before this hard man. She bore up to pass through and close it behind her.

Thin women in sorrow have both the faces and figures for bleakness and woe, but there is nothing quite as futile and shaking as the aspect of a fat woman in affliction. The small mouth unable to form into the classic lines of tragedy can but purse and quiver. Grief is bowed, but fat keeps the stout woman's curves constant, except that the flesh suddenly grays and looks as though the juices of life had gone out of it for all its roundness.

When the widow Laggan emerged from the surgery and entered the waiting room once more, all eyes were turned upon her, and the Reverend Peddie recognized the symptoms at once and got up and went to her, crying, "Oh dear—— Don't say that something ill has befallen Rabbie. Is he to remain in hospital?" And then he echoed the prior remarks of the widow. "Why, whatever would the town do without the presence of Rabbie across the sill?"

Safe within the circle of her own people, Mrs. Laggan could let the tears flow freely as she told of the sentence passed upon her friend. "Th' doctor said 'twould be better if he were to be put away just now. Och, why must those we love always go and we remain behind? 'Twill no' be the same any more wi'out Rabbie. I doubt not I'll be following him soon and 'twill be a' for the best." She dabbed at her eyes with a cotton handkerchief and essayed a smile. "Do ye remember how Rabbie wud block the door and all the gentry would raise up their knees to pass ower him?"

It was so small a thing that had happened, yet the waiting-room was stiff with the tragedy of it, and Mr. Peddie felt the horror clamped like a hand about his heart, squeezing that member until it felt in some similar measure the pain that was oppressing the widow Laggan. Mr. Peddie had one of those awful moments, to which he was prone, when he could not decide what it was that God would wish him to do, what God Himself would do, were He to stand there with them all in the presence of the agony of the widow Laggan.

For to Mr. Angus Peddie there was neither gloom nor sourness nor melancholy about either the God or the religion he served. Creation and the world created, along with the Creator, was a perpetual joy to him, and his mission seemed to be to see that his flock appreciated and was properly grateful for all the wonders and beauties of nature, man, and beast as well as the great and marvelous unexplained mysteries of the universe. He did not try to explain God, the Father, or the Son, but worked to help his people love and enjoy Him. A man of unusual tolerance and breadth of vision, he believed that man could deny God for a time, but not forever, since God was so manifest in everything that lived and breathed, in things both animate and inanimate, that He was universal and hence undeniable.

And yet, human being that he was, he felt the panic when his God chose to turn his back upon the likes of the widow Laggan and his own warm heart was riven with pity for her plight.

There stood a weeping fat woman dabbing at her eyes with a small cloth, the tears straggling unevenly over the curves of her cheeks and her triple chins quaking and jouncing. And in a moment she would walk out of there and begin to die.

Peddie felt the strong push of the impulse to rush into the surgery of Mr. MacDhui, crying, "Stop Andrew! Don't kill the animal. Let it live out its time. Who are you, who hate Him, to play God? But he resisted it. What right had he to interfere? MacDhui knew his business, and veterinarians, just as doctors, frequently had to make decisions and break news that was painful to people, except that to the vet was sometimes given the additional mercy of destruction to save pain and suffering. . . .

Mrs. Laggan said once more, speaking as though to herself, " 'Twill no' be the same wi'out Rabbie," and went out. Mr. MacDhui's beard came in through the door again and he stood there a moment regarding them all truculently, as though experiencing some remnant of the scene that had just taken place and the sympathy engendered for the old woman.

He asked, "Who's next?" and his countenance took on even a greater expression of distaste when the Glasgow builder's wife with the Yorkshire terrier half arose irresolutely from the hard, waiting-room chair and the dog gave a shrill yelp of terror.

A small voice said, "Please sir, could you spare a moment?"

Someone remarked, "It's little Geordie McNabb, the draper's boy."

Geordie was eight. He wore khaki shorts and a khaki shirt and the kerchief of the Scout Wolf Cubs. He had a round, solemn face with dark hair and eyes and a curiously Chinesey cast of countenance. In his grubby hands he clasped a box, and in the box palpitatingly reposed his good deed for that day. MacDhui strode over to him overpoweringly, overtoweringly, looming over him like a red Magog, thrusting his bristling beard nearly into the box as he boomed, "Well, lad, what is it you want?"

Geordie stood his ground bravely. Patently, inside the box there was a green frog with heaving sides. The boy explained.

"There's something wrong with his foot. And he cannot hop. I found him by the side of the lochan. He was trying very hard to hop but he couldn't at all. Will you make him better please so that he can be hopping again?"

The waves of old bitternesses had a way of rolling up inside Andrew MacDhui at the oddest and wrongest moment, causing him to do and say things that he did not mean to at all. Here he was in his waiting room full of clients, and it suddenly came over him as he stood bent over and looking down into the box, *Doctor to a frog with a broken leg, that's what you are, my great, fine fellow——*

And thereupon the old angers and regrets returned to plague and irritate him. Had there been justice in the world, all of these people in the room, yes, and the child too, would have been there to consult him about ailing hearts or lungs or throats or livers, aches and pains and mysterious cramps, sicknesses and diseases, which he would combat for them and put to rights. And there they were instead, with their pampered, snuffling, mewing, and whining little pets kept for their own flattery's sake, or because they had been too lazy or selfish to bring a child into the world on whom to lavish their love and affection.

The ailing Yorkie was quite near to him and his nostrils, already flaring with disgust of himself and all humanity, caught a whiff of the perfume with which his mistress had scented him. He therefore replied to Geordie McNabb out of the black cloud of anger enveloping him, "I have no time for such foolishness. Cannot you see that I am busy with a room full of people? Go put the frog back by the pond again and leave it be. Off with you now."

Into the dark, round eyes of Geordie came that expression reserved to children who have been hurt by and disappointed in their grownups. "But it's *sick*," he said. "It's no well. Will he not die?"

MacDhui, not ungently this time, steered the child toward the door and gave him a farewell pat on the behind. "Off you go, boy. Put it back where you found it. Nature will look after it. Now then, if you like, Mrs. Sanderson——"

2   If it is family you go by, then you will certainly be impressed with mine, for I am a relative of that Jennie—Jennie Baldrin of Glasgow—about whose life and times and adventures in London, aboard ship and elsewhere, a whole book has been written and published.

We are Edinburgh on one side of my family, several of my forebears not only having been employed at the university in the usual capacity as hunters, but one or two are said to have contributed to scientific knowledge and advance, and Glasgow on the other, the Jennie Baldrin side.

Jennie was my great-aunt and she was most distinguished and Egyptian-looking, with a small, rather narrow head, long muzzle, slanting eyes, and good-sized, rounded, well-upstanding ears, and in this I am said to resemble her closely, though, of course, our coloring is quite different. I mention this with excusable pride, since it shows that we trace our ancestry back to the days when people had the good sense to recognize us as gods.

That false gods are worshiped today—well, more's the pity, for in Egypt, in the old days when members of our family were venerated in the temples, times were better and people, by and large, seemed happier. That, however, is neither here nor there and does not concern what I have to tell. Yet, if you know that once you were a god, no matter how long ago—well, it is bound to show somewhat in your demeanor.

Nor does Jennie play any part at all in what is to follow, except that I suppose I inherited something of her independence, spunk, and poise, not to mention elegance, and I brought in her name only as a possible point of interest to you should you happen to be familiar with her story.

I, too, have had a most curious adventure and experience, one of the most interesting and marvelous things that ever happened, at least that part which concerns myself.

I will not keep you in suspense. It has to do with a murder.

But what makes this story different from any you ever read is that the one who is murdered is—ME.

The name I bear, Thomasina, came about through one of those ridiculous and inexcusable errors committed by so many people who attempt to determine our sex when we are very young. I was originally christened Thomas when I came to live at the home of the MacDhuis in Glasgow to be the pet of Mary Ruadh, then aged three. When the error became obvious the name was simply feminized to Thomasina by Mrs. McKenzie, our housekeeper, whether I liked it or not and without so much as a by-your-leave.

I do not know why people are quite so stupid at determining our sex when we are young. The difference is easy enough to see if you will just *look* instead of guess, and take a little trouble, for with boys, things are apart, and with girls they are near together, and that's the rule, no matter how small they might be.

Mr. Andrew MacDhui might have told at a glance, no doubt, since he was a veterinary surgeon. But he was a most queer man to follow the profession of doctor to animals, since he had little love for and no sentimental interest in them whatsoever, and hence never paid the slightest attention to me from the moment I came into the house, which I cannot say disturbed me. The disregard was mutual.

We lived in a large, rather gloomy house on Dunear Street, which Mr. MacDhui had inherited from his father, who was also a veterinarian when he died. The two lower floors were given over to the offices, surgery, and animal hospital and we lived on the two upper ones; Mr. MacDhui, his wife, and Mary Ruadh. They all had red hair. I have too, or rather ginger-colored with a white blaze on my chest. But what people really seem to find irresistible about me is that I have four white feet, and the very tip of my tail is white to match. I am quite used to receiving compliments upon my looks and bearing.

Although I was then only six months old myself, I remember Mary Ruadh's mother, Anne. She was beautiful and her hair was the color of the copper pots by the fireside. She was very gay and always singing about the house, which made it less dark and gloomy, even on rainy days. She was forever cuddling and spoiling Mary Ruadh and they would often spend time "giving one another whispers," which was a kind of love-making. It was not an unhappy household, in spite of Mr. MacDhui. But it did not last long, for soon after I came Mrs. MacDhui contracted a disease from a parrot that was being kept in the hospital, and died.

That was a bad time for me, I can tell you, and if it had not been for Mrs. McKenzie I do not know what would have happened to me, for Mr. MacDhui half went out of his mind, they said, and it certainly sounded like it, the manner in which he raged and carried on, and the love he had had for his wife he now transferred to his daughter, and half frightened her to death with it, and me too, I can assure you. He kept staying away from home and would not go near the hospital for days on end and things were getting in a bad state when he received a visit from an old friend of his from the country, a minister by the name of Mr. Peddie, and after that things got a little better and soon we had a great change.

It seems that Mr. Peddie and Mr. MacDhui had known one another when they were both students at Edinburgh University—

they might even have known some of my family there—and Mr. Peddie told Mr. MacDhui that there was a practice for sale in the town where he lived and advised him to go there.

So. Mr. MacDhui sold out his practice in Glasgow and the house on Dunear Street where he was brought up, and we all moved to Inveranoch on the west bank of Loch Fyne in Argyllshire, where my tragedy happened to me.

Mary Ruadh then was six years old, going on seven, and we lived in the last house but one near the end of Argyll Lane. Our next-door neighbor was Mr. MacDhui's friend, Mr. Angus Peddie, the minister, who kept a most disgusting pug dog by the name of Fin. Ugh!

Our house was really two houses, one next the other, but separated, and they were of whitewashed stone with slate roofs; they were rather long and narrow, two stories high, with tall chimneys at each end, on which there was usually perched a sea gull. In one of these we lived and in the adjoining one was the office, waiting room, surgery, and hospital of Mr. MacDhui. But of course we never went there, for Mary Ruadh was forbidden to do so. After what had happened in Glasgow, Mr. MacDhui had sworn he would never again have sick animals in the place where he lived.

I considered myself a good deal better off in Inveranoch than in Glasgow because Loch Fyne was an arm of the sea that pushed up from the ocean down by Greenock right up into the Highlands as far as Cairndow and brought with it gulls to watch in flight and the smell of the sea and fish and queer birds to chase that ran along the beach, behind which lay a wonderful dark and scary country of woods and glens and mountains of stone in which to hunt. I was never allowed out in Glasgow, but it was quite different here and soon I became a real Highlander and we Highlanders, of course, looked down on every one else.

Inveranoch was not as large a city as Glasgow, in fact it was quite small, with no more than a few thousand inhabitants, but to make up for that hundreds of visitors came there every summer for their holidays.

This was the busiest time for Mr. MacDhui, for the guests often brought their pets with them, mostly dogs, of course, but sometimes also cats and birds, and once, a monkey, and the climate did not always agree with them or they would get themselves bitten or stung in the woods, or pick a fight with one of us Highlanders, which was foolish since they were much too soft and then their owners would have to bring them to Mr. MacDhui for repairs. He seemed to take this in very ill part, for he was a man who hated pets and disliked being a veterinarian and preferred to pass his time in the back country with the farmers and crofters rather than keep office hours.

However none of this was any of my concern and I was fairly comfortable at this time and living a routine sufficiently to my own taste, except for one thing. Mary Ruadh had become a cat carrier.

If you will have had a little girl yourself you will know what I am talking about. If not, you may have noticed that, at a certain age, little girls always carry a doll around wherever they go, but some carry their cat. Often they do not even know they are carrying it as they walk or toddle about with it. They hold it around the middle clutched to their breasts, just below the shoulders, so that most of the cat dangles a dead weight, with head and forequarters hanging over the arm.

Mary Ruadh did vary this most uncomfortable and humiliating position sometimes by placing me across her shoulders like a fur piece, where I could rest and even be admired by people, who sometimes said it was difficult to tell which was Mary Ruadh's hair and which was me. I didn't mind that. Or she would carry me upside down in both arms, like a little baby. I hated that.

If you ask me why I put up with it, I cannot tell you, since my philosophy of life is quite simple. When you find yourself in a situation where unpleasant things, or things you don't like, occur more frequently than pleasant ones—walk out.

Well, there were other things too, which I wasn't going to mention, but as long as I am on the subject, I might as well. There was the being made to sit on a chair sometimes at tea with a napkin around my neck and pretend I was a person, or, rather, Mary Ruadh pretended. This got me a few caraway-seed cakes, of which I happened to be fond, and a couple of laps of cambric tea out of a saucer, but it didn't make up for the indignity.

When I had kittens they took them away from me and drowned them.

At night I was forced to sleep at the foot of her bed. Nor could I go away to my favorite chair after she fell asleep, for if she woke up and I was not there she would call for me and sob most heart-breakingly. Sometimes during the night, even when I was there, she would wake up and begin to cry softly in the darkness and murmur, "Mummy—Mummy!" for it seemed she remembered her too. Then she would reach down in the darkness and wake me up and hold me to her so hard, with her face buried in my flank, that I could hardly breathe, and you know how we *hate* to be held.

She would then cry, "Oh, Thomasina, Thomasina, I love you. Don't ever leave me." After a little she would become more quiet and I would wash her face a little and lick the salt tears from her cheeks, which made her laugh and giggle and say, "Thomasina— you *tickle*," and soon she would go to sleep again.

And I stayed on. Believe me, if it had been a little boy, I should not have done so, thank you very much. I should soon enough have run away and not come back, taken to the woods, or found someone else in town to live with, for I am perfectly capable of looking after Thomasina. Though I may look delicate, I am most resilient, have a hardy constitution, and can stand almost anything. Once a boy on a bicycle ran over me. Mrs. McKenzie came running out of the house screaming that I was killed, and Mary Ruadh cried and carried on so that it took an hour afterward to calm her, and all that happened was that the boy fell off his bicycle and hurt himself and I got up and walked away.

Well, and then there was Mr. MacDhui himself and there is plenty I could tell you about him, and none of it favorable. An animal doctor who didn't like animals, there's a good one. A bit too quick with the chloroform rag when people brought their sick pets to his surgery, was what they said. I'll tell you I wouldn't want him treating me. Mr. MacDhui was jealous of me because his daughter loved me so much, and he hated me. But what was even worse, he *ignored* me. Mr. High-and-mighty-around-the-house-as-though-I-was-not-there. Nose in the air; whiskers bristling all of the time. And the medicine smell of him. Ugh! It was the same one that came out of the hospital when you went past. When he came home at night and bent down to kiss Mary Ruadh his huge, bristly, red face with the medicine and pipe smell would come right close to mine, since Mary Ruadh would be carrying me, and it made me feel sick.

Naturally I annoyed him all I could, calling attention to myself by washing in front of him, taking care to be on *his* chair when I knew he would be wanting it, lying in doorways where he would be likely to trip over me, rubbing up against his legs and ankles, leaving hairs on his best clothes whenever I could find them, and jumping up on his lap when he sat down to read the paper and making smells of my own. He did not dare to be rough with me when Mary Ruadh was in the room and so he would just pretend I was not there and then get up suddenly to go for some tobacco and dump me off.

Add up all of these things and you might almost say it amounted to sufficient cause for me to move out. Yet I stayed on and was not too unhappy. I wouldn't have admitted it to anyone else, but if the truth be known, I was rather fond of the child.

I think it could have been because in some ways girl children and cats are not unalike. There is some special mystery about little girls, an attitude of knowing secret things and a contemplative and not wholly complimentary quality about the way they look at you sometimes that is often as baffling and exasperating to their elders as we are.

If you have ever lived with a girl child you will know that quiet, infuriating retirement into some private world of their own of which they are capable, as well as that stubborn independence in the face of stupid or unreasonable demands or prohibitions. These same traits seem to annoy you in us as well. For you can no more force a cat or a girl child to do something they do not wish to do than you can compel us to love you. We had this in common, Mary Ruadh and I.

Thus I did many strange things I should not have believed myself capable of doing. When Mary Ruadh went to school —this adventure of mine took place during the summer holidays— I suffered her to carry me all the way there, and to be pawed or fussed over by the other children until the bell rang and she went inside, when I was free to run home and look after my business.

But, believe it or not, when it came time for her to come home in the afternoon I would be sitting up on the gatepost with my tail curled about my legs, watching for her. True, it was also a fine vantage point from which to spit on the minister's pug dog when it went by, but nevertheless, there I was. The neighbors used to say you could always tell what time of day it was by the MacDhui cat getting up onto the gatepost to watch for her wee mistress.

I, Thomasina, waiting on a gatepost for a somewhat grubby, red-haired, and not even especially beautiful child.

Sometimes I wondered whether perhaps there was not another bond between us: we were each to the other something to cling to when the sun went down and nightfall brings on fear and loneliness.

27

Loneliness is comforted by the closeness and touch of fur to fur, skin to skin, or—skin to fur. Sometimes when I awoke at night after a bad dream I would listen to the regular breathing of Mary Ruadh and feel the slight rise and fall of the bedclothes about her. Then I would no longer be afraid and would go back to sleep again.

I have mentioned that Mary Ruadh was not an especially beautiful child, which perhaps was not polite, since she thought that I was certainly the most beautiful cat in the world, but I meant especially beautiful in the unusual sense. She was a rather usual-looking little girl except for her eyes, which told you of some special quality in her or about her when you looked into them. Often I was not able to do so for long. Their color was a bright blue, a most intense blue, but sometimes when she was thinking thoughts I could not understand or even guess, they turned as dark as the loch on a stormy day.

For the rest, you wouldn't call her much to look at, with her uptilted nose and freckled face and a long lower lip that usually stuck out, while her eyebrows and lashes were so light you could hardly see them. She wore her ginger-red hair in two braids tied with green or blue ribbon. Her legs were quite long and she liked to stick her stomach out.

But there was something else pleasant about Mary Ruadh: she smelled good. Mrs. McKenzie kept her washed and ironed when she was home and she always smelled of lavender, for Mrs. McKenzie kept lavender bags in with her clothes and underthings.

It seemed as if Mrs. McKenzie was forever washing and ironing and starching and scenting her clothes, because it was the only way she was allowed to show how much she cared for Mary Ruadh. Mrs. McKenzie was a thin woman who talked and sang through her nose. She would have mothered Mary Ruadh the way we will frequently look after somebody else's kitten as though it were our own, but Mr. MacDhui was jealous and feared that Mary Ruadh would come to love her too much if she were allowed to cuddle her. Oh, Mr. Bristle-and-Smelly was allowed to cuddle her all he wished, but nobody else.

I *loved* the odor of lavender. Smells, almost more than noises, seem to bring on the happiness or unhappiness memories. You might not remember what it was about a smell had made you angry at the time, or afraid, but as soon as you come across it again you are angry or fearful. Like the medicine smell of Mr. MacDhui.

But lavender was the happiness smell. It made my claws move in and out and brought the contentment purr to my throat.

Sometimes, after putting Mary Ruadh's things away after ironing them, Mrs. McKenzie would forget to close all the chests of drawers and leave one open. Then I would quickly nip inside and lie there full length with my nose up against a lavender bag, just smelling, smelling, smelling. That was bliss. That was when I was contented and at peace with the world.

3 Outside MacDhui's surgery Geordie McNabb went wandering away clutching his box, in which the injured frog reposed on a bed of grass and young heather. Occasionally he proceeded with an absent-minded hop, skip, and jump, his usual ebullient method of locomotion, until, brought up by recollection of the more sobering aspects of his situation, he slowed down to a mere trot or saunter.

He was not aware of going in any particular direction, but was only glad to be away once more from the ken of grownups who loomed over one, tall, bristly, and unsympathetic, and hustled one about with a pat on the bottom, an indignity unworthy to be bestowed upon a Wolf Cub.

But ever and anon he paused to look into the box and give the frog a tentative poke, reaffirming his diagnosis of a broken leg, which prevented it from hopping and carrying on frog's business. At such times he regarded the little fellow with a combination of interest, affection, and deep concern. He was fully aware that he had a problem on his hands connected with the eventual disposition of his charge, since take it home he could not, owing to house laws on the importation of animals, while at the same time to abandon it as recommended by the veterinarian was unthinkable. It was Geordie's first encounter with the chilly and uncooperative attitude of the world toward one who has taken the fatal step of accepting a responsibility.

His seemingly unguided wanderings had taken him to the edge of the town, that is, to the back of it, where the houses ended abruptly and the several farms and meadows began, beyond which lay the dark and mysterious woods covering the hill of Glen Ardrath, where the Red Witch lived, and he realized that he *had* thought of this fearful alternative as a possible solution but had quickly rejected it as altogether too frightening and dangerous.

Yet now that he was there by the bridge crossing the river Ardrath, that peaceful stream flowing into Loch Fyne, but which was fed by the tumbling mountain torrents that came frothing down out of the glen, the prospect of paying her a visit seemed awesomely and repellently attractive and exciting. For it was a fact that the townspeople avoided the lair, or vicinity of the Red Witch, who was also known as Daft Lori, or sometimes even Mad Lori, and most certainly small boys, fed on old wives' tales and fairy-book pictures of hook-nosed crones riding on brooms, avoided the neighborhood except when in considerable company.

But there were two sides to the estimate of the so-called Red Witch of Glen Ardrath, one in which the picture was supplied by the superheated imagination reacting to the word witch, and the other was that she was a harmless woman who lived alone in a crofter's cottage up in the hills, where she made a living by weaving on a hand loom, conversed with birds and animals whom she nursed, mothered, and fed, and communed with the angels and the Little Folk with which the glen was peopled.

Geordie was aware of both of these tales. If it was true that the roe deer came down from the flanks of Ben Inver to feed out of her hand, the birds settled on her head and shoulders, the trout and salmon rose from the sunny shallows of the burn at her call, and that in the stables behind the cottage where she lived there were sick beasties she found in the woods or up the rocky glen, or who came to her driven by instinct to seek human help and whom she tended back to health, why then it might well be worth the risk to deposit his frog with her. At any rate it appeared to be a legitimate excuse for the having of a tremendous adventure, whatever came of it.

He crossed the saddleback bridge over the river and commenced the climb to the forest at the entrance to Glen Ardrath, past the gray bones of Castle Ardrath, of which the circular inner keep and part of the stone curtain was all that had remained standing.

The home of the Red Witch was supposed to be situated a mile or more up the glen where the forest was heaviest and it took considerable courage for a small boy alone, even though panoplied as a Wolf Cub and filled with some of their woods lore, to enter the darkening area of lichened oak, spreading beech, and somber fir and to push his way through the head-high bracken. He tamed his apprehensions by looking for and identifying the summer wild flowers in full blossom of July that cropped up beside the path he was following; purple thrift and scarlet pimpernel, yellow broom and the pink of the wild dog rose that grew entangled with the white-flowering bramble which in the late summer and fall would yield the sweetest blackberries. He recognized purple columbine, red campion, and the blue harebell, the true bluebell of Scotland, growing in profusion in a glade that seemed made by the traditional fairy ring of trees growing about a circle carpeted with flowers and warmed by shafts of sunlight that penetrated through the branches of the trees.

From there the hill climbed more steeply, and he could hear though not yet see the wild rushing of the burn. He sat down there a moment to rest and took the frog out of the box and laid it on the moss, where it palpitated but did not move. Watching it, Geordie felt his heart swell with pity for its plight and helplessness and, putting it back into the box, determined to see the matter through without further delay.

At last he came in sight of the cottage he sought, and with the guile of the Red Indian, properly instilled into every Wolf Cub, he paused, flattened out to reconnoiter.

The stone cottage was long and narrow and had chimneys standing up like ears at either end. The lids of green shutters were closed over the windows of its eyes and it seemed to be sleeping, poised on the edge of a clearing of the woods on what seemed to be a small plateau, a broadening of the side of the glen, and where the burn, too, widened out and moved more sluggishly. Behind it and off to one side was another long, low stone building that had once been a barn, no doubt, or cattle shelter. Geordie hugged his box close to his beating heart and continued to study the surroundings.

A covin oak raised its thick bole a dozen or so yards before the cottage, and yet its spreading branches reached to the tiles of the roof, and the topmost ones overshadowed it. The great oak must have been more than two hundred years old and from the lowest of its branches there hung a silvered bell. From the clapper of the bell a thin rope reached to the ground and trailed there. And now that he was himself quiet, Geordie was becoming aware of movements and sounds. From within the cottage there came a high, clear, sweet singing and a curiously muffled thumping. This, Geordie decided, was the witch, and he trembled now in his cover of fern and bracken and wished he had not come. The singing held him spellbound, but the thumping was sinister and ominous for he had never heard the working of the treadle on a hand loom.

Overhead a red squirrel scolded him from the branch of a smooth gray-green beech; a raven and a hooded black crow were having a quarrel and suddenly began to flap and scream and beat one another with great strokes of their wings, so that all of the birds in the area took fright and flew up; blue tits, robins, yellow wagtails, thrushes and wrens, sparrows and finches. They circled the chimneys, chattering and complaining; two black and white magpies flashed in and out of the trees and from somewhere an owl called.

The voice from within rose higher in purest song, though no melody that Geordie had ever heard, yet it had the strange effect of making him wish suddenly to put his hands to his eyes and weep. The beating wings ceased to flail and the cries and the flutterings of the birds quieted down. Geordie saw the white cottontail of a rabbit, and the bristly round back of a hedgehog down by the burn.

Thereupon Geordie McNabb did something instinctively right and quite brave. He crept out from beneath his cover and advanced as far as the bell suspended from the covin-tree and the rope hanging therefrom. At the foot of it he deposited his box with the frog in it and gave the rope a gentle tug until the bell, shivering and vibrating, rent the forest with its silvery echoes, stilling the voice and the thumping from within the house. As fast as his stumpy legs could carry him, Geordie fled across the clearing and dove once more into the safety of the cover of thick green fern.

The peal of the bell died away, but the quiet was immediately shattered by the hysterical barking of a dog. A Scots terrier came racing around from the barn behind the house. A hundred birds rose into the air, making a soughing and whirring with their wings as they flew wildly about the chimneys. Two cats came walking formally and with purpose around the corner of the house, their tails straight up in the air, a black and a tiger-striped gray. They sat down quietly some distance away and waited. As Geordie watched, a young roe deer, a buck, suddenly appeared out of the underbrush, head up and alert, the sun shining from its moist black nose and liquid eyes. It moved warily, tossing its fine head, its eyes fixed upon the house, where the front door was slowly opening and with infinite caution.

Geordie McNabb's heart beat furiously and he came close

to giving way to panic and running for all he was worth. But his curiosity to see the Red Witch of Glen Ardrath, now that he had come this far and dared so much, and his need to find out what was to become of his frog, kept him there.

The door opened wide, but no Red Witch appeared, almost to Geordie McNabb's disappointment; only a young woman, hardly more than a girl, it seemed to Geordie, a plain girl, a country girl, such as you could see anywhere on the farms surrounding Invera-noch, in simple skirt and smock with thick stockings and shoes, and a shawl around her shoulders.

She could not have been a witch, for she was neither beautiful nor hideous, and yet little Geordie found that he could not seem to take his eyes from her countenance. What was it that drew and held his gaze? He could not tell. Her nose was long and wise, and the space between it and her upper lip seemed wide and humorous so that somehow it made you want to smile looking at it. The mouth was both tender and rueful and in the gray-green eyes there was a faraway look. Her hair, which hung loose to her shoulders in the fashion of country girls, was not bound and was the cherry color of a glowing blacksmith's bar before he begins to beat it.

She looked out of the door, brushing away a lock of the dark red hair from her forehead and the gesture, too, was of one who also is clearing away cobwebs from the mind. Geordie lay there on his belly, hidden by the ferns, loving her suddenly with all his heart, and he did not know why nor did he think of any spell cast upon him but only that she was there and he loved her.

The girl looked about her for a moment and then, to Geordie's surprise, gave a high, clear call on two notes. For a moment Geordie thought that the silver bell was still ringing, so clear and piercing was the call, but the sides of the metal had long ceased vibrating and it was only her throat that produced the marvelous sound.

It acted upon the buck, who came stepping nimbly out of the woods and walked slowly across half the clearing as she stood contemplating the animal out of her faraway eyes, with the rueful smile at her lips. The deer stopped and lowered its head and stood there gazing up at her mischievously and playfully so that she burst into laughter and cried, "Was it you then, at the bell again. For that ye'll wait for your supper——"

But the buck, as though suddenly alarmed, or sensing the presence of another, turned and bounded away into the forest. The cats came sedately forward, walking almost in tandem, and began to weave in and out her feet. But the Scottie dog ran to the box containing the frog and began to sniff it, thus calling her attention to its presence.

She crossed the threshold then and Geordie watched her run to the box with quick, lithe steps that had in them something of the movements of the deer. She knelt, her hands folded in her lap for an instant, and peered into the box. Then she reached out and removed the weary, injured, palpitating, little reptile.

She held it gently in her hand and the broken leg spilled from the side of it and hung limp. Carefully she probed it with a finger and looked into the beady yellow-green eyes of the frog, and the odd space between her nose and upper lip twitched most movingly as she lifted the frog and held it to her cheek for an instant while she said, "Was it the angels or the Little Folk who brought ye here to me? Puir wee frog. I will do what I can for you." Then she arose and disappeared into the house, shutting the door after her.

The cottage slept again, its eyes tightly shut. The two cats and the dog retired whence they had come. The whirring birds quieted down. Only the squirrel in the tree, who knew where Geordie was, continued to scold. Geordie felt as though the greatest load he had ever known in his life had been lifted from him and he was free at last. The frog was safe and in good hands. His heart filled now almost to bursting with a new and strange kind of joy and singing, he left the shelter of the bracken, and as fast as his legs would carry him hopped, skipped, and jumped along the path alongside the foaming burn, downhill toward Inveranoch and home.

That same summer's morning Mr. MacDhui, finishing with his waiting list of clients, motioned with his head to his friend Mr. Peddie, who had waited until the last, to go inside with his groaning animal. He followed him, remarking, "Come in, Angus. I am sorry you have had to wait for so long. These fools with their useless pets seem to take up all of my time. Well, what is the trouble? Have you been overfeeding the beast on sweets again? I warned you, did I not?" He seemed hardly aware he had included his friend in the category.

Mr. Peddie, who really did not have the proper physical aspect for it, contrived to look both guilty and sheepish. He replied, "Of course you are right, Andrew, but what am I to do? He sits up and begs so prettily. He is mortally fond of sweets." He looked fondly upon the pug dog, who lay belly flat upon the enameled examining table with an occasional belch disturbing his normal wheezing. He rolled his creamy eyes pleadingly in the direction of Mr. MacDhui, who, memory and experience told him, possessed the formula to pardon overindulgence.

The vet leaned down to smell the dog, wrinkling his nose in distaste; he probed his belly and took his temperature. "Hmph!" he grunted, "the same complaint—only aggravated." He stuck his chin out and bristled his beard at the divine and mocked, "A man of God, you are, speaking for the Creator, and himself having no more self-control than to stuff this wretched animal with sweets, to his own detriment."

"Oh," replied Peddie, squirming uneasily, his usually joyous moon face exhibiting the sadness of the scolded child, "not really

37

a man of God, though I do try. No more than an employee of His in the division of humans who must make up in love what they lack in brains and grace." He made a deprecating gesture. "So many good men go into the Army or politics, or law, He is often compelled to take what He can get."

MacDhui grinned appreciatively and looked at his friend with affection. "Do you think He really enjoys all this sycophancy, flattery, bribery, and cajoling that you chaps seem to think necessary to keep Him good-tempered and tractable?"

Mr. Peddie answered immediately and with equal good humor: "If ever God inveigled himself into error, it was when He let man imagine Him in his own image, but I rather think this was man's rather than God's idea, since it has been more flattering to the former."

MacDhui barked like a hyena, flashing his strong white teeth through the red line of his full lips. He loved the running battle with Peddie which had been going on between them ever since he had moved from Glasgow to Inveranoch at his behest, and which they carried on almost whenever and wherever they encountered one another. "Oh ho," he said, "then you admit that man has endowed God with a full set of his own faults and spends most of his praying time catering to them?"

The minister stroked the head of his little dog lovingly. "I suspect the real punishment for the sin in Eden," he said, "was when he made us human, when he took away the divinity He had loaned us and made us kin and blood brothers with"—and here he nodded with his head toward the suffering pug dog—"these. You must admit the sentence contains an element of humor, something for which God is rarely given credit."

For once Mr. MacDhui was caught without a retort, for with university cunning his friend had suddenly made use of some of his own best arguments.

"But you won't even admit that relationship," the minister continued, cheerful at having extricated himself from the position where MacDhui could lecture him, "whereas I love this little fellow foolishly and consider him as important as myself when it comes to indulgence. Tell me, Andrew, do you not at all come to love these suffering animals you treat? Does not your heart break when they look at you so helplessly and trustingly?"

MacDhui turned his aggressive beard upon the pastor and regarded him with mingled truculence and pity as he replied. "Hardly. Even if I am only a veterinarian, I am still a doctor. If every doctor permitted himself to become emotionally involved with each of his patients or relatives of his patients, he would not last long. I am not sentimental, nor can I abide this indulgent affection wasted upon useless animals." And he thrust out his beard again.

The Reverend Peddie nodded his round, smooth face as though in understanding and agreement and quite suddenly attacked from another quarter. He asked, "Was there then nothing you could do as a doctor for that poor old woman's dog—I mean Mrs. Laggan's? The one you persuaded her to have put away, and I doubt not have done so by now."

Mr. MacDhui turned as red as his hair and his eyes grew hard and angry. "Why, has she complained to you, or said anything?"

"Do you find that so strange then? No, she did not complain, but she could not conceal her desolation. I saw her eyes as she went out. She is now all alone in the world."

MacDhui continued defiant. "You thought I was hard on her, did you? Well, and what if I could have kept the animal alive for another three weeks or a month, or even two? The end result would be the same. She would still be alone in the world. And besides I offered to procure her another dog. People are always wishing me to find homes for all sorts."

"But it was *that* poor, wretched, wheezy dog she loved and whose presence and friendship gave her comfort—just as this little fellow here fills a part of my life. Don't you believe in the power of love at all to make our tour of duty here a little more bearable——?"

MacDhui shrugged and did not reply. He had loved and wooed and would have devoted his life to the profession of medicine and it had been denied him. He had loved Anne MacLean his wife and she had been taken from him. . . . Love was a snare and love was a danger. One was better off without it, if one could avoid it, which was not always possible, and he thought of Mary Ruadh and his love for her. Simpler perhaps to be a stick or a stone, or a tree and feel nothing.

Mr. Peddie was ruminating, with his brow knitted in a frown. "There must be a key, you know," he said.

"Key to what?"

"Perhaps it IS love. The key to the relationship between man and the four-footed, the winged and the finned creatures who are his neighbors in woods, field, and stream and his brothers and sisters on earth——"

"Tosh!" snorted MacDhui. "We are all part of the gigantic cosmic accident that put us here. We all started even, you know. We developed the upright position and the thumb and they lost. Bad luck for them."

Peddie regarded MacDhui keenly through his spectacles and said with a smile, "Ah, Angus—I did not know you had come so far already. To admit we were put here seems to me a weakening of your position you can ill afford. And who, may I ask, arranged this cosmic accident? For surely you are not so old-fashioned as to believe any longer that accidents just happen——"

"And if I ask you who, you will say God, of course."

"Who but?"

"Antigod. The system is wretchedly run. I could conduct it better myself." MacDhui reached up to a shelf and took down a small bottle of medicine. The pug dog emitted a gigantic belch, struggled to its feet, and sat up begging. The two men looked at one another and burst into roars of laughter.

4   I was checking a mousehole when Mary Ruadh came to take me away to go down to the quay in the town, in company with Hughie Stirling, to see the steamer arrive from Glasgow.

The interruption did not leave me in the best of humors, for I had put in a lot of time and work on that hole and felt that I was just about to achieve results.

It was the one by the larder, the important one. I had been treating it for days and it was a nuisance being dragged off. Mousehole watching to me was *duty*, and I always did it thoroughly and well. All of the other things I had to do for Mary Ruadh to keep her happy and contented, including submitting to being carried about by her everywhere she went, were her idea and not mine.

People are inclined to forget or overlook our primary purpose in a house—and out of purely selfish reasons, such as when they try to turn us into babies—and often, when made to live unnatural lives, we become spoiled and lazy. Even when every so often we bring them a mouse as a reminder and lay it at their feet, people are so conceited and stupid as to accept it as a *personal* gift, instead of realizing that we are calling attention to our reason for being there and paying up for board and lodging.

I suppose you think that checking a mousehole is easy and no work at all. Well, all I can say is YOU try it sometime. Get down on your hands and knees and remain in that position, concentrating and staring at one little hole in the wainscoting for hours at a time, while simultaneously pretending that you are not. Checking a mousehole isn't just giving it a sniff and going away as a dog would do. On the contrary. If you are as conscientious and dutiful as I am, it is a full-time job, particularly if there are two or three or you suspect one of them of having two entrances.

It isn't catching mice, mind you, that is the most necessary. Anyone can catch a mouse; it is no trick at all; it is putting them off and keeping them down that is important. You will hear sayings like, "The only good mouse is a dead mouse," but that is only half of it. The only good mouse is the mouse that isn't there at all. What you must do, if you are at all principled about your work, is to conduct a war of nerves on the creatures. This calls for time, energy, and a good deal of cleverness, which I wouldn't begrudge if I wasn't expected to do so many other things besides.

Just to give you an idea of what mousehole watching entails, after you have located and charted them and decided which ones are active and which extinct, you select one and go there, but, of course, never twice at the same time exactly. A mouse is no fool and soon learns to time you if you are regular. I find that hunch and instinct, or just plain feline know-how are the best things to guide you. You just KNOW at a certain moment; it comes over you as in a dream that THAT is the time to go there.

Well, first you take two or three sniffs and then settle down in front of it and stare for a while. If the mouse is in, he or she can't get out, and if they are out they can't get home. Either way it is worrying. And so for the first hour you just remain there staring. At the same time, when you get used to it you find that you can think about all sorts of other things, make plans, or wish, or remember who you were, or what happened to an ancestor thousands and thousands of generations ago, or perhaps think about what there is going to be for supper.

THEN, suddenly you close both eyes and pretend that you are asleep. Now, this is the most important and delicate part of the entire operation, for now you may rely only upon your ears and the receiving antennae at the ends of your whiskers. For this is when the mouse, if it is out, will try to get in, or try to get out if it is in, and just at the psychological moment when it thinks it has you, you open one eye.

I can promise you that the effect upon the mouse of finding itself suddenly stared at by that single eye of ours is absolutely tremendous. I am not sure what it is exactly, unless it is to be confronted with the evidence that you actually need only one eye to watch while the other one sleeps that is so upsetting to the mouse, but there it is. A few doses of that and it is on the verge of a nervous breakdown. Its nervousness soon communicates itself to its family; they hold a consultation and decide to move away.

This is the manner in which any responsible member of our species handles the mouse problem in the household, but as you can see, it calls for technique, practice, and time; above all, time. I managed to keep the house reasonably clear in spite of all the other things I had to do, room and parcel inspection, washing, exchanging news with the neighbors, and looking after Mary Ruadh, for which of course I got no thanks or appreciation at all from Mr. MacDhui, and little more from Mrs. McKenzie, from whom I had to listen to such complaints as, "Och, ye lazy Thomasina. The mice have been at the larder again. Do ye then no' ken a moosie when ye see yin?" which was supposed to be very cutting and sarcastic, but of course rolled right off my back.

So there I was, just settled down to put the cap on three solid days of nerve war, when Hughie Stirling came whistling outside the house, and the next thing I knew, Mary Ruadh in a blue pinafore with blue socks and blue shoes was picking me up and carrying me off through the town down to the quay. I had never been there before at steamboat time.

Hughie Stirling was the laird's son. He was almost ten, but already tall for his age. He lived in the manor, whose grounds reached almost to the back of our house, and he was a great friend to Mary Ruadh.

You can have boys, for my part. I find them nasty, dirty, cruel in the main, and unkind and heartless to boot, selfish little beasts, but I must admit that Hughie Stirling was different. He managed to keep himself clean and had a kind of noble look about him, with a lean face, dark, wavy hair, and light blue eyes, the farseeing kind.

Mary Ruadh tagged after him whenever she could, or he would let her, which was quite often, for he seemed to like to look after her. Most boys of that age will have no part of little girls at any price, but a few, like Hughie, seem to like having them about, particularly if they have no sisters, watching over them, picking them up, brushing them off and wiping away their tears when they fall or hurt themselves, and seeing to it that their noses were blown when it was necessary. Like Mary Ruadh, Hughie was an only child and so he liked to borrow her occasionally, and of course I went along over Mary Ruadh's arm, for she would not go without me. Hughie never seemed to mind this and appeared to understand it and not think it curious. Perhaps he appreciated my worth. I am not surprised to find this attitude in one of the aristocracy.

If I could live my own life, that is to say, if I were not "house," I should move to the water front and spend the days sitting on the jetties in the sun, sniffing the tar in the ropes with which the boats are made fast, and when the fishermen's skiffs came in, I would strut along the granite flagstones of the quay, with my tail aquivering in the air, and go down to greet them and see what they had brought in from the sea.

Next to lavender, I think the smells I like best are those of the sea, boats and heaps of old oilskins, sweaters, gear and tackle and rubber boots piled up in the boathouse, and the beautiful odor of fish; fish and seaweed, crab and lobster and the green sea scum that fastens to the gray-stone landing steps. And there is a wonderful odor by the sea in the very early morning, too, when the sun has not yet pierced through the mists and everything is soggy with damp and dew and salt.

And so once I was there with the children in the square by the quay where the statue to Rob Roy stands, I was not too ill-pleased, for there were many interesting and exciting things going on, except that when the steamer came in and blew its whistle it frightened me so that I fell off Mary Ruadh's shoulder and hurt myself.

That wants a bit of explaining, I know, for we always fall on our feet, particularly when we have time to turn over, but this all happened so quickly that I didn't.

The steamer was all white with a narrow black funnel, and how was I to know that the funnel was going to make a horrible noise? I was quite fascinated watching the ship come puffing up to the edge of the stone jetty, with bells clanging and orders being shouted, and much white froth of water all about it as it went first forward, then backward, then even sideways, and suddenly, without warning, the loudest and most frightful shriek burst from the top of the stack and I fell over backward.

Well, I suppose I could have saved myself, but it would have meant digging in my claws into Mary Ruadh's neck, for I had been lying across her shoulders. If it had been anyone else, I should not have hesitated to anchor my claws, you may believe me. But it all happened so quickly, the awful noise that seemed to split my ears open, and then there was a bump and I was lying on my side, hurting.

Mary Ruadh picked me up at once and rubbed it, and so did Hughie Stirling, and they made a fuss over me, though Hughie laughed and said, "The old whistle frightened her," and then to me, "You'll have to get used to that, Thomasina, if you're going to be a seagoing cat." It seems that he and Mary Ruadh were planning a trip around the world in a yacht he was going to have when he grew up and, of course, she had said she wouldn't go without me.

The rubbing made it feel better; Mary Ruadh cradled me in her arms and held me tight, and the next time it hooted I wasn't nearly so frightened and almost forgot the pain in the excitement of watching the mail sacks being tossed onto the pier, followed by the luggage of the visitors, which was covered with the most interesting-looking labels, after which the visitors themselves came ashore down a wooden gangway that had been run onto the side of the ship from the quay.

Many of them had children by the hand and that, of course, interested Mary Ruadh and Hughie and Geordie McNabb, who had joined us. Geordie is eight and a Wolf Cub and he goes all over by himself and sees everything. There were a half dozen or so dogs on a leash that came ashore, and a cat basket; overhead the gulls wheeled and screamed; taxicab drivers honked their horns and shouted at the people and all in all, except for my tumble, it was a most satisfactory landing. And Geordie had some interesting news.

He told Hughie and Mary Ruadh, "There's gypsies and tinkers come to Dunmore Field at the foot of the glen, across the river. Lots and lots of them with wagons and cages and caravans and things. They're camped beside the woods on Tarbet Road. Mr. MacQuarrie, the constable, went out to have a word with them."

"Oh!" exclaimed Hughie Stirling, "*that's* exciting! I wish I had been there. What happened?"

Geordie McNabb drew in a deep breath and his eyes became quite as round as his head because of the importance of answering the question put to him by the laird's son. I could see that.

He replied, "Constable MacQuarrie said as long as they behaved themselves and didn't give any trouble they could stay there."

Hughie nodded his head. "And what did they say?"

"Oh, there was a big man there and he had on a big leather belt and it had nails in it. And he put his hands in his belt and laughed at Mr. MacQuarrie."

Hughie said: "It's no' clever to laugh at Mr. MacQuarrie."

Geordie continued: "Another man, a little one wearing a waistcoat and a hat came up and he pushed the man with the belt away and said that they were grateful and would not give any trouble, but would just try to earn a few honest pennies. Then Mr. MacQuarrie asked what they meant to do with the animals in the cages."

"Oh," exclaimed Hughie, even more interested, and by now so was Mary Ruadh, and so was I. "What animals, in what cages?"

Geordie reflected before he replied, "Well, they had a bear and an eagle and a mountain lion and some monkeys and dogs and an elephant and horses, and——"

"Poooh!" remonstrated Hughie, "gypsies never have elephants."

Geordie looked as though he was sorry he had said it. "Well, maybe they didn't really have an elephant, but they DID have a bear and an eagle and a mountain lion and monkeys and they said they were going to let people look at them for a shilling."

"I say," Hughie burst out with enthusiasm, "if I can wheedle a couple of shillings out of Mummy, we must go——"

Geordie had not yet finished his account. He continued, "Mr. MacQuarrie said he supposed that was all right as long as they did not ill-treat the animals, or give a performance."

Mary Ruadh asked, "What's a performance?"

Hughie replied, "Standing on their heads and doing tricks, I suppose. I'll bet they're going to when the police aren't looking."

Geordie concluded: "The man with the belt started to laugh again, but the other gypsy with the hat and the waistcoat went over and pushed him with his shoulder and Mr. MacQuarrie went away. I tried to look under the cover of one of the wagons to see what the animals were like, but a big boy came and chased me. He had a whip."

All this Mary Ruadh recounted to her father that night, during the time he gave her her evening bath and he listened to every word she said as though she were as grown-up as he, which I must say, astonished me, for grownups have a way of talking to children—yes, and to us too—that is most patronizing, irritating and humiliating. But Mr. MacDhui just nodded and grumbled and grunted seriously, as he listened, all the time soaping the back of her neck and ears with the washrag. "Well, little pink frog," he said finally, "just see that you keep well away from those gypsies whatever they mean to do, for they were always a filthy thieving folk and you cannot tell me they have reformed their ways in the last generation just because the police are content to condone their presence, eh?"

I think that Mrs. McKenzie was shocked at the idea of Mr. MacDhui giving Mary Ruadh her bath, but much as I dislike the man, I, who have been a mother, can testify that no kitten ever received a more painstaking and thorough washing than did she at the hands of her father when he came home at night, for this was the moment in the day that he seemed to enjoy the most, and therefore was almost pleasant—though of course, not to me, for I was not allowed to come into the bathroom, but sat outside in the hall and looked in.

He sang to Mary Ruadh,—can you imagine?—in his loud and most disgusting voice, the silliest words ever. I remember them. They went:

> There dwelt a puddy in a well,
>   Cuddy alane, cuddy alane,
> There dwelt a puddy in a well,
>   Cuddy alane and I.

49

There was a puddy in a well,
    AN a mousie in a mill;
Kickmaleerie, cowden doon,
    Cuddy alane and I.

Now, I ask you, where was the sense in that? But somehow Mary Ruadh seemed to understand, and when her father bellowed, "Kickmaleerie, cowden doon!" she screamed and shouted and splashed with her bath toys until the water shot all the way out into the hallway where I was sitting.

Then Mr. MacDhui picked her out of the tub and gave her a tousle and a rubdown until her whole body was red, when he would say, "How now, little pink puddy! Now this fine blue towel really becomes you. What shall we have for tea? Kickmaleerie Mary Ruadh!"

But me, he never so much as deigned to notice.

After they had their supper in the dining room, with Mary Ruadh sitting on a pile of cushions so that she would be higher, they would go into her room across the hall, where he played with her or sometimes told her some ridiculous kind of story, or she would climb into his lap and laugh and gurgle ridiculously and play with his bristly face and pull his fur and tease him, or sometimes they would even join hands and dance around the room together, and if you think THAT is any way to bring up a child or a kitten, you won't get me to agree with you.

That night Mary Ruadh became so excited that she would not calm down to say her prayers that Mr. MacDhui always insisted upon. These were kind of a petition and rhyme that she had to say every night before she went to sleep, and sometimes *having* to do it made her very willful and naughty. Well, I know, for one thing, how *I* am when I am *made* to do something.

Then Mr. MacDhui changed quite suddenly from being kind and gay to becoming most stern and ugly. He pushed out his great red beard at his daughter and growled, "That will be all and enough of that, Mary Ruadh. You have had plenty of play. Now say your prayers at once or I shall have to punish you."

Mary Ruadh asked, "Daddy, WHY do I have to say my prayers?"

If she asked this once, she asked it at least four times in the week. I had to smile inside to myself, for of course I knew it was just to keep putting it off, just as when we are ordered to do something, we suddenly discover that we have a most important bit of washing to do.

His answer would always be the same: "Because your mother would have wished it; that is why. She said her prayers every night."

Mary Ruadh then asked, "Can I hold Thomasina while I say them?"

I had to turn away to conceal the smile on my face, because I knew the explosion that was coming from Mr. MacDhui.

"No, no, NO. You cannot. Kneel now and say your prayers properly this minute."

Mary Ruadh asked that same question every night, not, I think, to make her father angry, but rather as a kind of routine in case someday he changed his mind and said yes.

It always succeeded in making him quite furious, and whereas at other times he simply ignored me as though I did not exist, I am sure at that moment he hated me.

He then stood beside her bed while she knelt, folded her hands together in the manner that was prescribed for her, and began her petition.

"God bless Mummy in heaven, and Daddy, and Thomasina——"

I always waited to make sure that my name was mentioned well up in the list that included such odd bods as Mr. Dobbie the grocer, and Willie Bannock, and Mr. Bridie the dustman, of whom she seemed to be fond, and then I went over and rubbed against Mr. MacDhui's legs, purring and getting hairs on his trousers, because I was well aware that it infuriated him, but he didn't dare shout, or kick, or swear, or do anything about it, because by that time Mary Ruadh was in the middle of her rhyme, which went:

> Gentle Jesus, meek and mild,
>   Look upon this little child;
> Pity my simplicity,
>   And suffer me to come to thee—AMEN.

and which was a very important one so that he could not stir until it was properly finished, by which time I would be under the bed where he could not reach me.

But he seemed to forget that he was angry when the prayers were finished and she lay upon her pillow with her ginger hair tousled about and he looked down upon her after he had kissed her good night. I used to watch his face, and all the bristle seemed to go out of his beard for once, and his fierce eyes turned soft. It was even more than soft. Soppy! Then he would blow himself up with a deep breath, turn, and stalk out of the room, like somebody in a play.

But I just stayed under the bed and waited my turn.

When he was gone, Mary Ruadh would call, "Mrs. McKenzie! Mrs. McKenzie!" and when she came in she would say, "I want Thomasina!"

I wouldn't make it difficult for the poor old soul, but by that time would be cruising close to the edge of the cot. Mrs. McKenzie would reach down, pick me up, and put me into Mary Ruadh's bed. Mr. MacDhui, who had gone off to his study, always heard her doing it, and knew that it happened, but pretended that he didn't. . . .

Well, that was what THAT day in my life, in fact, many days

in my life were like—for in most respects one day was very like another—except for the pain I felt at the base of my spine from the bump I had received when I fell off Mary Ruadh by the statue of Rob Roy, as I have told you already, and which was followed by the morning of my assassination.

5 On Thursday mornings, Mr. MacDhui left his house before seven for farm calls in the immediate neighborhood so as to return in time for his office hours, which were from eleven to one, leaving him the afternoon, if need be, for more distant visits.

Before departing on this day, he rattled off instructions to Willie Bannock: "I shall be stopping at Birnie Farm to see a case of scour, and Jock Maistock suspects the blackleg amongst his Ayrshires, so see that there is an ampoule or two of vaccine in the bag. I shall be testing John Ogilvie's herd, and I may stop at the McPherson chicken farm, if there is time, and relieve the mind of the widow. If I am late getting back, tell the folk to bide."

He did not neglect the morning round through his modest animal hospital, with the indispensable Willie in his train. On this particular day the veterinary seemed more aware than usual of the irony of this routine, which convenience and necessity had dictated should be almost an imitation if not a burlesque of that in the great hospitals in Edinburgh and Glasgow. There, he knew, each morning the house surgeon, followed by an intern or two, a matron, and a train of nursing sisters paraded through the wards inspecting charts, having a thump or a look at a patient, diagnosing, prescribing, dropping a pleasant or cheery word at each bed, dispensing hope and courage along with medicines, and leaving the ward behind him brighter, happier, and at ease, each human armored more strongly for his or her fight against injury or illness.

MacDhui, looking with a mind's eye turned resentful, could see himself in this healer's role as he had since he had been a boy, a doctor whose mere presence in the sickroom was enough to banish sickness and bar the angel of death. Since it had been denied him, he denied in turn the warmth and love which is so much a part of the cure of any ailing animal.

They were immured in scrupulously clean cages in which paper or straw might be changed by Willie a dozen times a day, properly diagnosed, drugged, bandaged, fed, watered and thereafter ignored by him. Pausing before each cage, he regarded each inmate as a specimen and a problem from whose exhibition of symptoms or reaction to treatment there was further knowledge or experience to be gained. But as fellow creatures, prisoners like himself aboard the same revolving ball of rock, dirt, and water, brothers and sisters in one great family of the living, he did not consider them at all.

They seemed to feel this as he went by and remained quiescent, regarding him with sad or morose eyes, or giving vent to minor-keyed complaints, whines, mews, snuffles——

They went through the aisle of cages, with Mr. MacDhui appraising and ordering dosage and treatments as always, to Willie's intense admiration, for Willie was mortally in awe of this great, red, pagan deity who could cure wee beasties. Nor were there any to be "put away," which came as a great relief to the attendant, for one of his duties was to play the part of executioner when MacDhui decided that an animal was better off dead than alive, a decision from which it appeared nothing could turn him once it had been made.

It was a job Willie hated, but he never presumed to question the orders of his chief, and with gentleness, chloroform bottle, and rag, got the unhappy business over with as quickly as possible and put the remains on the heap out back of the house, where he would not have to see them until the day's end when the incinerator was fired and all waste matter from the hospital burned, including small corpses.

"Try a larger dose of the Number 4 formula on Mrs. Sanderson's dog and I'll have another look at it when I get back. I don't expect I shall be late. If that confounded parrot keeps up its abominable noise, you have my permission to wring its neck."

He took his bag, into which Willie, who knew every ailment at each farm and what was required almost before MacDhui told him, had packed syringes, plungers, clysters, sprays, disinfectants, vaccines, dressings, sutures and needles, gauzes and plasters, as well as various stock items against emergencies, went out, climbed into his jeep, and drove off.

Willie waited until he saw him reach the end of Argyll and turn the corner into the High Street before, with almost unseemly haste, he hurried back to the animal hospital, where he was received with a perfect pandemonium of enthusiastic barks, whines, howls, shrieks, squawks, mews, and general animal hurrah for a loved human.

Willie, who just about came up to Mr. MacDhui's shoulder in height, was seventy, and fifty of those years he had devoted to the love and care of animals. MacDhui had inherited him from the man from whom he had bought the practice. Spry and alert, he had a friar's atoll of white hair about his skull and melting brown eyes that gave away his character and kindness of heart.

This was The Hour. Dogs stood up frantically on their hind legs inside their cages, pawing and shouting at him, birds shrieked, cats stiffened their tails and rubbed their flanks against the cage doors in anticipation, even the dogs too sick for greater demonstrations managed at least a waving and a thumping of their flags.

"Now, now—" Willie said, surveying the pandemonium with

the most intense satisfaction. "One at a time now, one at a time!" He stopped first at the cage of a fat dachshund, who went hysterical in his arms when he took him out, screaming, wriggling, licking his face, singing a passionate obbligato over the general chorus of enthusiasm. "There, there, now, Hansi—dinna excite yersel' so, or 'twill appear on your chart, no less, and the doctor will read that I've had ye oot for a spell. Ye'll be going awa' tomorrow or the next day——"

Thus he went from cage to cage, bestowing love, the secret medicine which surely effected as many cures as the doctor's drugs, or helped them along. Cats and dogs that were well enough he had out for a hug, or a bit of play, the sick had their ears and bellies rubbed, the parrot his head scratched, the lot of them, pampered, petted and spoiled until each had had its turn and been calmed down, when the regular routine of care and medication went forward.

The morning was misty and the smell of sea salt mingled with coal and peat smoke was in the air from the breakfast fires as Mr. MacDhui drove through the streets of gray-stone or whitewashed houses, tall, narrow and slate roofed, down to the quay where the waters of the loch were gray too, and a blue fishing boat with a stumpy mast and the forward well loaded with lobster pots, floats, and gear chuffed out of the harbor.

He breathed the smell of mingled sea and land, wild sea and rugged woodland and man and habitation smells, with no particular enjoyment, nor did he look to the flight of gulls or the curl of the tide lapping the shore; the beauty of the blue boat on the gray mirror of the loch in the pearly morning mist, already shot through with the light of the mounting sun, was lost upon him. He turned the jeep northward onto the Cairndow road, crossing the river Ardrath by the old saddleback bridge and, when he reached Creemore, took the left fork up into the hills.

When he had climbed somewhat, he could see the gypsy encampment lying at the foot of a fold in the valley to the south and noted from the smoke and the number of wagons that it was a large one. He recalled what Mary Ruadh had told him of it as seen through the eyes of Geordie McNabb, and the run-in that Constable MacQuarrie had had with them, but he shrugged the whole matter off as none of his business. If the police chose to let them remain there, that was their affair. There would no doubt be the usual neglect of their horses and livestock among these people, who in some instances even in this day and age continued to live themselves like animals, but as long as the police were satisfied he did not care. This the curious paradox of the animal doctor who did not love animals.

But he would have denied vehemently and truculently, and had, in just such an argument with Mr. Peddie, that he was a cold or loveless man, and with much outjutting of his beard had cited his affection for his daughter Mary Ruadh as the keystone of his life. He admitted to loving little or nothing else but her.

The minister, with whom he liked to tussle philosophically just because he was so unpredictable, and whose range was from the erudite through the theological to the poetic, had surprised him by indulging in flights of the latter in his reply.

He had maintained that in his opinion one could not love a woman without likewise loving the night and the stars that made even more of a mystery of her presence, or the soft air and sun that warmed and made fragrant her hair; that you could not love a little girl without loving, too, the field flowers, limp and wilted, with which she returned from a foray into the meadow, clutched in a damp hand. And he had said that, too, you would have to feel love for the mongrel she adored or the cat that she carried and even for the stuff of the frocks that clung to her body. He said that if you loved the wild sea lashed in storm, then you could not help loving the mountains too, which, with their swelling hills and jagged and snow-topped peaks swirled by the wind like sea froth, imitated the waves and presented to one's gaze the miracle of an ocean petrified in mid-storm. He declared that you could not love the bright, hot, lazy summer days without loving also the rains that came to cool them; that one could not love the flight of birds without loving, too, the flash of the trout or salmon in the dark pool, that one could not love man, any or all of him, without loving the beasts of the field and the forests, or the beasts without loving the trees and the grasses, the shrubs and the heather and the flowers of meadow and garden.

And here, dropping the rhetorical style into which he had drifted, and truth to tell, held MacDhui rather speechless with astonishment, he slyly descended to a more ordinary and matter-of-fact routine of speech and said that it was difficult to understand how a man could love all or any of these without loving God as well, from any point of view, philosophically, practically, theologically, or just plain logically. The result, of course, had been the usual scornful and indignant snort from MacDhui, who declared that Peddie was better and at least more plausible as poet.

Mr. MacDhui turned in at the wagon track leading to the Birnie farm and, parking the jeep, entered the stone stalls of the stables with an expression of deep disgust upon his face. The stench was overpowering. Fergus Birnie, a wizened farmer, was almost as dirty as his cowsheds. He greeted the veterinarian sourly at the entrance and complained, " 'Tis the lask come back again. The medicine ye gied me was gey unchancy. Ye swyked me wi' it, Mr. MacDhui, and I'll thank ye for the shillings back I laid oot for it."

MacDhui minced no words. With his red beard thrust into the farmer's face as near as he could bear the smell of him, he bellowed, "Ye are a filthy dog, Birnie. Yer cattle are in diarrhea again because ye live dirtier than any swine wallowing out yonder in their ane glaur. I've warned ye often enough, Fergus Birnie. Noo I'm taking awa' yer license for the herd and the selling of yer milk until ye change yer ways."

He went outside and removed a small metal plate from the door of the barn and put it in his pocket, while Birnie stood there regarding him blankly. "I'll be back here within the hour," the veterinarian said. "Call your misbegotten sons over here and wash down these stables and sheds—and yourselves along with it. And wash those cattle until they are clean enough to buss. If there's so much as a smitch of dirt about here when I return, I'll charge ye to Constable MacQuarrie for endangering the public health and it's to jail ye'll all go."

He drove on to the Maistock farm back in the hills, a well-run place, where he complimented Jock Maistock for giving him an early warning of symptoms of the dreaded blackleg in one of his long-horned, fringe-browed Ayrshire cattle. He ordered the suspected animal slaughtered at once, vaccinated the remainder of the herd against the disease, and placed a temporary quarantine on them until time should reveal the extent of the immunity obtained.

He called in at the McPherson chicken farm and calmed the fears of the widow McPherson that she was in for an outbreak of the gapes, a disease of fowls caused by worms in the windpipe. The laboratory report had been negative and the suspected chicks were suffering from a harmless respiratory attack and were already perking up in their isolation pen. MacDhui certified them for release.

He called in at the farm of a wealthy experimental cattle farmer who was trying out a herd in the hills, and gave the cattle the tuberculin test, visited several other small farms and crofters' cottages for minor complaints, and on his way back looked in again on Fergus Birnie's stalls.

Fear of loss of bread and butter had worked upon the farmer, and stables and cattle were in passable condition, clean enough at least for the vet to get on with the treatment. He inoculated each animal, promised to restore the license when the disease had abated, provided the standard of cleanliness was maintained. With a final threat to drop in any day unannounced to check up on them, he climbed into his jeep and headed down the twisting, winding track to the main road back to the valley and Inveranoch.

Yet he dawdled with his driving, hunched about the wheel, dwarfing it with his great bulk, since he was in no hurry to get back. For of all there was to and about his work and profession, this was the part he liked the best, poking about in the rugged hill country above the loch, visiting the farms, and practicing a medicine that was almost human medicine in that it was designed to aid in the protection of human beings, and where the beasts he was called upon to treat were doughty breadwinners and servants of man, from the clever, bright-eyed sheep dogs to the black-faced sheep they herded and the stalwart hardy breeds of Highland cattle.

Here, too, he was received almost with the same respect as Dr. Strathsay, who came out likewise to the back country to deliver their children, set their fractures, or treat occasional illnesses. To the crofter who lived by his sheep, pigs, fowl, or cattle, Mr. Mac-Dhui was a man of importance. A person could well recover from a sneeze or feverish cough, a hand or foot cut with ax or scythe, but a dead animal that could not even be sold for meat was money out of pocket, and an infection which might condemn an entire herd to slaughter was a catastrophe. To them Mr. MacDhui was a man of value and in most quarters he was treated with deference.

Thus it was with reluctance that the animal doctor found himself again in Inveranoch, where his office waiting room would no doubt be filled once more with both locals as well as visitors from as far off as Liverpool, Birmingham, and London, with their useless and pampered pets.

It was a quarter past eleven when he drove the jeep around to the back and, entering the premises from the rear, turned his bag over to Willie Bannock along with a quick account of the morning's doings back in the hills, washed his hands, still talking and giving his assistant no chance to speak, and donning a fresh white coat, made his usual entrance, beard outthrust, into the doorway of the waiting room.

He noted that, as usual, every bench and chair was occupied, the locals in their sober clothes, coveralls or work aprons, the city dwellers more flamboyantly clad, including a lady in a most grand and fashionable hat holding a chocolate-covered Pomeranian with rheumy eyes. And, as always, the sight inspired the same choler and truculent impatience it seemed to bring on every day at this hour. He hated them and he hated his work.

Yet he looked them over and looked again and this time became aware of a startling presence among the group of waiting clients. Seated quietly and most upright on the edge of the last chair at the far end of the room, the very last in line, was his daughter, Mary Ruadh.

MacDhui colored red at this challenging evidence of disobedience, for the child was under strict orders and Mrs. McKenzie knew it too, that she was never to come next door to the surgery, hospital, or consulting room, as many of the diseases suffered by animal patients were likewise infectious and communicable to man. One such tragedy in his life had been sufficient.

As he stared with rising anger, he noted that what had seemed to be an extension of her red-gold hair tumbling down her shoulder was her ginger cat held in her arms close to her breast, its head cuddled under her chin in the manner of a child. Before he could inquire sharply as to what kind of play or nonsense this was, and in direct contravention to his orders, Willie Bannock was at his elbow whispering: "The puir puss has some unco' ailment. It can walk nae mair. The chiel has been biding anxiously for your return."

Mr. MacDhui said, "You know as well as I she is not to come here. Well, since she is here then she must await her turn like the rest." To the woman seated nearest the door he said, "If you will take your dog inside now, Mrs. Kechnie, we'll have a look at those ears," when a great noise and hubbub was heard without in the street, approaching nearer and a moment later the door swung open and it burst in upon them.

It revealed itself to be composed of small children in various stages of excitement, housewives from neighboring cottages, wiping their hands on their aprons, several men likewise attracted by the noise, and at its center the minister, Mr. Angus Peddie, old Tammas Moffat, the blind man who was licensed to sell pencils and shoelaces at the corner of High and Fore streets, and Constable MacQuarrie. In the constable's arms, muddied and bloodied, still in his harness with the guide handle, lay the quivering form of Bruce, the seeing-eye dog that had been provided for Tammas through subscription by the parish at the instigation of Mr. Peddie.

The noise caught Mr. MacDhui as he was closing the door and he returned quickly. "Now, now—what's all this? I'll have no crowding in here. Come, now, out with you, all of you who have no business here, everyone except Mr. Peddie, Tammas, and the policeman. Angus, what has happened?"

"Run over, sir," the constable replied in place of the priest, who busied himself clearing the followers on out of the room. "It happened only a few moments ago, one of the visitors, speeding. We'll have him under lock and key in short order, but in the meantime I'm afraid the dog's done for. Both wheels went over him. We brought him here as quickly as we could."

Mr. Peddie returned, fluttering anxiously. "He's still living, Andrew. Perhaps you can still do something——"

The old blind man was in a state, his knees trembling and his head shaking from side to side, stunned by the accident, lost without his dog, bewildered by the people about. He moaned, "Where is he, my Bruce? Where is he? We were about to cross the street. I heard a noise and a shout. Where is he? Is he dead? What will I do? What will happen to me?"

Mr. Peddie took him by the arm. "Gently now, Tammas. Don't take on so. The dog is still alive and in good hands. Mr. MacDhui will do the best he can for him."

The blind man groped for an instant and then quavered, "Mr. MacDhui? Mr. MacDhui? Is that where we are?"

"Take the dog inside," Mr. MacDhui ordered Willie Bannock, who carefully relieved the policeman of his quivering burden. The veterinarian glanced at the dog as it went by and wrinkled his nose; the life seemed all but crushed out of it.

"Is it Mr. MacDhui?" the blind man said again, and turning his sightless face to him, put out his hand, touched and held his arm. "I'm an old man. I cannot be doing without him. Save my eyes for me, Mr. MacDhui——"

The plea went into the bowels of Mr. Veterinary Surgeon Andrew MacDhui like a knife thrust and turned there, for with three words—"save my eyes"—the blind man had brought back again all of the frustration and failure of his forty-odd years of living. He would have given the next forty to have heard those words spoken to him as a doctor of medicine, to have been called upon to give of his skill, love, and devotion to the saving of human sight, or health, or life itself instead of being asked to put together again, like Humpty Dumpty, the fragments of a dog.

Something of what was passing through his mind communicated itself to his friend, Mr. Peddie, either because of the tortured misery the minister thought he glimpsed at that moment in the face of the animal doctor, or because he himself was so well acquainted with MacDhui's story, since they had known one another since their schoolboy and student days in Glasgow.

It was to the young Peddie that the boy MacDhui had confided his ambition to become a great physician just about the time that the former had decided for the ministry, and they had argued and discussed the respective merits of their chosen professions then, boasted, bickered, and let their ambitions soar.

And it was only Peddie, the young divinity student, who saw fall the tears of grief, rage, and frustration when the tyrannical father cut short his boy's hopes and ambitions and compelled him to follow in his own profession of animal medicine.

"He means——" Mr. Peddie began, but MacDhui quelled him with a look.

"I know what he means," he said. "The dog is three-quarters dead and ought to be put out of his misery, but—I'll save Tammas's eyes if I can——" Then to all of those in the waiting room he shouted, "Go home. Come back tomorrow. I have no time for you now."

One by one they picked up their pets and filed out. MacDhui said to Peddie, "There's no use your waiting. It will be sometime before I can tell. Get Tammas home. I'll let you know——" He went into the surgery and closed the door behind him.

The constable led the blind man out. Peddie was about to follow when his glance fell upon the child sitting quietly in the corner hugging her cat to her and he went over to her in surprise.

"Hello, Mary Ruadh. What are you doing here? Why aren't you out playing?"

She looked up at him confidingly, for they were old and trusted friends, and replied, "Thomasina's very sick. She can't walk at all. I'm bringing her to Daddy to make well."

Mr. Peddie nodded and absent-mindedly stroked the head of the ginger cat and scratched it under the chin as he always did when he came upon the two together. The accident to the blind man's dog, though he had not witnessed it, had been a shock to him, and, too, he had felt the depth of pain of MacDhui's reaction.

Mr. Peddie nodded again and said, "Ah well, I've no doubt he'll put her right again," and went out after Constable MacQuarrie.

6 On that fatal day I awoke, as usual, at dawn and prepared to engage in my accustomed routine—a yawn, a good stretch lengthwise followed by a round humpbacked one, and then escape from the house.

I had a secret exit and entrance, of course, but I could use them only when nobody was about or they wouldn't have been secret any more. These escape routes are the first things we work out in whatever house we find ourselves living. People actually believe they can shut us up. Well, there are few places or houses we cannot get out of if we really want to do so.

I liked to be about early in the morning to see the sun come up, to attend to eliminations, have a quiet once-over-lightly wash to get my fur looking presentable, inspect things on our lane, and exchange a bit of gossip with friends and neighbors sitting on their doorsteps or engaged upon similar errands. This was one of the pleasantest hours of the day and I used to look forward to it. It was wonderful to be free and with no people about. Yet I always managed to be back before Mary Ruadh awakened.

But not that day. I opened my eyes at the usual hour when the curtains drawn over the windows turned from black to gray, tried to stretch, and discovered that I was unable to move my legs. Such a thing had never happened to me before. I was so frightened I simply lay there trembling from head to tail.

I thought perhaps it might be a bad dream, for we have them quite often, dreadful ones in which we are being chased and cannot run fast enough, and I lay there quietly for a little, waiting for it to go away. But it didn't, and as it grew lighter, I realized that there was something wrong with my vision as well. I was unable to see the room or the corner of it, or the window, sharply; objects seemed to be unclear and when I tried to look harder they seemed to vanish. I appeared to be swimming in and out of things.

The next thing I remembered I was lying in Mary Ruadh's arms and she was saying, "Sleepyhead Thomasina. I have been awake ever so long and you are still sleeping. Shall I give you a whisper, Thomasina? I love you!"

I had no time for such sentiments. . . . I was sick, sick, sick and for all I knew, might be dying. There was no use my trying to tell Mary Ruadh that something queer had happened to me, that I could not make my legs work and sometimes could not even see her even though I was lying in her arms. Those are the times when people are our despair, so dense, obtuse, and insensitive are they, and unable to understand even our simplest communications. Another cat would have known at once, at the first sight, the first sniff, the first and smallest impulse transmitted from my antennae to hers, that I was dangerously ill.

The dreadful morning wore on until sometimes I was certain it could only be a nightmare. Mrs. McKenzie came to get Mary Ruadh up, but since the child always carried me about everywhere, I was left to lie there while she was helped to dress; then she came and got me from the bed and carried me into the next room and later lifted me into the dining room and put me on the chair next to hers while she had breakfast and Mrs. McKenzie gossiped with the dustman.

And when I cried Mary Ruadh only said, "Haven't you a lot to say this morning, Thomasina, you naughty sleepyhead——"

At last Mrs. McKenzie finished her interminable chatter, placed my bowl of milk and cereal by the back door in the kitchen, and called, "Come, puss, and get yer porridge——"

I lay on the chair where Mary Ruadh had last put me, unable to stir except for my head and the tip of my tail. I didn't want anything to eat. I only wanted them to find out there was something the matter with me and help me. I cried to them as loudly as I could, but not much sound came out. Mary Ruadh said, "Lazy Thomasina! Go and have your breakfast. Oh, very well then, I'll carry you, you lazy old Thomasina."

She picked me up and went with me to the bowl and put me down next it, where I fell over onto my side. I tried washing, but I was not even able to make the proper movements with my head and tongue. Mary Ruadh said, "Thomasina, you MUST drink your milk," imitating the way Mrs. McKenzie used to say the same thing to her. "If you don't drink your milk, you naughty Thomasina, I shan't take you to the burn this afternoon to watch the trout with Hughie Stirling."

I tell you, it isn't much fun to be lying at death's door, AND at the same time be scolded and told you are to be punished. . . . For there was nothing I liked so much as to squat among the flowers on the bank of the brook that flowed into the river not far from the ruins of Castle Ardrath and watch the trout lying on the bottom, fanning themselves with their fins.

I think I could sit and watch them for days. I never caught any. I did not even try to scoop them out with my paw, though I am sure I could have done so had I wished. I was just happy to lie as still as they. Sometimes when one moved away from the sunny shallows and swam into a deeper portion where it would be merely a faint shadow against the bottom, I would get up and follow it and looking down into the clear water, try to make it out. The children would wander off, exploring, but I would just stay there watching the fish. Tears began to roll from my eyes as I thought that I had probably done this for the last time.

I lay on my side, helpless, no sound coming from my mouth as I tried to call for the help that was not forthcoming.

At last! Mary Ruadh came over to me and tried to set me on my feet, saying, "Thomasina, you MUST eat your breakfast!" and when I fell over onto my side again she became alarmed and when it happened once more called, "Mrs. McKenzie! Oh, dear Mrs. McKenzie; do you come here at once, please, and see what is wrong with Thomasina. Please, Mrs. McKenzie, do come at once."

The housekeeper hurried into the kitchen and knelt at my side. She, too, tried to set me on my feet and when I fell over she said, "Och, Mary, I'm feart oor puss has some unchancy illness. The puir wee thing canna stan' on her ain fower feet."

Mary Ruadh picked me up, half crushing me, crying my name over and over, the tears rolling down her cheeks. "Thomasina—Thomasina—poor Thomasina——!" Like a fool, I purred. I couldn't help myself. Mrs. McKenzie enveloped us both in her arms and said, "Dinna greet so, lassis, for it's mair nor his hert can stan' tae hear ye. Ye maun rin, Mary Ruadh, an' take Thomasina next door tae yer ain feyther, the doctor, wha'll nae doot ken goo tae pit richt whitever ails her. He'll shairly no rail gin ye come there this yince an sae sair an errand."

Mary Ruadh ceased her crying at once. The tears stopped as if by magic and she smiled down at me. "Do you hear, Thomasina? We will go to see Daddy and Daddy will make you well again."

I must confess I did not share her optimism, and quite frankly I did not relish finding myself in the hands of this great, red brute of a man who could not bear the sight of me, and entrusting what was left of my life to him. But there seemed to be no other choice. Had I been able to walk, I should have crawled away to some hole or corner by myself.

Mrs. McKenzie led us next door, Mary Ruadh carrying me, and as soon as we entered I smelled the same medicine smell that was always on Mr. MacDhui and it turned me sick and faint.

I was swimming again, in and out, and I saw blurred, as though looking into the loch when it was stirred by the wind, a room filled with people, some with cats and some with dogs, but I was feeling quite too awful to care much about them. Mary Ruadh sat down on a chair while Mrs. McKenzie explained to Willie Bannock what had happened. I heard Willie say that it was the doctor's morning to be away at the farms, but as soon as he returned he would tell him and the best thing for Mary Ruadh to do was bide there.

Willie Bannock said he did not dare examine me himself, for the doctor would have the rest of his hair off his head if he did, but Mary Ruadh was not to worry, for the doctor was quite the cleverest man in the world where beasties were concerned and would cure me if anyone could. I felt cheered for the first time. I always liked Willie Bannock. Had I but known the part he would be called upon to play!

And so we settled down to wait and I slipped in and out of consciousness, or was it sleep, or was it death? I could not tell, but each time I found that I was still on Mary Ruadh's lap, the lavender scent of her clothes stronger even than the medicine smell, I purred a little.

Have I grumbled a good deal about my lot, about being dragged and carried hither and thither like an old rag doll by Mary Ruadh? Have I done a lot of complaining over being slave to a child and an unwelcome guest in the house of a man who could not seem to bear the sight of me, and whom I disliked cordially? Well, now that the time had come when I might have to leave them, I did not wish to do so.

For to die is to go away from all the people and things that you like; it is a journey from light into darkness, from excitements and play and tastes and smells, voices and affection and the here, into the quiet, endless sleep.

No more to sit in the warm yellow sunlight and wash down one's back with smooth, rhythmic, *satisfying* strokes, never again to stalk through the jungle of meadows of high sweet grass and field flowers, to flash into the air after a grasshopper, butterfly, or buzz-bug, no longer to crouch patiently at the mousehole, whiskers forward, eyes eager, body tensed and waiting, ready to wriggle the back quarters and spring; no more the sweet comfort of the drowse by the fire while outside the rain drums on the slate roof, or the white, wet snow falls silently; not ever again to enjoy that sheltered half sleep through which one hears the reassuring movements of the humans in the house, the sighs, the rustle of newspapers, the click of needles, the sound of human voices. An end forever to the satisfying bowl of warm milk, or the dish of porridge or haddock leavings, the comfort of the leg and ankle against which to rub, the stroking hand, the gentle fingers that understood and scratched where it most itched; not any more to steal the forbidden catnaps in the chests of drawers, to lie on the soft fragrant clothes and smell the sweet lavender.

To die is to depart, to go away from these things forever and become one with the generations that have preceded us since the beginning of time, a whispered memory in the bones and whiskers of the generations to come.

I could admit it now; my world was too beautiful to leave. Life is not easily laid down. Many of our kind have known hard and cruel times, living in cities and towns, starving, cold, wet, beaten, kicked, and set upon, fighting daily for their miserable existence. Yet how, even in those circumstances, we cling to life when even death might seem preferable to the misery and friendlessness of those chilled and lonely lairs, never having known the warmth of a fire, the hearth of a home, or a human hand to fondle us.

How much more, then, did I not wish to go away, to become but one more link in the long, dark chain of another's memory.

Was I still alive, or already dead? It seemed that there was a great noise and hubbub and to-do; I heard the howl of an animal and thought that Anubis, the great jackal, had come to escort me on the final journey. But I was awake and saw the room crowded with people shouting and gesturing, and I thought once that I glimpsed the blue of Constable MacQuarrie's uniform, and the big red bush of Mr. MacDhui as he waved his arms and shouted.

A wave of reassurance swept over me. I thought to myself, Aha! Word has got about now that I am ill, and the whole town, including the constable, has collected to plead with old Red Bristles to make me well for the sake of Mary Ruadh and all the others who have loved and admired me.

And I thought too, Why, Mr. MacDhui cannot *AFFORD* to let me die. I am too *important*. I am necessary to the happiness of the daughter he says he loves so much and over whom he makes such a fuss. Oh, you are safe, all right, Thomasina. No one is going to let anything happen to you.

I could see that; I was swimming into darkness again, but I didn't mind, for I was satisfied. The excitement apparently occasioned by my illness was no more than my just due for the manner in which I always comported myself.

It was sometime later—how much I do not know—that I came awake again in Mary Ruadh's lap, but it was a different kind of awake. I no longer swam in and out of dreams. All was now clear-cut and steady. It was as though my ailment had either worked its greatest harm and was relenting, or, having prepared to kill me, gave me a moment's truce before the end.

Whichever, I now heard, saw, and felt more sharply than ever that I could remember.

It began with the angry voice of Mr. MacDhui, roaring from the door through the empty room to where Mary Ruadh still sat, but now quite alone, with me clutched to her breast.

"Mary Ruadh! What are you doing here still? Did I not tell you to leave at once and never come back here again? Have

I not forbidden you ever to set foot here? Must I remind you about your mo——"

Mary Ruadh was not frightened at all. She interrupted him firmly. "Daddy! Thomasina is *Sick!* Mrs. McKenzie said you would cure her."

"Blast Mrs. McKenzie! Why doesn't the woman mind her own business and do as she is told? Besides, I ordered each and every one to return tomorrow. I have no time for anything now. Be a good girl and go home."

His white coat was smeared with blood like a butcher's; he wore rubber gloves and had a small knife in his fingers. The expression of his face was most wild and fearful and his beard and hair were matted with sweat. He was a sight to inspire terror in anyone, but Mary Ruadh was not at all impressed. She said, "I won't go home. Thomasina is very sick, Daddy. She can't stand up or eat or anything. Please, Daddy, make her well."

Mr. MacDhui fell into talking to her as with an adult, as he so often did with her. "I beg of you again to go home, Mary Ruadh. I am in the midst of a most important operation to save the life of an animal who serves as the eyes to a man who is blind. Which is more important, the eyes of a blind man or that wretched cat?"

"Thomasina," Mary Ruadh replied firmly and properly to this ridiculous question, and Mr. MacDhui for a moment was so exasperated that he could not even speak. But then, strangely, he seemed to calm for a moment and he stared down at his daughter quite differently, as though perhaps he might be seeing us both for the very first time.

"Very well, then, bring the beast in; I can spare you a few moments while the dog is resting. But take your face away from her until I find out what it is that ails her. Do you think that I want to lose you too?"

We went through into an office. The door was open into another room where there was a bright light and a white table with something on it. Mr. MacDhui said, "No, no, Mary Ruadh—you cannot come in here. Give me the cat and wait there."

He took me from her. Mary Ruadh gave me a last pat and said, "There, now, Thomasina. Don't you worry. Daddy is going to give you some medicine to make you all better again. I'll give you a whisper: next to Daddy I love you best in all the world."

Mr. MacDhui took me inside and closed the door. There was a big dog on the white table in the middle of the room. He was bloody. His mouth was open and his tongue hanging out. I saw his eyes and felt sorry for him even though he was a dog. Willie Bannock was there, his apron like a butcher's too. He was giving the dog a damp sponge at which to suck. Nearby was a can and a rag from which came a sweetish, sickish smell. I felt frightened and wished that Mary Ruadh were there.

There was another and smaller table at one side. Mr. MacDhui placed me there on my side. Willie Bannock said, "Och, the wean's wee puss. She was grieving ower it sair——"

"She gave me no peace until I would bring it in. Well, now that it is here——"

But first he went over and gave a long look down at the dog, who rolled up his eyes at him and looked back. Then he came over and touched me. Do you know, his hands were not brutal and cruel at all as I had expected, but kind and gentle. They felt all over my body and pushed deep into my belly and back, where they found a fearful pain that made me cry out. Then he pulled back my lips from my teeth and held my eyes open while he looked into them. He gazed at me for another moment, shrugged, and said something to Willie Bannock that I did not understand but which sounded like "meningeal infection." Then he added, "We had best destroy her——" I understood that last, you may be sure, and went cold with fright and lay there shivering and twitching under his hand.

"Och!" said Willie Bannock, "the wean wull take it gey hard.

Micht it not be some hurt the puss has suffered? If ye would let me——"

"Be still," Mr. MacDhui ordered. "Have we not enough on our plate at the moment? The animal will be better off dead. Mary Ruadh will get over it, or have another——" He went to the door leading to his office, opened it, and stood blocking it so that I could not see Mary Ruadh. But I heard him say, "I am afraid your cat is very sick, Mary Ruadh."

"I know that, Daddy," she replied. "Mrs. McKenzie said so. That is why you must give her some medicine to make her well again."

He said, "I am not sure that I can, Mary. I think perhaps the best thing would be if we were to put her away. Even if she recovers from this attack she may always drag her hind legs. I think you will have to say good-by to Thomasina, Mary Ruadh."

Can you imagine me lying there hearing this?

Mary Ruadh did not understand. "But I don't want to say good-by to Thomasina, Daddy. You must give her some medicine right away and then I will take her home and put her to bed and nurse her."

The dog on the table in the center of the room gave a cough and a moan. Mr. MacDhui turned his head to look at it for a moment. Then he said to his daughter, "That you cannot. Try to understand, child. When people fall ill, sometimes they get well, and—sometimes they die. With animals it is different. It is kinder to put them out of their misery and this is what we will do with Thomasina. We will put her to sleep."

Mary Ruadh understood at last and threw herself at her father, trying to get past him to me. "No, no, Daddy! You *mustn't* put Thomasina to sleep. You must cure her. Mrs. McKenzie SAID you would cure her. I won't let you put her to sleep. I won't, I won't, I won't!"

I heard Willie Bannock say, "The dog's breathing easier, sir."

"Ach!" cried Mr. MacDhui angrily, holding her back. "Do not be a naughty girl and stupid besides. Cannot you see that the cat is already half dead and will like as not die anyway and that I have enough on my hands at the moment without bothering with such——"

Mary Ruadh began to scream. Mr. MacDhui's neck turned as red as his hair with choler as he struggled with her and bellowed, "Mary Ruadh! Go home at once——"

Willie Bannock said, "Sir, if ye would gie me leave tae look after the wee puss, maybe I micht——"

Mr. MacDhui turned on him. "I'll thank you to mind your own business and do as you are told. Take that chloroform can and put that damned cat out of its misery and there's an end to it and we'll get on with the dog. . . ."

An end to it! My end! The end of me, ME! The finish to my life, my thoughts and hungers and desires and pleasures, my *existence!*

I could hear Mary Ruadh struggling to reach me and was helpless to assist. Oh, had I been able I should have jumped upon Mr. MacDhui's back and bitten his neck in two.

"Sir——" said Willie Bannock.

"Get on with it as soon as I have the door closed," Mr. Mac-Dhui ordered.

"Daddy, don't, please—oh, please, please!" sobbed Mary Ruadh. It was a most terrible scene.

Willie Bannock called out to her, "Dinna ye greet so, Mary Ruadh, for ye're bursting ma ain hert. The wee puss will no suffer a bit and that's the promise o' Willie Bannock."

"There now, that's right." Mr. MacDhui tried to comfort her. "Willie will put her to sleep as gently as can be and it will be all over in a moment. Come, now——"

There was a queer kind of silence, as though the child was no longer struggling, or even crying. Then I heard her say in a strange way I had never heard her speak before, "Daddy—Daddy—if you put Thomasina to sleep, *I'll never speak to you again as long as I live——*"

"Very well, then," Mr. MacDhui shouted, "I will not bide defiance. Go home!" and slipping quickly inside the room, he closed the door and locked it.

Then I heard the pounding of Mary Ruadh's fists upon the panel of the door, and her frantic screams.

"Daddy—Daddy—please don't kill Thomasina! Oh, please don't! Thomasina—— Thomasina——"

Mr. MacDhui jerked his beard at Willie Bannock—"Get on with it then, Willie"—and began to peer down at the dog again. Then he picked up some kind of instrument, and I knew that Mary Ruadh and I had gone out of his mind.

Willie Bannock came over to me, uncorking the canister, poured out some of the sweetish-smelling liquid onto a cloth and held it over my nose, and I, too, no longer cared about Mary Ruadh or what would happen to her, or anything but me, me, ME, for I was going to die and I did not wish to, I wanted to live, to live, to LIVE, even if I were to be sick, crippled, an outcast, I wanted to live——

I couldn't breathe; I was choking, my senses began to swim. I heard Mr. MacDhui shout, "Come, come, man, don't be all day about it. I need you over here——" Mary Ruadh's fists were still pounding on the door from without—I heard one last despairing cry, "Thomasinaaaaaaa!"

And then it grew darker and darker and quiet, and all quiet and all dark, and I, Thomasina, was no more.

7   At the rear of the animal clinic and hospital of Veterinarian Andrew MacDhui of Inveranoch-by-Loch-Fyne was an incinerator and a refuse heap. Toward evening it was the duty of Willie Bannock to dispose of the contents of this refuse heap consisting of waste from the hospital as well as the corpses of defunct animals that had either perished in the course of illness or were done away with at the advice of Mr. MacDhui.

A stickler for hygiene, the veterinary would order these corpses placed outside upon the refuse heap immediately, to await the attention of Bannock via the incinerator, a most modern electric one, complete with smoke arrestor. A high fence enclosed this area from the prying eyes of neighbors, and a lower one partitioned the grounds behind the little hospital from those of the dwelling next door, where Mrs. McKenzie waged her perpetual battle to wring a few herbs, flowers, and vegetables from the soil.

Mrs. McKenzie's formal gardens were often the subject of some banter on the part of Mr. MacDhui and even the Reverend Peddie when he came to spend an evening with his friend, but both were also just men who praised her flowers and occasional radishes, onions, and carrots when there was a yield. Thus death and life were close neighbors in the back areas of the twin houses on Argyll Lane.

The rear of the hospital was, of course, strictly off limits for Mary Ruadh, but with due care and appreciation for the sacredness of Mrs. McKenzie's horticultural ventures she had the run of the yard back of her own house and often played there.

There was yet an hour before lunch and Mrs. McKenzie was still at her ironing in the upstairs spare room devoted to her department of sewing, mending, frilling, etc., and so she did not hear Mary Ruadh when she returned empty-armed from the tragedy that had befallen her next door. Tears fell in a steady stream from the eyes of the child and she sobbed, not in paroxysms, but without end, as though to weep was now the normal state of being for her, as before it had been to laugh, gurgle, or smile, as though she would thus weep forever after.

For all her tears, there was a certain grim purposefulness in her movements, and as she entered the house she hushed her sobbing until it was no more than a whispered exhalation of the breath that expressed her misery.

Closing the door behind her softly, she hearkened for a moment to the doleful kirk-humming and ironing noises that proceeded from above and betokened what Mrs. McKenzie was safely about. Then she continued on through the dining room, into the kitchen where Thomasina's untasted bowl of milk still remained on the floor, left there by the housekeeper in anticipation of her return from the doctor, cured and with an appetite.

Filled with the necessity and daring of her determination, Mary-of-the-red-hair stepped over it without so much as a glance and went out the back door, proceeding at once to the fence that divided the area from the one next door. It was higher than her head. She searched about until she found a wooden box or two and soon made a steps onto which she climbed, and looked over. There, atop the refuse heap, stretched out as limp as an old, discarded fur piece, lay the remains of Thomasina, the eyes closed, one lip partly withdrawn from the white teeth.

With a cunning never before in her life called upon, but which seemed to be there, ready-made for her need, Mary Ruadh appraised the rear windows of both houses. No figures appeared at any of them. Mrs. McKenzie's ironing continued to occupy her, as the sound of the doleful melodies testified—she always sang hymns when she ironed, probably an association between the hot iron and the probable hell-fire to come—and if her father and Willie Bannock were about, they were still in the operating room, which was in the front part of the house.

Swiftly the little girl scrambled over the fence and, hanging by her hands, dropped onto the ground on the other side. Then she ran to the heap and took her dead from it, like the Scottish women of old who came forth after dusk when the battle was over and the clan corpses lay stark upon the battlefield, sought out and claimed their men, and silently lifting them in their arms, carried them away for burial to some secret grave that would not be found or desecrated.

Mary Ruadh draped Thomasina about her shoulders as she had so often done in life, quickly arranged another steps of boxes, kicking them away when she had done with them, and climbed back into Mrs. McKenzie's garden, removing the evidence there too, with a care to spare the housekeeper's show of asters, stock, and sweet William. There was a door in the rear wall of the garden and, clutching the still-warm body of the cat to her breast, she quickly let herself out through it, closing it quietly behind her before she began to run.

The lane was at the south end of the village, where the tide crept upon a pebbled shore and small sand runners and sea birds pecked, yet nearby, at no more than a hundred yards distance and swelling upward from the sea, there was a copse of pale gray ash, smooth-boled beech, and gnarled oak. It was for the shelter of these woods lying at the entrance to the grounds of the dark-stone manor house that Mary Ruadh ran as fast as her legs could carry her and her burden, as though if she did not reach it quickly, her grief would overtake her and catch her naked in the open where she could not hide.

At the foot of a giant oak, so ancient that its roots, like the veins on the hands of the very old, stood out from the ground to form ridges of moss-covered shelter for a small body, Mary Ruadh flung herself beside the limp remains of her friend, for on that day that had begun so ordinarily and usually, like any other day, she had lost all she had.

It was not only her cat, her dear companion and friend of whom she had been bereft, but also her father.

Now, however, she wept over the immediate, beating the earth with her feet and fists and burying her face again and again in the soft, still flank, crying aloud over and over the beloved name of Thomasina until her wailing filled the grove and reached the ears of Hughie Stirling and brought him over to where she lay, to discover the cause.

Hughie, the son of the laird who lived in the large manor house in the park on the slope a mile or so from the shore, was a boy of nine, attractive, with blue eyes of unusual clarity and color beneath dark brows and long lashes with curly, crisp dark hair, high brow and cheekbones, and square chin of the Campbells, to whom the Stirlings were related. A leader in the parish school, which he attended with youth of all degree and scale in and about Inveranoch, he was enjoying the lazy days of summer-holiday freedom.

Clad in shorts and white T shirt, Hughie went over and knelt by the side of the child and examined the still figure of the cat. "Hello, Mary Ruadh. I say, whatever has happened to Thomasina? Is she dead?"

Mary raised her tear-stained face to see her friend and protector kneeling above her. She poured out her heart to him. "She was sick and Daddy killed her," she wailed. "She couldn't stand up this morning and when I took her to Daddy to be cured he made Willie Bannock put her to sleep. She's dead."

The boy examined the cat more closely and gave the body a tentative prod. Even then, the sweetish scent of the chloroform still clung to it, and he wrinkled his nose. His quick mind saw and understood what might have happened. Raised among animals, dogs, cats, horses, livestock, and in an atmosphere where they were less sentimentally regarded, he knew how quickly a beast could be stricken with a sudden illness and an agony which made shooting a mercy. He said, "Maybe it was all for the best, Mary Ruadh. Maybe Thomasina was so sick your father couldn't help it——"

The child turned upon him a look of mingled despair and sudden hatred, and Hughie, more sensitive than most, was at once aware of his error, yet helpless in the new onrush of tears and sobs, as, confronted with this last blow, the seeming disloyalty of her friend, she cried, "Daddy didn't even try. He just went and had her killed," and then added, "I hate you too——" In a paroxysm of grief she buried her face in the ground and dug into the moss with her small fingernails.

At a loss for what to do, Hughie first pronounced a valedictory over the departed: "She was a good cat," he said, and then added, "Don't cry so, Mary Ruadh, you'll do yourself a hurt. Maybe Thomasina is in heaven already with wings and is having a lovely time chasing winged mice."

The little girl glanced at him for a moment with slightly less hostility, but the tears and sobs that wracked her slender body continued. Hughie could not find it in him to care greatly about the cat, for his world was full of assorted cats who lived in the barns and stables or snoozed in the kitchen behind the stove and one was like another, but the awful grief afflicting Mary Ruadh touched and frightened him. . . . He was near enough her age to understand the greater tragedy of her loss of trust in her father along with the companionship of her pet. Plainly there was nothing more to be done for Thomasina, but he was deeply concerned over Mary Ruadh. He had heard of people dying from a broken heart. Unless something were done to help her, his playmate, over whom he had exercised a kind of benevolent watch throughout the summer and who was strangely dear to him, might lie there until she wept herself to death over the corpse of her cat.

So much a man already was Hughie Stirling that in this crisis he remembered that where one could not console the next best thing was to distract. He said, "I'll tell you what we'll do, Mary Ruadh. We'll give Thomasina the best and most wonderful funeral any cat ever had. Mary! Mary Ruadh! Do you hear me? We'll give Thomasina a grand burial this very day. I know just the satin box at home that will do for the casket. We'll put in the young heather for her to lie on, which is as soft as down—well, almost, anyway. Are you listening to me, Mary Ruadh?"

She was. The agony of sobs began to diminish and when she raised her head and tear-brightened eyes from the gray-green sward of old moss and roots, the anger and mistrust had gone from them. There was definite interest.

Hughie pressed the advantage thus won and at the same time began to fire his own vivid imagination, for even as he invented and improvised to divert the unhappy child, the idea began to sound most promising and might result in a "do" that would be talked about by his companions in Inveranoch for a long while to come.

"Look you, Mary Ruadh," he cried, "we will have a procession through the town as long as when Lachlan Dougal was buried and you shall wear widow's mournings and walk directly behind the casket, weeping."

Mary Ruadh was now frankly interested in the proposal. She picked herself up and knelt facing Hughie, so that the body of

Thomasina lay between them, unnoticed. "Will I wear a veil and a black shawl? Mrs. McKenzie has a black shawl."

"Of course," Hughie assented, delighted with the results he was achieving and more and more carried away with his idea, "I'm sure I can find you a veil of mother's. We'll have the funeral this very day in the afternoon. I'll ask Geordie McNabb, and Iain will bring his brothers and sisters and others from the school."

Mary Ruadh asked, "Can the dustman come?"

"Well, no," Hughie replied, "he'd very likely be working——" Then as the child's face fell, he had another brilliant inspiration. "Do ye ken Jamie Braid, the son of Sergeant Braid, father's piper? He's been learning the pipes and already has unco' skill. We'll have *him*. Can ye no' see Jamie in his kilts with his ain wee pipes (Hughie when he became excited was apt to drop somewhat into the local way of speech), wi' the ribbons flying and his bonnet set saucily upon his knob, piping MacIntosh's Lament?"

Mary Ruadh was quite enchanted now. Her eyes were as round as half-crown pieces and tears no longer flowed from them.

Hughie continued: "Well, and I'll wear my formal kilts with skean dhu and sporran and every one on the street will turn his head as we go by and say, 'There goes the poor widow MacDhui, a-burying of her dearest Thomasina, God rest her soul, foully done to death——'"

"Really truly, Hughie?"

"Oh yes," the boy promised, "and I'll tell you something more." He was now beginning to be intoxicated by his success, not only in distracting his unhappy friend, but at the same time organizing a splendid afternoon's entertainment, far better than the somewhat tame picnic he originally projected. "We'll make a headboard!"

"What is a headboard?"

"Well, it's a kind of a thing like a gravestone when you are in a hurry. It tells about the person who is buried there." Here his own blue eyes widened and he ran his fingers through his crisp, dark hair, seized by the throes of literary composition and quite forgetting his prior judgment rendered upon the assassination, namely that Mr. MacDhui probably had no alternative but to put the cat out of its misery. "We'll print on it, 'Here lies THOMASINA—*MURDERED* July 26, 1957.' "

Mary Ruadh's gaze was brimming with worship. The word "murdered" had the proper ring to it and filled her with a curious satisfaction. She looked down now upon the still form of Thomasina; gloomy retrospect enveloped her once more as the memory of the morning's events returned and out of it she pronounced sentence: "I'm not going to speak to Daddy ever again."

Hughie nodded absently. Mary's family vendettas were her own affair and none of his concern as long as they did not impinge upon the grandiose funeral, the details of which any Highland chieftain or even modern local inhabitant of Inveranoch would have been proud.

He went on creating: "I'll play the part of the minister and make the speech at the graveside—'ashes to ashes and dust to dust' and then all about what a wonderful person the deceased was and how sorry everybody is that she has gone away to her heavenly reward. And after that we'll cover over the casket with earth and lay our wreaths and flowers on the mound and we'll come away from the grave to a merry tune skirled by Jamie Braid, after which we'll have a feed of some kind, a real draidgie, and all be gay and cheerful again. Well, what do you say to that, Mary Ruadh?"

By way of reply she put her arms about Hughie's neck, leaning over Thomasina to do so, and hugged him, for he had brought something interesting and exciting at least momentarily into her life; something was about to happen in which she would play a major role and she was quite enchanted with the program.

"Good lass!" Hughie said, produced a reasonably clean handkerchief, wiped the tear stains away from her face and held it for her to blow her nose. Then he brushed her pinafore where leaves and moss had clung to it, ran his fingers through her bright hair and, setting her then upon her feet, said, "There you are, then. I'll be taking Thomasina home to prepare the casket; I'll find Geordie McNabb and he'll wake over her whilst I'm having lunch and getting everything ready. Jamie's brother Ewan will go and tell the others. We'll all meet here when the tower clock strikes three, and form up for the procession."

Nearly a head taller than she, he stood smiling down at her, mightily pleased with himself and with her as well. It would be a great "do" that afternoon, probably the best of the whole summer, one that would be remembered and spoken about by him and all his friends and companions for long after. He picked up the remains of Thomasina and flung them unceremoniously over his shoulder and, turning Mary in the direction of her home, started off with an affectionate pat on her shoulder. "Off you go now. And remember, wear your mourners and don't be late. A funeral's no good at all without the widow or weeping relatives. And this one is going to be quite the best ever."

Mary Ruadh now trotted off obediently. She did not so much as turn around to give the departed and departing Thomasina another glance. *That* Thomasina, the one she had carried about with her and nursed and played with and cuddled to her at night, was "gone away" never to return, which was her understanding of death, for it had been explained that her mother had "gone away" when she was very little. Gone away, then, meant not there any more. Yet the yearning remained, and her left arm, over which Thomasina was usually draped, felt strangely unweighted. She had had no experience of knowing what to do with a love when once the object of its power and intensity of feeling was no longer there to receive it.

And then there was something else besides the death of a person, since Thomasina was in many ways more real to her and human than many of those surrounding her, and that was the death of a love, which had happened almost simultaneously and was still going on within her.

The gentle, the all-wise, all-knowing, all-powerful, all-loving father had "gone away" too. In his place there remained only the mountain of a man with the bristly red beard, thunderous voice, and iron arms who had set her on the other side of the door while inside his office the murder of Thomasina was taking place. As Mary Ruadh thought of the lovely word that Hughie had used and which was to become a permanent part of Thomasina's memorial, a slight smile of satisfaction played about the corners of her otherwise innocent mouth. The grownup who had brought about the disaster of Thomasina's departure was still to be dealt with.

8   Mr. Veterinarian Andrew MacDhui missed the funeral procession of his late victim that afternoon, for he was engaged in proceeding through another part of the town in the company of his friend, Mr. Angus Peddie, to bear good news to blind man Tammas Moffat, that, in a sense, he would "see" again.

Mr. Peddie dropped in upon the animal doctor shortly after three o'clock to learn what had happened to the Seeing Eye dog he had been instrumental in securing for Tammas, who was one of his oldest parishioners. He was a wonder, was Mr. Peddie, and known all over the town for being able to smooth-tongue a person out of a contribution when there was a need. His way was to appear to be letting you in on something, like a hot tip on a horse, or a winning pools combination; he made you a cheerful and excited co-conspirator and before you knew it, you had parted with a pound note, or ten shillings, or whatever you happened to have on you at the moment. And blessed if later on, when the results showed, you didn't feel as though you *had* won something.

The minister found Mr. MacDhui looking tired but satisfied when he entered his consulting room. Peddie said, "I stopped by, Andrew, to ask whether there was any news of Tammas's dog—good or ill——"

MacDhui savored for a moment the pleasure of the reply he had to make, before indulging in it, but the smile of gratification would not stay from his full lips; his strong teeth showed through the red bristles of beard and mustache as he replied, "Well, I have saved Tammas's eyes for him. The dog will manage. In three weeks it will be good as new."

Mr. Peddie said, "Ah. Oh, splendid, splendid. I knew it would be so. I was expecting it."

MacDhui cocked his head at his friend. "Your faith, Angus, flatters me, but I might tell you——"

"Oh," Mr. Peddie said innocently, "I wasn't referring to you in this instance, I meant——"

MacDhui barked a savage laugh. "Hah! Your Higher Power, of course. Well, my friend, if you knew how many times the slender thread of your faith came near to being snipped. It's almost a miracle the beast is alive——" He checked himself as he realized what he had said.

Peddie nodded cheerfully and said, "Well, yes, that's what I asked for. In matters of faith, narrow escapes don't count. It's the results really that matter, isn't it? As for what you would do, I had not the slightest doubt. Shall we go and tell the good news to Tammas? He was in a great torment of worry when I left him. It is a terrible thing to be blind and alone. The dog was his comfort as well as his guide."

"Eh?" MacDhui asked. "What do you want me along for? You can tell him——"

"It was to you he said, 'Save my eyes,'" Peddie replied, "yours was the hand and the skill——"

"Oh, was it? I thought you just said——"

"Well, actually, it was you who said it. But then you wouldn't be the first to confuse the Power and the instrument. Come along, Andrew, it will do you good to see the old man's joy."

MacDhui grumbled in his throat, but he put on his old tweed jacket with the leather patches at the elbows and pockets, loaded a great black pipe, took up his twisted blackthorn, and said to Peddie, "Want to have a look at him first?"

He took the minister to the hospital part of the house. The dog lay on clean straw, his hindquarters encased in bandages and plaster. But his fine eyes were alert and keen, the pointed ears picked up, and he beat a rat-tat-tat on the floor of his cage with his brush at their coming, whined and scratched at the door with his forepaws.

"What a beautiful sight," Mr. Peddie said, and feasted his eyes on it.

"Don't pamper or spoil him," MacDhui said to Willie Bannock, who was hovering nearby. "He's been trained for but one man."

Tammas Moffat lived on the other side of town, the poorer section, and as the two men walked thither chatting, the faint wind-borne skirl of pipes in lament reached the ears of Mr. Peddie for a moment and he paused, cocking an ear. "That's strange," he said, "I thought I heard the sound of MacIntosh's Lament. But there's no' any burial today I know about."

It was the faraway mourning of the little pipes of Jamie Braid, the sergeant piper's son, in funeral procession for Thomasina that had reached his ears. Mr. MacDhui hearkened for a moment and then said, "I hear nothing," and they continued on.

Tammas Moffat had a room on the second floor of a two-story house of whitewashed stone and roof of gray slate in a section of such tenements, drab new council houses and the remains of several wartime Nissen huts. Several small children were playing in the dust before the house; a gray and white gull with but one leg perched on the chimney and an old woman in cap and apron was sweeping the doorstep.

"Is Tammas Moffat in?" Mr. Peddie inquired.

She paused in her sweeping long enough to say, "I have nae doot ye'll be finding him at home. I have not heard him stirring."

"Thank you. We'll go up then. The veterinary here has good news for him about his dog."

"I'm sure your news will be welcome. He was badly put out when the poor bonnie creature was hurt. I haven't seen a sight of him since he came home."

They entered and went up the dark, narrow stairs, Peddie leading. There was no sound in the house whatsoever, though from below they could hear the dry susurrus of the sweeping and the rumbling of the baker's van and then the beat of the gull's wings as it flapped off the chimney.

Mr. Peddie paused irresolutely, halfway up the stairs. He turned to look back at the veterinary. "Andrew——" he said.

"Well——?"

The minister did not continue, and the silence became oppressive. The rotund little man was much more of an instrument of communication from outside sources than his outward appearance indicated or most people suspected. He was an extraordinarily kind and sensitive man, so sensitive that at that moment he felt his soul go sick within him.

"Andrew," he said again, but changed his mind when the looming bulk of his friend pressed him on and he merely said, "Well, we will see, then." He proceeded to the top of the stairs and with heavy, lagging footsteps walked to the end of the landing and knocked at the closed door. He waited for a moment, with ever-waxing certainty, and when there was no reply, opened the door gently and went in, followed by MacDhui.

"Oh dear," said Mr. Peddie softly. The blind man was sitting in an armchair facing the door. His head had not fallen forward but somehow remained in the position of listening, the strained, anxious listening for footsteps that had been his attitude when death had come to him.

Mr. Peddie bent down and looked up into the sightless eyes to see whether there was any sign of life remaining, but MacDhui hurried forward and placed his head on his chest to listen, and then took his wrist to try to find a pulse. The sere arm was still warm, but there was no heart within the body.

"He's gone," MacDhui said. "He cannot have been dead for more than an hour or two."

Peddie nodded. "Yes, I know. I—knew."

MacDhui suddenly emitted a harsh and horrid laugh that exploded through the silent house. "I saved his eyes!" he brayed. "Where is your God now?"

He shocked Mr. Angus Peddie into anger. The minister drew himself up to all of the dignity his size and form could muster, his round face flushed, lips quivering, eyes behind the spectacles hot with indignation.

"Be quiet, Andrew," he cried, "and be damned to you for your impertinence."

"Aye, you can damn, but you cannot answer me. What was the good of it all? What is the use of the work I have done? What kind of God do you worship who permits the dog to live and the man to die?"

"Is God your servant then, or is He God?" cried the minister, in most un-Peddie-like outrage. "Must He admire your work and flatter your vanity like a father to a child, or is He to go about His business?"

"Tosh! Is this then your great design that we are supposed to worship and believe in and give thanks for?"

Ruffled and angry, they faced one another across the unheeding form of the old man, who sat like one in quiet judgment upon their folly and the humanity of it.

MacDhui shouted, "What has he to be thankful for?" his beard thrust out toward the top of Peddie's head.

The minister was the first to recover. He said, looking at the dead man, "He was an old man; he died peacefully; he died with hope in his heart." He looked up at MacDhui and said, with such contrition in his mild eyes that MacDhui was similarly moved, "I should not have lost my temper, Andrew, I am sorry."

MacDhui said, "Well, nor am I proud of shouting at you over this poor fellow. I am sorry I was impertinent to you——"

"Oh, you weren't to ME," Peddie said. "That wasn't what I meant. It has unstrung us both, except I knew as we climbed the steps that it would be so." With the greatest gentleness, he closed the eyes of the blind man.

He paused momentarily in the middle of this act as he was struck by a thought that seemed unrelated at the time and which yet he knew somehow was not. He said, "Mary Ruadh was in your waiting room this morning. She told me her cat was ill. Whatever became of it?"

To MacDhui, the morning's scene sprang to life again with painfully vivid clarity. He saw and heard again the hurt and moaning dog upon the table, with Willie Bannock sponging its tongue and muzzle, and his daughter standing outside the door with the dying cat in her arms. For, he told himself again, it had been dying and no doubt of that, and mentally his tongue formed the exact long medical term for the nature of its illness. No one knew whether it was communicable or not, and there had been Anne, his wife. He smelled again the sweetish scent of the chloroform rag as Willie Bannock had carried out his orders and destroyed the animal, and in his ears once more was the helpless drumming of Mary Ruadh's fists upon the panels of the door and her fearful cries. He wished he could get the sound of the thrumming of those tiny hands upon the door from out his ears.

He replied, "I had the animal put away. I suspected a meningeal infection. Better safe than sorry. Besides, I was attending the dog and couldn't take the time. I have no doubt the beast was better off dead."

A frown clouded the serene face of Mr. Peddie, and he pulled at his lower lip with his fingers, a trick he had when he was greatly worried. "Oh dear," he said. "Oh dear!" For he seemed to be feeling into the future again; sometimes he wondered whether he was not in some manner related to the Norms the way occasionally for him the carpet of tragedy seemed to unroll, long before those came along who were to tread it. The cat was dead then, and the child would be desolate and there would be far-reaching consequences.

"Oh dear me," he said again, and, still fingering his lip, walked out of the room and down the stairs, with Andrew MacDhui following him, uncomprehending.

9   The procession led by Jamie Braid, the sergeant piper's son, wound its way through the town by way of Rob Roy's Square and across the quay northward, skirting the shore where, guided by Wolf Cub Geordie McNabb, it crossed the river by the old saddle-back bridge and then turned westward into the mouth of Glen Ardrath, passing on the way the gypsy encampment in the valley, with its many caravans whisping smoke out of crooked pipe chimneys.

Jamie was a thin boy and so tall for his age of eleven that he seemed to be proceeding on stilts, though they were actually the long shanks of his legs striving to reach into his body. His face, too, was thin so that when he puffed out his cheeks to inflate the tartaned bag beneath his arm he appeared to have a crab apple stored in each one, while his eyes threatened to bulge from their sockets. But he had a fine head of thick, wavy brown hair and his Glengarry was cocked bravely upon it at the angle proper to his father's late regiment. There were streamers attached to it and streamers and ribbons, too, from his pipes, and his kilts rose and fell as he walked the slow piper's tread he had learned from his father.

Behind him, bearing the sacred pennant of their Wolf Cub troop, marched Geordie McNabb with several of his fellows in uniform, lending the military touch. Next came the hearse itself, drawn by four of the younger girls of the first class of the Inveranoch elementary school, hitched tandem fashion in pairs. This was a fine bit of improvisation on the part of Hughie Stirling in the brief time between luncheon and the appointed hour for the cortege to form. Having to compromise between a caisson and a cart, the casket containing the mortal remains of Thomasina reposed on the body of an old toy express wagon he had routed out of one of the potting sheds.

The casket itself was a large wicker comfit case lined with satin that Hughie had seen in his mind's eye as left over from Christmas and stored away against the day when it might be turned into a sewing basket or something else useful. The children had lined it with young heather to make a bed and upon it had laid Thomasina curled into a lifelike position as though merely sleeping, and over all, as a covering, and in lieu of the flag with which the military draped its coffins, a length of the Stirling tartan had been flung.

Directly behind the casket marched Mary Ruadh in her weeds, on the arm of Hughie Stirling, who had seized upon the occasion—and in the face of certain retribution to follow—to make of himself the glittering star of the production.

Thus he had filched his formal attire from the chest where it reposed in moth balls waiting to be called forth reverently by The Games, or a visit from someone royal. There was genuine Mechlin lace at his sleeves and his jabot was a thing of frothy splendor against the short-cut black velvet jacket with the silver buttons bearing the crest of the Stirlings. He wore dirk and sporran and white gloves; his bonnet was set on the back of his crisp, curly hair and he carried an authorized prayer and psalm book. Rarely had such a handsome lad been put together, or one who lent such tone to a funeral.

Mary Ruadh was draped in Mrs. McKenzie's best black wool shawl, which, being too long for her, was wound first around her shoulders and then her waist, with a curiously oriental effect.

Hughie, on his successful raid through the grownups' quarters of the manor, had unearthed a purple veil of his mother's, or more likely his grandmother's, since it was the kind ladies used to wear when they went motoring in the open juggernauts of the twenties, and this was now draped about Mary Ruadh's head in the manner of a summer thundercloud through which gleamed the red-gold of her hair, like the sunshine attempting to break through the storm. The effect was both startling and striking, if not exactly funereal.

And finally, trailing behind the principals and dignitaries, followed those adherents of the Stirling coterie, members of the school, plus a scattering of summer-visitor children raised by word of mouth and bush telegraph, who came in what they had, or thought appropriate to the burial ceremony of the best cat in Inveranoch, and as the imposing cortege moved onward, it attracted quite a few more to walk in its wake, so that it numbered a good twenty by the time it burst from the northern boundaries of the town and headed for the glade in the glen that Geordie McNabb had suggested as the burial ground.

The town itself took the masquerade in its stride and as indicative of the changing times when youth no longer walked solemnly in the steps of its forefathers as well as a to-be-endured manifestation of that summertime madness which descended upon Inveranoch with the influx of holiday visitors. A nearsighted old gentleman standing by the side of the road removed his ancient, flat-topped, curl-brimmed bowler as the cortege went by, several people smiled indulgently, and that was about all the stir created by the affair.

But if this was but innocent children's fancy and play to the onlookers and a delightful afternoon's make-believe for the participants, there was one to whom it was not, and who in a small way was trailing the remnants of the complete innocence of childhood out behind her as she proceeded on the arm of the exquisitely beautiful Hughie Stirling. This was Mary Ruadh MacDhui, for after all it was not only her cat but her alter ego that lay in the silk- and heather-lined casket beneath the Stirling tartan, and which was now on its way to being buried forever.

The place of interment had been chosen by Geordie McNabb, who remembered it from the visit he had paid to the Red Witch with his injured frog, and approved by Hughie Stirling. The proximity to the strange weaver of Glen Ardrath known as Daft Lori held no more terrors for Geordie, for he had looked upon her, but it did add a fillip of further adventure for the others.

Thus the little Wolf Cub guided the procession to that faery circle in the woods, the glade formed by beach and ash and presided over by an enormous graybeard of the forest, an ancient oak beneath which surely Rob Roy, the outlaw, wrapped in his cloak of invisibility from the King's men, had slept on many a summer night.

It lay some thirty yards or so off the main path that climbed up into the glen, but away from the burn, whose rushing descent made cool music to background the doleful droning of the pipes. A shaft of the late-afternoon sun like theatrical illumination, penetrating the glade, cast its spotlight upon the colorful pageant of the children.

It splintered on the silver buttons of Hughie Stirling's jacket and the silver chain of his sporran, and a darting arrow of reflected light caught in the eyes of Daft Lori almost a quarter of a mile away, higher up in the darker, deeper woods above, where she roamed in quest of mushrooms and varieties of herbs. She wore a skirt and shawl of green wool that she had woven herself and her red hair was bound up in a green cloth. Over her arm she carried a light basket in which reposed a small knife and trowel.

She was as sensitive, alarmed, and wary as a young deer at this unusual invasion of what had come to be regarded as her territory. Not even picnickers came to this part of the glen. The wind now brought the cry of the pipes to her. She glided forward cautiously, moving from tree trunk to tree trunk, ever closer until she paused behind the smooth bole of a copper beech clinging to the hillside a hundred yards or so from the glade, into which she now had an almost unobstructed view.

She thought at first it was a faery rout, a visit from the Little People of another age, for she believed in them, and in gnomes and pixies, nymphs and brownies, elves and hamadryads, and angels too, and frequently communed with them. She caught flashes of the gay colors, the lace, velvets and tartans, the ribbons and streamers; the pipe music smote her with melancholy and sadness and, because of the distance, she did not at first recognize the intruders as children.

But later it became plain to her, and though she could not hear their voices clearly or immediately distinguish what was toward, or fathom the meaning of the curious ritual they seemed to be performing, she remained quietly concealed in her vantage point until at last the meaning of it all was revealed.

In the Scottish thoroughness of his organization, Hughie Stirling had even thought to provide a gravedigger, one of the young sons of the gardener at the manor, who had marched, spade over shoulder, in the procession and proudly too, and now his moment of importance had come, as Hughie intoned solemnly, "Gravedigger—do thy job."

The lad made the earth fly in the glade and soon had prepared a creditable shallow pit into which the wicker basket was lowered as the principals and mourners stood about the graveside enjoying themselves thoroughly. Mary Ruadh watched the proceedings silently, with round, serious eyes, and no one could tell what she was thinking.

Hughie Stirling, somewhat out of his depth with ritual, scattered some earth over the top of the basket, saying, "Return unto the ground from which you wast ta—I mean *thou* wast taken, for dust thou art and unto dust returneth, amen," and then remarked, "I think we ought to sing something——"

No one had thought to bring a hymnbook; none of them was strong on doxology. One of the girls struck up a tentative quaver, appropriately nasal, but was not followed and subsided in embarrassment. It was bullet-headed Geordie McNabb who came to the rescue, his years as yet unencumbered by theology or ritual, and having been asked for a song, launched into the "Bonnie, bonnie banks of Loch Lomond," in which they all joined with the fine fervor of familiarity. The strains of it drifted up the glen and reached the ears of the Red Witch of Glen Ardrath herself, resembling a hamadryad, watching from behind her tree.

When the last chorus had been rendered, Hughie cleared his throat preparatory to delivering the valedictory he had been composing in his head during the march and wherein he felt more at home.

He said: "Brethren, friends, and fellow mourners at the graveside. We have come here to bury Thomasina and to praise her. Thomasina was the beloved cat of our own grieving Mary Ruadh MacDhui here, who I am sure you all know. Anyway, here she is. Thomasina was a good cat. She was one of the best cats in Inveranoch. I suppose it would not be too much to say that she was one of the best cats in all Argyllshire. Those of us who knew her well were proud to be her friend and now that she has been taken from our midst her place cannot be filled and we all feel for her sorrowing mother."

Several of the visitors were so overcome by this eloquence that they burst into applause at this point to be quelled by a stern, "Not yet, you cutts." When they had subsided he continued.

"Thomasina never did anything wrong such as catching birds or biting or scratching anyone. If she caught a mouse in the cellar she would bring it to Mary Ruadh to keep, instead of eating it herself. She was never cross or bad-tempered. She was also very clean and was always washing herself. She liked Mary Ruadh best of all, but she would also let other children pick her up and play with her, which most cats, as you know, will not do. She could purr louder than any cat I ever heard and the expression on her face was very becoming to her. She had a few faults, but I will not mention those here. Her mortal remains now lie at our feet, but her soul has already ascended straight to heaven, where it will sit at The Right Hand and will wait there until Mary Ruadh's soul comes to join hers when they will be together again, forever and ever, amen!"

The amen having given the direct clue that he was finished, all of the children now responded to the magnificence of this speech with prolonged rounds of applause that awakened the echoes until the pattering appeared to bounce from side to side of the rocky glen. Hughie Stirling bowed modestly and said, "We'll fill in the grave now, but first, Mary Ruadh, you ought to attempt to throw yourself weeping across the casket like the bereaved always do."

Mary Ruadh said succinctly, "I don't want to. I want to go home."

It had been a long day and tremendous things had happened to her, how tremendous she was not yet even aware. The procession and the funeral had been exciting and diverting; she had enjoyed being the center of attention, but now she wished to be at home, where her sense of loss could be more sharply identified than here. The connection between her and the object in the basket was no longer clear, since she could not see it, the glade was foreign and the sun was beginning to sink. Teatime was coming on, tea in the warm, friendly surroundings with Mrs. McKenzie about, her dolls on their chairs and Thomasina opposite her with napkin tied about her neck and the little bit of pink tongue showing between her lips as it always did when there were goodies to be shared. The picture in her mind was so vivid that it startled her momentarily into tears that had not yet flowed since the burial had begun. She knew in her heart that Thomasina had gone away, or had been "put away" and that she would never see her again, but she could not do her mourning here and in front of them all. It was at home she had her rendezvous with misery.

It had all been rather much for one small girl to grow so old in the brief span between morning and afternoon. . . .

Truth to tell, Hughie Stirling was wanting his tea too, and in a shed back behind the manor there was a cache of food, the funeral feast or draidgie he had organized, and it was getting on. Too, he had noted the glint of tears again in the eyes of Mary Ruadh and so he remarked reasonably, "All right. You don't have to. Sometimes the bereaved bears her sorrow nobly and silently without unseemly show of emotion. Fill in the grave, Gravedigger."

The earth rattled against the top of the wicker basket and loosely filled the shallow trench, forming a small mound. The gravedigger, too, was anxious to be getting home. While Hughie Stirling set up the previously prepared headboard some of the children collected wild flowers, and as Jamie Braid intoned an appropriate pibroch, they circled the grave and deposited them thereon.

"Now," ordered Hughie, "you play something cheerful." Obediently from Jamie's pipes skirled the strains of the Campbelltown Reel, and he stepped out, bending his long stork's legs high at the bare knees, puffing and swelling. Hughie Stirling took Mary Ruadh by the hand and they and all the rest filed from the scene and vanished down the glen path in the direction of Inveranoch.

Nothing stirred in the glade for what seemed like a long time; the rays of the sun now seemed directed upon the greensward stage from the wings rather than the flies and threw elongated shadows out of which the girl known as Daft Lori came gliding, a green wraith, hardly to be seen, hardly to be heard.

She trod the ground lightly and timidly, first about the edges, then, drawn by curiosity, she crossed the little clearing and kneeling swiftly on the ground beside the newly turned earth she studied and read the inscription composed by Hughie Stirling and painted on the headboard marker, somewhat plagiarized from sentiments he had encountered on the gravestones of Inveranoch churchyard.

"Here lies Thomasina, born Jan. 18, 1952, FOULLEY MURDERED July 26, 1957! Sleep Sweetly Sainted Freind."

All fear and perplexity now went from Lori's countenance, while a smile of sympathy and understanding illuminated her face and sweetly rueful mouth. Yet a moment later her expression changed to one of uneasiness again as she reread the marker and the words "FOULLEY MURDERED." They seemed to cast a chill upon her and upon the glade and turn it from a place of innocence where a children's summer masque had taken place to one where something evil seemed to lurk. She shuddered and rose to her feet, took a few steps, and then turned back, unable to tear her eyes from the grim legend.

She knelt again by the graveside, her hands folded, her plain face and clear brow contracted with concern as she bent over it. A children's play burial had taken place there, of that there was no doubt, but who and what had been buried there? She wished she knew what she should do. For an instant her fingers closed over the trowel reposing in the basket on her arm, yet still hesitated. Whatever lay beneath the ground was dead, and it was with the living that she had to do. She continued to kneel there undecided.

10 All in all, it had been a bad day for Veterinary Andrew MacDhui and he returned home to supper late and in ill-humor after awaiting the arrival at the blind man's home for Dr. Strathsay, the older of Inveranoch's two locum tenens, and also in company with the Reverend Peddie, giving police testimony on the discovery of the body of Tammas Moffat.

The death caused no surprise. Tammas was eighty-six. It was Dr. Strathsay's preliminary guess that the old heart had failed from strain and shock, which the autopsy would later confirm, but MacDhui could not find interest in such details. The man was dead and there was an end to it; he need not have died, for MacDhui had brought his Seeing Eye dog back from the brink, performing, as he had indicated, a miracle of modern canine surgery. Tammas had passed on without ever knowing this. MacDhui was not pleased with fate, or circumstances, or luck, or whichever it was that appeared to doom him to play just the opposite role to that of his youthful ambition, to be a healer and doctor to humanity.

He was still preoccupied as he swung open the low wooden gate leading to his house and marched up the narrow flagstone walk, and halfway there he paused uncomfortably as though he had forgotten something, looking about him, then searching his pockets and thereafter his mind, but for the life of him he could not think what it was, or why he had thus stopped. It was only later he remembered. Mary Ruadh had not been there to greet him on the pathway, her ginger cat hanging over one arm like an extension of her hair.

Nor was there any charging of small feet accompanied by shouts of "Daddy—Daddy!" as he crossed the threshold. However the odor of food cooking cheered him somewhat and he went to his quarters for a scrub-up and thereafter proceeded to the dining room where a startling sight met his eyes.

Mary Ruadh was seated at the table set for two. She was still clad in mourning dress—that is to say, Mrs. McKenzie's black shawl wound about her middle and the purple cloud of veiling, now draped about her head and shoulders madonna style.

In the background Mrs. McKenzie was seen through the door to the kitchen in the throes of those final hurried operations of opening and closing oven doors and potlids that indicates food is about to be got onto the table. She glanced in anxiously through the door when she heard Mr. MacDhui enter and then quickly ducked back to her tasks. Mary Ruadh did not look up at all when her father came into the room, but sat staring before her, her hands in her lap.

MacDhui called out cheerily enough, "Hello there, chicken: what's all this? What are you dressed up for, Queen of the Night?" He cocked his head and beard at her and said, "Becoming, though not exactly cheery in view of the kind of day I have had. How about putting it off now that we are about to have supper?"

The child raised her head and with a steady and unwinking gaze, looked at him, through him, and beyond him, and did not reply.

Mrs. McKenzie put her head in through the door, an anxious and worried expression upon her long, narrow face and called, "Mary Ruadh, are ye no fer sayin' good evenin' tae yer feyther?"

She shook her head in silent negation. Her father chose the

wrong moment to be jocular, and an even worse allusion. "What's the matter, child? Cat got your tongue?"

Two tears welled forth from the eyes of Mary Ruadh and rolled down her cheeks, and her small face puckered for a moment as though she were about to break down. Had she done so, it might have been better, for the huge man would then have gathered her to him, hugged and cuddled her, chucked her under the chin and comforted her and in the familiar warmth of his arms and affection, her new resolve might have melted then and there and been dispelled.

But the tears were not followed by others, the crying wrinkles smoothed from the young face, to be replaced by an expression of stony distaste as she stared her father down.

The veterinarian called in the direction of the kitchen, "Mrs. McKenzie! I say, Mrs. McKenzie—what ails the child?"

The housekeeper came into the room, nervously wiping her hands upon her apron, looking with worry as well as some trepidation upon the likes of a Mary Ruadh such as she had never encountered before. The plain but rather sweetly odd face of childhood innocence, the perpetual breathlessness of one who lives half in, half out of childhood's dream world, had turned hard and curiously adult in its concentration. It was as though a changeling had suddenly entered the house. Mrs. McKenzie was a simple soul and quite out of her depth in the presence of primitive emotions.

She tried to explain: "The puir bairn's in a swither o'er the death o' her pussy baudrons. She canna thole to be wi'oot." When the veterinarian stared at her blankly she added, "The weans had a funeral for her this afternoon. The procession was a grand yin wi' Jamie Braid, the sergeant piper's son from the great hoose blowin' the deid march. I dinna ken whaur they laid her awa'——"

Impatiently Mr. MacDhui said, "Aye, aye, but that is nought but a lot of children's play and gilaver. I wish to know why she will not speak with me? What has got into her?"

Mrs. McKenzie looked from the glowering child to the glowering man and plucked up her courage. "The bairn maun be ower fashed. O' course she couldna mean it, but she said ye mur—I mean tae say, she said ye put away her puss baudrons Thomasina, and she will no speak tae ye again 'til ye bring her back."

MacDhui stared unbelieving, a flush mounting from out his shirt collar and rising to join the flame of his hairline. In the tragedy of the blind man and the part he had played in it, the episode of the chloroforming of his daughter's cat that morning had been pushed clean out of his head.

It is most certain that under other circumstances, relaxed in his home as he was inclined to be after a hard day's work and in the company of the child he adored, MacDhui would have handled her otherwise and, with sympathy and understanding, cozened her out of her rebellion.

But the reference to what had happened that morning triggered once more, it seemed, the whole train of his frustrations brought on by that fatal plea of the blind man. It was those eyes he had been working on when his daughter had brought in her sick cat to shake him from his dream. He saw again the stark, stubborn, and stricken face of the child when he had pronounced the death sentence upon her pet, as he had felt compelled to do upon so many others that did not seem worth trying to save. Once more he heard the helpless beating of her small fists upon the surgery door and her exhausted, hysterical sobbing. Into his mind again came the haunted eyes and face of old Mrs. Laggan and her fat, wheezy, miserable dog, and the gentle words of his friend, the Reverend Peddie: "But it was *that* poor, wretched dog she loved——"

And he saw the picture of Tammas Moffat prepared to wait into eternity, sitting in his chair listening with his sightless eyes turned toward the door.

And so he turned upon his child as he did upon clients who tried his patience, red beard thrust forward belligerently, eyes hot, voice harsh, and shouted, "What nonsense is this, Mary Ruadh? I'll not have it, I say. I told you your cat was so ill it would likely have died in a day or so anyway. Now then, go at once and remove those garments and then return to the table and be yourself."

To his surprise, the child arose obediently, left the table, and went to her room. MacDhui suddenly felt as foolish and contrite as he had the moment he had found himself shouting at his friend Peddie across poor Tammas Moffat. When she returned a few minutes later without the offending clothes and took her place once more he said disarmingly, "See here now, Mary Ruadh, I'm sorry about Thomasina, but there's no restoring her and that's a fact. Now, how would you like another cat for your own, a wee kitten? When I looked in upon grocer Dobbie on the way home he offered me a choice out of six his mother cat brought in. And one of them was snow white without a mark. Now what do you say to that?"

Mary Ruadh said nothing. She did not seem to have heard. Mrs. McKenzie fluttered in the doorway with the tray. "Well, bring it in then, bring it in," MacDhui ordered impatiently. While they were eating he tried again. "Well then, a dog perhaps for a change, to be all your own, eh, Mary Ruadh, and follow you about wherever you go? Or perhaps a Siamese. Now there's an idea and I believe I know where I might lay hands on one. Come, Mary Ruadh, speak up."

The child turned her silent, stubborn gaze upon her father, and in her eyes was the look of one who regards a stranger. She compressed her lips tightly. MacDhui felt himself swept by that exasperation verging upon blind, helpless rage that adults experience in the presence of a willful and headstrong child whose contempt is written clearly and plainly upon its face. With an enormous effort he controlled himself, said no more, and fell to eating his supper, but with small appetite. Silence hung heavily over the room, and in the kitchen he had a feeling that Mrs. McKenzie was going about on tiptoes.

Mary Ruadh ate too, but listlessly and without looking at her father. Sinkingly MacDhui thought, What if she were really never to speak to him again—ever ever again? What was one to do? What would he do? What *could* he do? But it was, he told himself, preposterous and impossible, all over that damned cat that he should have turfed out of the house long ago as a potential carrier of disease germs and a general nuisance. The love she had lavished upon the beast should be reserved for a human—she treated it almost like—— With an effort MacDhui wrenched himself away from remembering Mary Ruadh's mother holding the child in her arms and the look upon her face before she died. And for one fearful instant he asked himself the question, denying it with all the inner vehemence he could muster—whether he had put the cat away out of jealousy——

At this point the uncomfortable and unhappy silence was broken shatteringly. "Please, Mrs. McKenzie," Mary Ruadh said, "may I have some more apple pudding?"

This unexpected end to the painful quiet, and the child's addressing herself to the housekeeper, he found a hundred times more unbearable and exasperating than if she had not spoken at all. Yet the first words she had said since he had returned home that evening appeared to him to offer an entering wedge. Thrusting his beard across the table at her, he said, "Have you not had sufficient apple pudding, Mary Ruadh?"

The child stared at him across the table and remained silent. At the kitchen door Mrs. McKenzie hesitated with the basin in her hands, not knowing whether to bring it or not.

"If you wish more dessert, Mary Ruadh," MacDhui said meaningfully and with all the pregnant emphasis and self-satisfaction of the chess player who, seeing game in hand, announces his first "check!" to his opponent, "If you wish more, you will ask it of me."

Again the child turned her gaze upon her father and this time added the insult of a longer study, quiet, thorough, contemplative, and hostile.

The figure and person of her father was there, the great, warm, smelly man to whom she cuddled, in whose beard and neck she buried her face, in whose arms there was safety, whom sometimes when she felt overwhelmed with love for him she could not hug strongly enough or devour sufficiently with kisses. Yet none of these feelings were present in her now.

For she was now looking upon the person who had ordered the life of Thomasina taken and the remains flung out upon the refuse heap, and who, now that she was punishing him for it, was not playing fair. And this was perhaps an even harder blow, for in the world in which she lived and played, the world of Hughie Stirling and Geordie McNabb, and even the simple world of Mrs. McKenzie, the great and unforgivable crime was injustice. The line between fair and unfair was sharply demarcated. Adults as well as those of their own age who crossed it were judged.

She was still too young to know the word "blackmail," but at her father's words she was filled at once with an understanding of its power and essential loathsomeness and she felt herself smitten to the heart with a sadness and disappointment almost deeper than any she had already experienced that day. First it was her cat which had been killed and now her father, for the look that she was giving him was his execution. In the short space of a few hours the two beings that she had most loved in all the world and who had made up the sum of her security and happiness had been taken from her.

Thereupon Mary Ruadh took her double loss with the quiet and deceptive stoicism of which the sensitive child is capable when deeply hurt. Withdrawing her damning gaze from her father she said, "No, thank you, Mrs. McKenzie, I don't think I want any more apple pudding."

Andrew MacDhui flung his napkin to the floor, scraped his chair angrily back from the table, and without another word turned and slammed out of the room and the house. She had defeated him. To his "Check!" she had replied with "Checkmate!" He knew that she had been aware of the logical extension of his gambit to, "If you wish anything to eat, you will speak to me and ask ME for it"—and that he would not browbeat her into compliance, for in those stony eyes and grimly clenched lips he had read her unshakable determination to be starved rather than speak to him.

Hot flushes of rage surged through him as he flung himself along the foreshore of the loch in a kind of desperation effort to work off the anger of the wish to pick up the child and shake her. It was MacDhui's first experience with that peculiar kind and intensity of rage that comes to a parent when he encounters some trait or facet of his own character mirrored in his child.

The sea loch was bathed in that unreal light of Northern lands where the clock calls for darkness or dusk to settle, but night refuses to fall and the falsely greenish glow of day lingers long after the sun appears to have sunk beneath the horizon. The loch was not moving, for the tide was slack. A heat mist covered it so that it seemed less a body of water and more a low-lying cloud through which extended the barren rocky mountainsides and peaks rising from the opposite shore. To the north MacDhui could see the lights of Inveraray and the crown of The Cobbler, that massive mountain barring the road to the Trossachs, colored by an afterglow.

It was the hour of stillness, but the scene had nothing to say to the disturbed and unhappy man who walked with such violence that the calm of the Highland twilight could not penetrate to bring him ease or relief from the events of the day. And a good deal of his temper stemmed from the fact that these exacerbations should have happened to him, for by and large he considered himself a good man and not deserving of the attentions of ill-intentioned fate, or just plain bad luck. Since he did not believe in God, he must needs ascribe it to one of these, or else face the fact that he brought it all upon himself, and such acknowledgements were not for Andrew MacDhui.

At last he walked himself into a more quiet state. His passions cooled and he turned his footsteps homeward, telling himself that this was in all likelihood not the first time there had been a row between a father and a child; by morning it would have all blown over; she would have forgotten it and things would again pursue their normal course.

11 My name is Bast-Ra.

I am the cat goddess of Bubastis.

My other titles are "Lady of the East" and "Lady of Sept," that is, of the star in the eastern heavens known as Sept. And I am known as Sekhmet-Bast-Ra, the tearer and renderer, destroyer of Apophis, the evil serpent at the foot of the celestial tree.

My father is Ra, the sun, my mother Hathor, the moon. Nut the sky goddess is my sister; my brother Khonsu, exorciser of evil spirits.

I am a most powerful and important deity.

I was goddess in the temple of Khufu in the year 1957 of the Twelfth Dynasty, and the thirteenth in the reign of Sesostris I, may his ka never grow less. And when I died, my mummy was wound round and round with plaited linen ribbons, and dyed one red, the other blue; a mask was made for my head, with golden eyes and whiskers of golden wire and the ears stiffened so that they stood up as they had when I was alive and worshiped and called sweet and dear, and holy and all powerful.

The coffin case in which my mummy was placed was of carved sandalwood and was so cunningly carved that it resembled me to the life so that when my priestesses looked upon it they wept and said, "That is indeed Bast the Beautiful, our beloved," for so I was known. And the coffin was painted in lemon yellow and white and cinnabar, for such was my coloring of mottled lemon and madder, with white feet and breast and with green eyes, and therefore the eyes of the coffin were two emeralds.

Harps and trumpets played and the sound of the sistra were heard above the weeping; the priests shaved their heads and eyebrows when they brought me to my vault, but my ka ascended and remained in the keeping of Isis-Hathor, lady of heaven.

I was born and lived a goddess. I died. I was resurrected and born again.

The months of my festivals in Bubastis were April and May, and in my honor the inhabitants of the city gathered in a great fleet of ships with banks of oars flashing in the sunlight; the boats were painted blue and crimson and the sails dyed in purple or ocher and the vessels of the priests and priestesses gleamed with gold and silver, all, all in my honor, so great a goddess was I.

And as they sailed up the two branches of the Nile that enclosed my island city, they played upon drums and tabors and castanets, the heavenly voices of my priestesses rose above the silvery shivering of the sistra.

And I, within the sanctuary of my temple, waited and dozed and slept and dreamed those dreams that were to become the destinies of men, spinning those strands that enmeshed them from the cradle to the grave. For I was and am Bast, the living goddess.

My temple was the most graceful of all those in the city, and light and airy, with the inner court surrounded by a grove of trees whose branches gave cool and pleasant shade. My temple buildings were more than two hundred yards long and the same in width and the columns of my inner sanctuary were of porphyry. My priestesses were chosen from the most beautiful and pure maidens of Bubastis and they served me night and day.

All this is changed now. My temple is a small stone house. I have but one priestess. Her name is Lori. She has not the beauty of my twelve priestesses of the Nile, for her skin is fair, her eyes as light as mine, and her hair the color of the copper ingots that used to lie gleaming on the wharf at Bubastis. But she is kind and sings to me beautifully.

I am in a different country and a different era. It is 3914 years since last I dwelt on earth. It is the year 1957 once more, the fourth of the reign of the great Queen Elizabeth II in the ninth Dynasty of Great Britain. I live in the cold northland of Scotland. It is here in a forest hut by a brook close to an arm of the salt sea that my ka has been returned to me and I live again. The others of our household do not believe in me and laugh when I tell them I am a goddess. Even my name is changed, for my priestess calls me Talitha. But I am Bast-Ra. I still dream the dreams of the destinies of men and spin the strands of fate by which they are ensnared. And someday they will know my power here as they did in my first incarnation by the banks of the Nile.

It is a curious thing to be a goddess, all knowing, all powerful— and to be a cat as well.

Sometimes in my temple sanctuary in Bubastis I used to laugh softly to myself at the cleverness of men. Oh, so, so clever! They walk erect, they use their hands and wear clothes; they have invented speech and writing, they can send messages from afar, fight wars, sail the waters, ride the land, store up food and wealth and rule the earth, and yet they prayed to us.

For all of their being men and lords of the earth, they came a-begging to us of favors, burned incense to us, brought us gifts, sang to us and danced and staffed us with priests and servants.

When I heard them approaching, tambours beating, sistra shivering, trumpets braying, when I smelled the incense from afar and heard the measured tramp of feet and the voices raised in songs of praise, and thought ahead to the address of the supplicant; "Oh, great Goddess Bast, oh, Bast-Ra, oh, great Sekhmet-Bast-Ra, child of the gleaming lady of heaven, protector of thy heavenly father the sun, oh, perfumed one, wondrous one, look with favor

upon this humble supplicant and grant him this one prayer——"
it was hard for me to repress a snigger.

But at other times, deep in my heart, I pitied them.

For it must be painful to be at once so great and yet so small, to be lord of all and yet master of nothing, to walk the earth as conqueror and yet never for a moment to live without fear.

But I, Bast-Ra, feared no one or nothing because I was a goddess and lived in a shrine, and because of me, all cats in the land might walk free of fear. Whoever harmed one of us was punished by death, imprisonment or banishment, for those were times when men were wiser and trod softly in the presence of their superiors.

In the days of my godhood when even my father the sun god Ra was referred to as The Great Cat, I represented the beneficent powers of the sun; I concerned myself with the fertility of the fields and the fertility of women; I was beauty and voluptuousness; the hieroglyph for my name was the picture of a jar of perfume; I comforted those maddened by the moon and contended with the desert jackal for the soul of the world.

For the jackal is a liar and the Dog of Evil. Our world was directed by the gods of which I was one, and not a bird, not a lamb might be injured without justice being visited upon the perpetrator for his violence. In the eternal struggle between good and evil, those who believed in the gods knew that in the end virtue must triumph and we must win. Storms darkened the air, winds wrought their havoc, thunders and lightnings split the heavens, yet in the end the sun returned and sailed its bark across the arc of the sky, the moon and the stars came out again, and all was right with the world once more.

Those were the days of my power, when I could blast, forgive, arrange, preordain, punish, reward, grant favors and protection, produce sunshine for picnics and moonshine for lovers, when men swore "By Great Bast," and I could work wonders when I felt so inclined.

All this seems changed now and my powers are diminished, for no one believes that I am a god or worships me or prays to me, not even Lori, though she loves and serves me and in her way performs those rites of morning and evening that I require. To remain a god, to keep the god-power, people must believe you are and that you hold it, as they did when I reigned in the temple of Khufu in far-off Bubastis. There was in us all, in the scarab, the mouse, the crocodile, the cow, as well as us cats, the sacredness which gave us the Power to be not as man or beast, but as God, the power to hearken to the groans of man, his fear and despair, and twist the skein to alter the threads of his destiny. For so he believed. We lived, we died, we gods and goddesses, but the Power stayed and so will remain as long as there is yet one who believes and calls upon it.

It was strange that my priestess Lori did not know me for who and what I was, for she was a human whom the Power once at some time had touched. She lived more in my world than in hers. It was the world of little beasts to whom she was nurse, mother, friend, and priestess, serving them. Like us, Lori saw and communed with things out of the past, the little forgotten creature-gods that once had been man's friend and allies on earth, elves and pixies, naiads of the brook and hamadryads of the trees, brownies and kobolds, nixies and sprites, faeries and things of the air, visible and invisible. And she saw and conversed, too, with that new heavenly host, angel and archangel, cherub, cherubim, and seraphim.

Besides which, my Lori was a weaver. She spun wool into thread and gathered the thread into skeins, the skeins she wove upon her hand loom into cloth, and the cloth she returned to the sheep farmers and herders up in the hills and they gave her food in exchange and enough money for her needs and sometimes they brought her things for the hospital where she tended the sick and injured beasts who came to her, or that she found in the woods;

bandages and medicines, and simple grease and tallow from which she made the salves and unguents that she used out of the herbs she found and collected in the forest.

In Lori's household, in Inveranoch of Argyllshire, Scotland, in the summer of the year 1957, I, Bast-Ra, goddess of Bubastis, who reigned in Egypt in the year 1957 before the coming of the Christ god, I set up my sanctuary and entered into my temple again.

I remember the day when my ka descended from heaven out of the hands of Hathor and entered a body once more, and Lori brought me forth.

She set me down before the little stone cottage that was to be my temple and said to the others, "Here is a new friend for you, she shall be called Talitha." The others were very ordinary beasts, three cats, a kitten or two, a jackdaw, a mangy Scots terrier, an old sheep dog, a hedgehog and a squirrel. The cats spit at me, the dogs barked, the jackdaw screeched, the hedgehog rolled himself into a ball, and the squirrel chattered and scolded.

Lori said, "Come, tis no' a kind way to welcome a stranger. Are ye not ashamed of yourselves?"

One of the cats, the yellow Tom with a scarred face, whose name I later learned was McMurdock, put his back up, but Wullie, a plain-looking ordinary black with no breeding whatsoever, but who was the oldest there, remembered something of manners and came forward and said, "Well then, before we welcome you, who are you and where do you come from? Also what do you want? As you can see, there are quite a lot of us, there is hardly enough to go around now and we could do very well without another, thank you."

I replied, "I am Bast-Ra the sacred, the beautiful, the lustrous and the all powerful. I am Sekhmet-Bast-Ra; my father is the sun, my mother the moon; his name was Amen-Ra, hers Isis-Hathor. The world rides upon the arch of my back. I am sacred and venerated and called 'Lady of the East.' "

The two kittens stopped playing with their tails and ran to their mother, a long-haired tabby named Dorcas, and Wullie said, "Can't say I ever heard of them, but I'll admit you talk big for one small, ugly she-cat——"

The anger of the gods flamed up in me and in another instant I should have summoned Horus the falcon to plummet from the sky and peck out their livers. But I decided to give them one more chance before blasting them.

I fluffed up my tail and fur and stretched to my full height. "I am Bast-Ra, the divine, goddess of Bubastis, bow down before me and worship; pray that I do not smite you from the face of the earth, fools, blasphemers, unbelievers, prostrate yourselves, look not upon my divine countenance lest my glory blind you."

I was greeted with roars of laughter, I, the sky goddess returned to earth. They shouted with laughter, holding their sides and rolling on the ground. The magpie flapped its wings and screamed, the squirrel ran up a tree, and the dogs became hysterical, the Scotty coming at me in short rushes, pretending to nip at my tail, until, not even bothering to blast him, I hit him a practical one on the nose that gave him something to think about.

But the others were still shouting and rolling about, thumping one another on the back and wiping their eyes. Dorcas hurried her kittens away, while making motions toward her head as though I were mad. McMurdock said, with his back suddenly arched, "You try any blinding around here, my lass, and you'll get what for."

There was then nothing left for me to do but to blast these impious ones, shiver, shrivel, burn, and slay them and let their carcasses be fed to the sacred crocodiles. I called upon Sopdu and Anubis, Maahes and the great and fearful serpent Apophis and his brothers, Besit and Mehen, Ammut who devoured the souls of the condemned and Aden, the demon of sickness.

Yet none came and nothing happened to the blasphemers.

The earth failed to open and swallow them up. They remained there unharmed, howling with sacrilegious laughter.

It was my first experience with those who did not believe. I was about to be beside myself with indignation, outrage, and shame when Lori settled the matter. She picked me up, saying, "Well, if they won't be having you or be polite, you shall be my ain puss then," and she took me inside the little temple where she dwelt and where I was the only one allowed, though I was not permitted to go abovestairs where she slept. Instead she made me a shrine in a basket by the side of the fireplace in the room next, where her loom was kept, and I accepted her as my priestess and soon busied myself to find out where I was and to what kind of life I had returned.

It was a strange and very sacred place, this forest temple, for few if any humans ever seemed to come there and then only when they brought a sick dog or injured wild thing to be healed. The shepherds from the hills, and the crofters from the wild country up glen sometimes came across some little beast of field or forest that had been caught in a trap, or suffered an injury. Then they rang the silver Mercy Bell that hung from a branch of the great covin oak that stood outside my temple, and Lori came forth to learn their needs.

They seemed to be afraid of Lori as indeed they should be of one who was a priestess now devoted to a true goddess. Rarely a shepherd would stay to have a wound upon his dog's leg or foot bound up, but mostly if they had some small wild thing they would leave it at the foot of the rope beneath the bell and vanish before Lori appeared. Lori never answered a knock at her door, or a shout, but only the silvery ringing of the Mercy Bell, which reminded me of the shivery glitter of the sistra of the priestesses, shaken in my honor in that Bubastis, removed from me by nearly four thousand years. Later Wullie, who was a most knowledgeable cat, even if plain and common, told me that Lori had found the bell in the woods far up in the glen and that it had once been used by Rob Roy, the outlaw, to warn him of the coming of the King's men.

There were three rooms on the ground floor of the stone house I called my temple; the kitchen, then the one with the fireplace, which was my shrine, and the big bare room where the loom was kept. There was a room up the stairs, a kind of loft where Lori slept, but I was not allowed to go up there even though I was a goddess.

Behind the cottage there was a small barn of stone with a slate roof and here it was that Lori had her hospital for hurt things and there were several places on the roof where the tiles were off that McMurdock showed me, where one could climb up and peer down inside and watch Lori as she tended the sick and the wounded. There was a rabbit and several shrews and field mice, some birds that had fallen out of their nests, and a young stoat that had an injured foot. There were many vacant pens and small wire cages, but Mac tells me that often it is quite full.

Oh yes, it is "Mac" and "Wullie" now, and even Dorcas, who is a snob, is quite friendly and lets me wash her kittens sometimes; the dogs have learned to keep their places. I never spoke of Bubastis again, or my godhead, and nothing more was said, even though the jackdaw would sometimes flap his wings when he saw me coming and screech, "Hi there, Goddess, old girl." The dogs thought it was very funny, but I must say the cats rallied round and didn't even seem to mind that I lived in Lori's house.

But I knew who I was and who and what I had been and that someday I would show them my power and what a goddess can do when she is determined. The Power would return and I would spin and weave like Lori and once again twist the threads of human destiny and bind the cloth of life.

My ka felt at peace and satisfied with my new body. There were no mirrors in Lori's house, but from what I saw of myself looking into the pool made by the burn near to the house, I was beautiful and not unlike in color and markings what I had been when I was the adored of all and man's hope and guide in my temple by the Nile.

There I had inspired love in my priestesses, who, in private, when there were no priests about or temple officials, used to stroke me and cuddle me and scratch me under my chin and let me listen to their gossip, where you may be sure I learned a great many things I used in my goddess business, and this was the case with Lori too, for she spoiled and hugged me and, when she was at her loom, sang to me, for she soon learned that I loved to be sung to and was used to it. Her voice was high and sweet like the reed flutes of Bubastis and sometimes when I shut my eyes I could fancy myself back there again in my sanctuary, listening to the music of my worshipers come to adore and petition me.

I was not unhappy in my new incarnation as Talitha. Lori was attentive and kind. There was sufficient to eat, but it was forbidden to go out and catch something even if I had wished to do so, for Lori could not bear to see harm come to any living thing and through that alone I should have recognized her as a priestess and one of us.

And so, soon, my life was proceeding peacefully and happily and would have no doubt continued to do so but for the coming of the Man with the Red Beard——

12 Mr. MacDhui was marching truculently through Dumreith Street, bareheaded, thrusting through the summer drizzle, having just paid what he considered an utterly useless call upon a spinster who kept her cat in a child's crib, when a black umbrella sailed up alongside him, and he heard the quick patter of feet attempting to fall into stride and keep pace with him.

"Would you wish me to try to have a word with the child?" Mr. Peddie asked, with no preliminaries or greetings, and then added seemingly inconsequentially, "You know it will be time soon for her to be thinking of attending the Sunday school."

The second speech served to distract and take the sting out of the first query, and the roar that had been gathering within MacDhui deflated, since he was not sure whether he had been presented with one idea or two.

"I am not at all sure I want her to attend the Sunday school," he growled, but then considered in softer vein, "I suppose, after all, her mother would have wished it and seen to it if she were here." And a moment later, "Confound it, man, why do you have to come a-bothering me at this time with such business?"

It had been an unhappy fortnight for Mr. Veterinary MacDhui, living as an outcast in his own house, eating his meals in the chill of his daughter's stony glare and silence, and listening to the nervous remarks of Mrs. McKenzie trying to fill the breach.

He had not again attempted the blackmail of compelling her to ask him for food. She had called his bluff from the first and *that* battle was lost. None of his attempts to break her silence had succeeded. She had suffered him to bathe her, but when he demanded that she say her prayers she had sealed her lips tightly, driving him from the room in a rage. His temper was not lessened when later he heard her saying them for Mrs. McKenzie. Nevertheless he had listened to the list presented for God's blessing. He rather expected the omission of "Daddy," but when he did not hear his name immediately after "Mummy in heaven" it came nevertheless as a shock. He considered prayer to be mumbo jumbo and supplication unworthy of the dignity of man. Standing there in the hallway between his room and his daughter's, he was filled with a miserable sense of desolation and a queer fantasy of a change being made in the books of heaven, a notation that he need no longer be considered when blessings were being dispensed.

"Really, what I would speak with her about," Mr. Peddie confessed, seeing that he had disarmed his friend somewhat, "was her not talking to you. It is an unhappy affair when a father and a daughter so young are separated by a wall of silence in their own home—whatever the cause——"

"Whatever the cause—whatever the cause," MacDhui repeated savagely, "whatever WHAT cause? There is no cause but her own stubbornness." He turned a frown and a glare upon the little dominie, but found the black umbrella momentarily interposed. He shouted down through it, "If I have failed, do you suppose you can do any better? She has the stubbornness of—of—of myself, I suppose, come by honestly. You will not succeed."

"Have you tried the child with another animal?"

"Oh, aye. The other night I brought home a beautiful beast, as beasts go, a Siamese kitten, an animal of breeding and pedigree. When I placed it in her lap she brushed it off onto the floor and ran screaming to Mrs. McKenzie and buried her face in her apron.

She screamed until I took the animal out of the house and put it in a cage next door. The neighbors thought, no doubt, I was taking a strap to her. It might be better perhaps if I did——"

"You cannot beat a child into loving you," Mr. Peddie remarked.

MacDhui nodded gloomily. Was love then such a tenuous thing as to be destroyed by pique or anger or disappointment? At that moment he felt the ache in his arms for his child, and his heart was filled with longing for the wondrous softness and fragrance of the skin at her temples when he pressed his lips there. And yet he knew that when she stared at him, the eyes hard in the young face and the lips tightly pressed together lest any vagrant sound escape, he would be possessed by the black rage of frustration and hatred for this female counterpart of himself. What was the tie that had bound her to that wretched cat?

And it was true, the neighbors were talking. The gossips had spread the tale of the silence in the house at the end of Argyll Lane and that Veterinary MacDhui's daughter had not spoken to her father since he had needlessly chloroformed and killed her pet cat. It just went to show, the gossips further said, that when people remarked that Mr. MacDhui was altogether too quick with the chloroform rag it was the truth; if, indeed, he would show no mercy to his little girl's own pet, what use to bring an animal around to him? Besides which, he was a surly, crotchety, and ungracious man who was like to bite your head off if you so much as spoke a word.

MacDhui was well aware that this was bad for business and that there had been a noticeable falling-off in clients in his waiting room as word had got around that since the affair of his daughter's cat he was no longer paying proper attention to his work. The story even seemed to have spread to some of the outlying farms where, if not loved, he was at least respected. Calls for his services during the past fortnight seemed to have been fewer and farther between.

"I do not know—I do not know—I cannot understand it." Mr. MacDhui groaned aloud, as though his friend were not there. "I would bring the brute back to life for her if I but could"—and then with a sudden angry shake of his shaggy head—"but, by God, I would chloroform it all over again if she brought it to me in the same state——"

"Some children are lonely," Mr. Peddie said. "It may have taken away somewhat her loneliness."

Although the minister had left unsaid the concluding thought, "She is motherless," nevertheless MacDhui heard the sentence in his inner ear as though it had been spoken. Had he been jealous of the animal and her affection for it? Had this made him less than careful in diagnosing the beast's ailment and too quick to dispose of it? Well, it was over and done with now. And a child should not be lonely with plenty of playmates. She always seemed to be about with some small fry or other from the neighborhood.

He had not noticed how alone she had been since the episode of the cat, that she had lost interest in her friends and in play and each day had taken to longer periods of silent brooding. Often when Mrs. McKenzie thought she was out with Hughie Stirling or Geordie McNabb she would be off by the loch shore, sitting on the beach looking into the water, unseeing, or shut away by herself in her room, grieving for her dead.

Her friends fell away too, for children are more sensitive and quick to observe changes or odd behavior in companions of their own age than are adults; quick too, to write them off and respect their moods. After several rebuffs, when Mary Ruadh had silently shaken her head and refused to accompany them to the quay, or go berrying, or attend a picnic with Hughie Stirling on the manor grounds, they had ceased to come. Imperceptibly Mary Ruadh had begun her withdrawal from a world that had suddenly manifested itself as harsh, cruel, and unjust.

Mr. MacDhui groaned again and said aloud, "Aye, but what's to do? I felt certain that after a time she would tire of the game, but, if anything she seems to grow more adamant. It is as though I were not there when she regards me——"

Mr. Peddie, who did not believe in putting things off, said, "I will go and have a word with her now and see if I can get at what lies behind her behavior."

They walked in silence to the end of Argyll Lane together, where Mr. MacDhui with a final "You'll get nowhere—I promise you" went into the cottage housing his hospital and dispensary, while the minister padded up the stone path next door and entered the veterinarian's home. He found Mary Ruadh sitting on the stairs looking, but he saw at once that her gaze was directed not without, but within. Also he was surprised to see how pale she was and she seemed to have lost weight as well. Certainly she was not the healthy, cheerful child he had seen over a fortnight before, holding her sick cat.

Mr. Peddie put aside his hat and umbrella with gravity of demeanor, eschewing forced cheerfulness, and went and sat down a few steps below her. A father, with a brood of his own, he was familiar with some of the intricacies of a child's mind, though not all. He opened with the safe gambit of the weather. "Foooosh," he sighed, "will this mizzle of summer's rain never end? It keeps a parson's clothes from drying and makes little girls stay indoors. Wouldn't you like to come over to our house and blow bubbles with Fiona and my young Andrew?"

He could see upon her the struggle to return and from how far, how very far away she seemed to have to come. When she had at last parted the curtains of her dream and stepped through them she regarded him solemnly and wordlessly and silently shook her head in the negative.

Looking up at her, Mr. Peddie suddenly felt himself indescribably moved at the sight of this small, plain, red-haired Mary Ruadh, a little girl sitting alone upon the stairs in a stone house with no dolls at her side, no companions, and no four-footed friends. And because he was himself an instrument, he was astonished to find himself in the presence of that deep soul-sickness which heretofore he had encountered only in adults and which he was attuned to perceive, as some doctors can enter a sickroom and diagnose the illness by the atmosphere.

"Mary Ruadh," the round little man said, kindly but seriously, "I know that you are grieving sore for your cat Thomasina——" The child's stare turned quickly to a hostile glower. Then she looked away from him, but Mr. Peddie continued, "I recall Thomasina almost as though she were here at the foot of the steps. Let us see whether I can remember correctly, and if I do not you shall tell me so."

Mary Ruadh looked back at him tentatively, unsure, but with this much of her attention he began: "She was so long"—holding his hands to illustrate—"so wide, and so high and her fur was the color of mixed ginger and honey biscuits in alternating stripes, but on her chest she had a pure white blaze in the shape of a triangle, something like this——" and he made one with his fingers.

Mary Ruadh shook her head decisively. "It was round—like this!"

The dominie nodded. "Now that I reflect and you remind me, it was round, and she had three white feet——"

"Four."

"And a white spot at the very tip of her tail——"

"Yes, but a little one——"

"Very well, then," Peddie continued. "Her head was most beautifully formed, and her ears were rather delicate and pointed and large for her head, but they stood up straight and made her look most alert and knowing."

The child was watching him closely now, taking in every word, checking every point. Her expression had softened. Color had come back to her pale cheeks and her eyes were alive again.

"Now her nose. How well I seem to remember her nose; it was the color of the terra-cotta tile on the roof of the vestry and there was one little speck of black on it."

"Two," corrected Mary Ruadh, and held up two fingers with a triumphant and dimpled smile.

"Hm, yes, two," admitted Mr. Peddie. "I seem to see the other now just a little to the south of the first one, but hardly to be noticed unless one looked most carefully. And now we come to her eyes. Do you remember her eyes, Mary Ruadh?"

She nodded excitedly but waited for him to go on with the description. He said, "Surely they were the most beautiful thing about Thomasina. They were like emeralds in a setting of gold. And her tongue was the most delectable pink, just the color of my polyantha roses when they first begin to bud in the spring. I remember once seeing her sitting opposite you at your tea table at a tea party, with a white napkin about her neck and with just the tip of her tongue showing. I said to myself, 'Hullo! Thomasina has been eating my polyantha and one of the petals is still showing.' "

Mary Ruadh laughed so that Mrs. McKenzie, at a sound that had been too long absent from that house, stuck her head through the kitchen door to see. "But it wasn't. It was her tongue all the time," the little girl cried.

Peddie nodded. "Didn't I feel the fool when I found it out. And I do remember what perfect manners she had, how she sat up like a real lady at the table, not a-lapping of her cambric tea until she was bidden, and when you offered her a biscuit she bumped it three times with her nose before accepting it."

"She liked caraway cakes the best," Mary Ruadh commented, and then asked, "Why did she bump them?"

"Well," the minister replied reflectively, "you may have your choice. Either she was smelling of them first as a kind of precautionary measure, *not* a very polite thing to do at a company tea, or she was being most polite, and each bump meant, 'For me? —Oh, but you are TOO kind!—Ah well, then, if you *really* insist. . . .' "

"She was being polite," Mary Ruadh decided, with a firm and knowing shake of her head.

"And I remember also how beautifully she moved, how lithe and graceful her long body was and how relaxed when you wore her around your neck sometimes, almost as though she were asleep."

"Thomasina slept with me in my bed at night," Mary Ruadh said. The glow had spread to her eyes now——

"And do you remember her little private call to you, what it sounded like? I heard it once when I passed your house and you were both without and she wished for your attention."

Mary Ruadh thought deeply, a fist pressed under her small rounded chin, and then gave more than a passable imitation of the seldom heard love call of the late Thomasina: "Prrrrrrrrrow."

"Yes," Mr. Peddie agreed, "it was 'Prrrrrrrrrow!' exactly. And so you see, Mary Ruadh, Thomasina is not really dead at all. We have reassembled her, you and I, and here she is before us both again as large as life."

The child fell silent again as she stared at him, her young brow furrowed beneath the lock of ginger hair that fell over it, not quite comprehending.

"She lives on," the minister explained, "in your memory and mine. Don't you see that as long as you and I are here to think of her and remember her as she was in all her beauty, she cannot ever die? You have but to close your eyes to see her. No one can ever take this memory from you, and sometimes when you are in bed asleep at night, she will come to you in your dreams, only ten times more beautiful and loving than she was before. Come, close your eyes and tell me; do you not see her now as we have described her?"

Mary Ruadh screwed up her eyes and her face with the effort. She said, "Yes." Nevertheless when she opened them she looked into those of Mr. Peddie with a clear and direct gaze and said quite simply, "But I want her."

The minister nodded and said, "Of course, and now that you have learned how, you have but to call her to your mind and she will come. When you are older, Mary Ruadh, you will know love of a different kind, and bereavement and grief and all that is a part of the difficult journey through life. And you will remember perhaps a little bit of what I have been trying to tell you today—that there is no wound of sorrow and mourning so great that loving memory cannot help to heal it. Do you think you understand this, Mary Ruadh?"

This time the child did not reply but only regarded him solemnly. Mr. Peddie then ventured to the crux of the matter. He said, "Thomasina lives in your father's mind as in yours and mine. If you were to put your arms about his neck and give him an old-fashioned whisper that you loved him, you and he could remember Thomasina together just as you and I have done and that would make the memory picture even brighter, for he would perhaps remember things we have left out——"

The child gave this suggestion a moment's grave consideration and then shook her head slowly and firmly in the negative. "I can't," she declared, "Daddy's dead!"

Taken aback, it was now Mr. Peddie's turn to stare at this strange child, for in spite of his knowledge and experience, he was shocked at the sudden and unexpected turn the conversation had taken. "But, Mary Ruadh! How can you say such a thing. Your father is not dead. . . ."

"Yes, he is," the little girl insisted gravely and unemotionally, and then added succinctly, "I killed him."

"Ah," said Mr. Peddie softly—for he was beginning to see which way the wind was blowing—"That was not very kind. How did you kill your daddy?"

Mary Ruadh reflected the precise details, savoring them again with a pleased and slightly malevolent expression on her face and gave them to the nonplused minister, who was beginning to suspect that in spite of being a father and a minister of the gospel, his understanding of child psychology left something to be desired.

"I put him on a long white table," she narrated, "and poured something out of a bottle onto a rag and held it over his nose. Daddy wriggled awfully at first, but I sat on him and held the rag there until he didn't wriggle anymore, but was dead. Then I put him out on the dust heap, but later I put him in a basket lined with silk and put on my mournings and we all went and buried him and Jamie Braid played the lament, but I was glad he was dead and did not cry at all."

The Reverend Peddie tried once more. "Then who is this man who comes home in the evening and sits across the table from you with his heart breaking because you will not greet him, or speak to him, or kiss him good night?" he asked.

Mary Ruadh reflected on this question seriously for a moment before she replied, "I don't know," and then added with unequivocal finality, "I don't like him."

Angus Peddie, who in his youth had been a considerable sports enthusiast and player of games, knew when he was beaten and also how to accept defeat with grace. He sighed and arose from the stairs, retrieving his hat and umbrella. Then going to her, he said, "Perhaps we will talk about this further some other time, Mary Ruadh," and gently kissed the pale cheek, nor did she try to avoid his doing so, and he took his leave.

But he noted and remembered that the paleness had returned to the face and the lackluster quality of the deep blue eyes and that when he had last looked back upon her she had looked not like a child but a little bowed old lady, and he made up his mind to suggest to Andrew MacDhui to have a word with Dr. Strathsay the next time he saw him, to suggest that he drop by, perhaps, and have a look at the child just in case there was something organic troubling her as well. Mr. Peddie was a well-read man and knew something of the severity of the traumas that could result from imagined as well as genuine catastrophies. A young lady of seven who on one and the same day had had her symbolic mother chloroformed practically before her eyes and thereafter had revenged herself by the mental murdering of her father, might understandably require the services of the family physician, if only to ascertain the extent of the damage done. The veterinary, however, was not in his office when the minister stopped by to tell him the results of his attempt and confess his failure, having gone out to a back-country call, and thus other matters intervened and in the end old Dr. Strathsay was not summoned until it was too late.

13   Andrew MacDhui soon was left in no doubt that gossip about him and the affair of his daughter's cat was all about Inveranoch and hurting his business with the locals. Now a hush would fall upon a knot of gabblers in front of the post office when he entered or left, or at the chemist's; he was conscious of drawing looks askance and could hear the whispers when his back was turned.

Some of them reached to his ears and were to the effect that if he could not or would not cure his own child's little pet, why then he could not be the doctor he was supposed to be and a pity to take one's own dear little thing to him, only to have him recommend to put it away. And furthermore, if his own child would neither speak to him nor have any dealings with him in his own home, as everyone knew was the case, there must be something very black indeed about the man and even more than met the eye at first.

Irritation, anger, shame, and frustration had further caused a deterioration in the behavior of MacDhui toward his clients and patients and made him the more truculent, bullying, short-tempered, and argumentative. He spoke in even a louder, more rasping tone and seemed to be looking for veiled insults or allusions in the most innocent remarks, until even the summer visitors thought him a most peculiar and unpleasant man, but since there was no other veterinarian within miles, they had to bear with him when their dogs acquired summer mange or suffered a sting from an insect or a bite from some bad-tempered local animal.

But this was not the case with some of the townspeople who knew of the woman known as Daft or Mad Lori who lived by herself as a recluse up in the glen, talked with the Little Folk and the angels and had a way with winged and four-footed creatures that assuredly was not quite of this earth. Hence the silver Mercy Bell attached to the covin oak outside the little cottage rang more frequently now, as former clients of the animal doctor made the pilgrimage to the lair of the so-called Red Witch of Glen Ardrath.

And thus inevitably, through whispers of these pilgrimages, Daft Lori swam into the ken of Andrew MacDhui as either a rival or a nuisance who must be dealt with.

He had heard of her, of course, but merely as a kind of local character, boasted of by the town, like Rab McKechnie, who when sufficiently drunk could recite the poetry of Bobby Burns from memory by the hour and would take it into his head to do so outside the Queen's Arms, his favorite pub, or old Mary who went about the streets picking up bits of paper and string. Lori had long been accepted as a kind of fixture and curiosity, about whom no one really bothered except to regale a visitor with the story of the witchwoman who dwelled in a wild glen up the mountain side, who conversed with the spirit, understood the language of the animals, and frightened little boys and girls, who mortally feared to approach anywhere near to her cottage.

Occasionally such a visitor shopping in the grocer's or chemist's or dry-goods emporium might encounter a quiet young woman with red hair and wide-spaced greenish eyes, plain-seeming, but if one looked again, revealing a great sweetness of expression, without ever guessing or even surmising that this might be the Red Witch herself, Daft Lori McGregor down from the hills on one of her rare excursions into town to lay in needed supplies for herself and her four-footed companions and patients.

But Mr. MacDhui had never encountered her, for Inveranoch was a largish town and their paths were unlikely to cross. Nor had he ever felt any curiosity about her, since local wonders or freaks are never as interesting to those who live close to them.

But now it was whisper, whisper, whisper. A word dropped here, or there, snatches of gossip picked up by large-eared Willie Bannock, whose loyalty to his employer remained undimmed, snatches of sentences overheard. "Oh, aye, there's nae doot she has a way wi' the wee beasties. The touch o' her hand to its head is enough to set an old dog a-dying to frisking like a pup," or, "They say she's a powerful one wi' spells, and dangerous if crossed"—and again— "Ring her silver bell o' maircy and she'll nae turn a sick animal frae her door, nor will she have so murkle's a farthing for her pains. The wild beasts of the forest feed frae her hauns. . . ."

Mr. MacDhui thought of these things with waxing indignation as he drove his jeep on one of his back-country rounds of sanitary inspection, passing the gypsy encampment that still remained in the meadow at the foot of Glen Ardrath.

The smoke rose into the misty morning air from the horseshoe of wagons and caravans drawn up at one end of the field, brightly colored garments fluttered from wash lines, and a farrier was shoeing a horse, for MacDhui could hear the distant metallic beat of his hammer.

At one end of the encampment was a row of wagons that had been converted into cages for the containment of wild animals, but as yet there appeared to have been no attempt made to exhibit them.

The gypsies apparently had been making character with the police, at any rate there had been no complaints. The women told fortunes with greasy packs of tarot cards; others derived an income from the sale of tin and copper utensils, at which, as followers of the ancient gypsy trade of *Calderai* or tinkers, they were adepts. The townspeople remained aloof and suspicious, but the summer trippers, failing to observe the dirt and primitive cruelty and bestiality behind the color of the encampment seen against the stark Highland background, thought them romantic.

Driving along the road that led upcountry into the hills, MacDhui looked dourly upon the encampment; he had no use for foreigners and they were dirty. Besides, through gossip with the farmers in the neighborhood, he knew more about this band probably than did the police. There was a bear trainer in their midst, a big, drunken brute of a fellow, probably a descendant of those gypsies known in the Balkans as bear drivers, and characterized usually by their cruelty to their animals, and later they were planning to give some sort of show or performance to lure the summer visitors, judging they were far enough out of town not to attract the attention of the police.

Whatever, it was none of MacDhui's business. If the police were up to their duty, he felt they would have cleaned out the nest long ago, denied them permission to camp, and sent them on their way to infest some other community. But shortly thereafter occurred the incident which drove all reflections upon gypsies from his mind and furnished him at last with out-and-out corroboration of the gossip that had been reaching his ears with regard to the witchwoman who was said to have a way with sick animals and was not averse to practicing.

On a rocky trail between Glen Ardrath and Bannockstyle, a farm hamlet further up in the hills, the veterinary encountered a tow-polled gad boy employed by one of the farmers, driving a curve-horned, dappled Ayrshire cow ahead of him with prods of a long gad pole cut from an ash sapling.

MacDhui pulled up his jeep, leaned therefrom, and addressed the boy in the vernacular: "Hello there, young Jock. Where are ye gaun wi' Fermer Kinkairlie's Roselle," MacDhui knew the name, pedigree, and markings of every cow, bull and plow horse in the district.

The boy stopped likewise and gave the veterinarian that cold, unswerving Highland gaze indicative of that independence that considers any question an intrusion. After reflection he decided to reply, for as a matter of fact he was more than a little uneasy because of his errand and glad of a chance for a word with his interrogator.

He intoned in a shrill, high-pitched voice, "Yin milchkye's gone off. She wis drony last nicht and this mairnen Fermer Kinkairlie says her clushets are as dry as a toom whuskey bottle and nae mair to be had frae yin than the ither."

MacDhui snorted. "Did ye think then to restore her by running her aboot the country like a fox hunter? I am well come then and will have a look at what ails the beast."

The lanky, straw-headed gad boy looked alarmed as MacDhui made preparations to descend from the jeep with his bag and backed to the cow. "Na na!" he cried, " 'Tis not you that's wanted. I'm tae lead her tae the Red Witch o' the glen, says the fermer, for what's to do, and he's gi'en me the siller to pay her. 'Twill be bogle-wark, I don't doot, and I'm no much of a one for dealins wi' the evil eye. D'ye ken this Daft Lori? Wad she be putting a spell upon me?"

Outrage exploded in a roar from MacDhui. "Faugh! Are ye all daft yersel's? Has Fermer Kinkairlie taken leave of his senses? Ye'll draw pints o' beer from yin kye's clushets sooner than a drap o' milk from the word o' some loony auld spaewife back in the glen!"

A stubborn look came into the lad's face. "Aweel, I ken ony what the fermer said. I'm nae ower liking the errand mysel'! I'll make the sign so, a' the time I'm in her sight——" and he made a fist, with his thumb and little finger extended.

MacDhui bawled, "Be off with you. I'll call in and have a word with the fermer and we'll see who's to be called for ailing beasts about here——"

Farmer Kinkairlie was a rugged, stocky man with one of those large shaggy heads that looked too large for the body it topped. He was a pipe-sucker and a reflector-before-replying kind of man who knew his own mind and his rights and was not afraid to speak out. MacDhui, when he wheeled his jeep angrily into the forecourt of the farm where he found him hosing down his cow byre in sanitary enough fashion, accomplished nothing with abuse, shouting, and threats.

"Mon," Farmer Kinkairlie admonished the irate veterinarian, "ye'll bairst a blood veesal wi' sic choler." He let the smoke of his pipe curl up about his head while he contemplated Mac-Dhui, continuing, "Yon coo nae has ony disease reportable under the Acts of the county. 'Tis a matter between me and her whaur I send her when her milk fails."

MacDhui, calming some manner beneath the man's demeanor, said, "Yer richt, Kinkairlie—I had no cause to shout at ye. But I don't know what's got into you all of a sudden, all of you. You've been glad enough of my services in the past, without turning the pages back to medieval superstition and sending to a warlock when a cow dries up."

The farmer was not mollified. He sucked at his pipe for so long that MacDhui thought he was never going to speak. Finally he said, "Aweel, Meester MacDhui, times change. Pairhops they're changing back again. For yin thing, they're no' so altered that I let any mon come here and tell me my business, no more do I pit my nose in yours. If you see onything here to rant aboot, sanitarywise, speak up, otherwise I'll thank ye to remove yer presence from the premises, since I have nae sent for ye——"

For an instant, MacDhui towered over the smaller farmer, a burly, menacing figure, red beard thrust forward, knotted fists thrust into the pockets of his leather jacket, eyes glaring. But the little man stared him back, and in another moment MacDhui felt that pipe smoke would be blown into his face, so he left off, turned on his heel, packed himself into his jeep, and roared forth from the farmyard. There was nothing to be done with Highlanders and no use wasting your breath upon them, once their minds were made up.

However the woman known as Daft Lori was another matter and with her MacDhui meant to deal as swiftly as might be.

When he entered his surgery Willie Bannock was busied with preparing sections for microscopic examination and had nothing to say. MacDhui scrubbed himself, donned his white coat, and thrust his head in through the door of the waiting room, but there was no one there but the Reverend Mr. Peddie with his pug dog Fin, who was wheezing, belching, and rolling up the whites of his eyes in his usual distress. The roly-poly little minister was himself looking sheepish and ill at ease to be back with his pet.

MacDhui waved his friend inside the surgery, frowning at the empty waiting room, unaware of the incongruity of his emotions; he was angry when it was full, and now put out when it was empty. He did not chaff Peddie this time but automatically reached up to the shelf and took down the familiar bottle of medicine.

Truth to tell, he was glad to see his friend, for he felt that if anyone were able to tell him something about the mysterious woman who lived in the glen, it would be the minister. He and Peddie had not encountered one another since the week before, when the dominie had briefly reported his failure to move or influence Mary Ruadh and had suggested that MacDhui let time take its course for the moment and in the meantime have the child looked over by the local practitioner as a precautionary measure. The veterinarian had taken the first bit of advice but not the second.

MacDhui came at once to the crux of the matter he had so definitely established that day. "See here, Angus," he said, "do you know anything about a half-witted woman by the name of Lori, who lives somewhere up in the glen and pretends she is a witch?"

The minister sat down. He had been expecting this query for some time. Now that it had come he hoped he would be able adequately to deal with the situation. Before he replied he uncorked the bottle and trickled a little of the liquid into the side of his dog's mouth to ease its gastric disturbance, patting its back and round stomach until it brought up a resounding belch, which brought a smile of relief to the little clergyman's face as well as to the wrinkled black countenance of the dog. Some of the sweetness of the smile still lingered at his lips as he replied, "I do not think she is half-witted, Andrew. Withdrawn, perhaps, in the modern sense of one who has found a world that is preferable to our own. And certainly she is no witch."

"Ah! Then you do know of her. Well, there must be some reason she is known as Daft Lori. And whatever, she is practicing veterinary medicine without a license and it must cease. This morning I encountered one of my clients sending a cow to her for a spell to cure dried-up clushets. And I suppose you did not fail to notice that my waiting room this morning is not exactly overpopulated. Well, I believe this woman is responsible."

For all his experience in dealing with human beings, Peddie was baffled as to how to remove the scales from the eyes of one who was so willfully blind to his own failings and shortcomings. To show him the truth would only lose him a friend. He saw the gulf between his MacDhui and himself over this point not so much as a flaw in character as rather a classic example of the difficulties to be compounded through living in an accident-created pilotless world rather than a God-created and directed one. To Mr. Peddie, who was a profound theologist as well as a simple man, atheism carried its own punishment; the unbeliever seemed almost to be carrying about a built-in rod. But he knew too well that this was no time to voice such an opinion. And so he asked merely, "What is it you propose to do?"

"The simplest thing, I suppose, would be to turn her over to the police, or make a complaint to them. There are severe penalties for practicing medicine, veterinary as well as human, without a license."

Mr. Peddie for the first time looked uncomfortable. "Dear me," he said, "I think that might be most ill-advised. Lori, you know, has never taken a penny for anything she has ever done to help anyone. I should not, if I were you, appeal to the police."

The stubborn chin came out. "And why not? Is there a law, or is there not? Is a man to give a lifetime to study and work to be undermined by some creature who takes it into her head to spoil and pamper animals, or brews stinks out of herbs? I think not."

Mr. Peddie sighed. "The law is indeed the law. That has always been the trouble with it. But you see, the police happen to think highly of Lori because she is a good woman, a really good person, and in the line of their duties they come in contact with so many persons who are not. Thus they would be prejudiced. . . ."

"You mean they would refuse to do their duty when called upon?"

"Oh no. Not our police. They are staunch men with a true Scots sense of duty, only——"

"Only what? If I charged this woman with . . ."

"Yes, yes, of course. But let me put it to you this way." Here Mr. Peddie paused to gather Fin to him, holding the pug dog upside down and cradled in his arms like a baby, or a small, black-faced pig, and no one could have managed to look more ridiculous, the white eyes of the dog, rolling adoringly out of the background of the minister's dark clothing, the legs spraddled wide as Peddie gently massaged his stomach, and yet such was the man's presence and inner gentleness, that no one but he could have managed to look so unridiculous as he outlined his parable.

"Mrs. Clachan says to her neighbor Mrs. Culross, ' 'Tis a chill and a sore throat I am suffering from this morning, Mrs. Culross: I can hardly get around on my two legs to do my work from the misery of it—and all the washing piling up.' Mrs. Culross asks, 'Look you, Mrs. Clachan; have you ever tried Evans' mixture? It's the grand cure for just such a complaint as you are speaking of. Six months ago when I felt a chill coming on, it had me on my feet in no time. I believe I still have a half bottle of it in the cupboard beneath the stairs. Let me fetch it for you.' "

Mr. Peddie turned his dog over and moved his massage to the end of the spine whence the corkscrew tail began bringing a look of most ineffable bliss to the animal's face. He continued: "She does so and Mrs. Clachan, who was suffering from nothing more serious than a severe case of washing piling up, partakes of some of the mixture, feels her stomach warmed and her head slightly addled due to the high percentage of spirits in the stuff, and gets on with it, cured. Is Dr. Strathsay to bring a suit against Mrs. Culross for practicing medicine without a license?"

He paused for a moment to let the idea percolate through his friend's skull and then concluded, "No, friend Andrew, you would not look well in court, bristling and blustering against a woman who, the police would report, had done no more than help out a lonely shepherd or crofter with a sick or injured animal or given some child or woman advice about a dog or cat that needed worming."

MacDhui snorted, half in acquiescence, half in disgust. "Yes, yes," he said, "I suppose you are right. Women are always objects of sentimental favoritism. Well, then you must go since you know her so well."

"Oh," Mr. Peddie replied, "as for that—I do not know her at all well. No one does."

"Eh, what? But this is nonsense, Angus. Somebody must. She must have come from somewhere, or have some story——"

Mr. Peddie mused for a moment and murmured half to himself, "Must everyone?" and then answered, "I suppose in a way they must, but it seems a pity. Her name is Lori McGregor. The crofter's cottage and barn in the glen had been deserted for years. She came there one day, but no one knows from where—or ever asks. She is a weaver. Perhaps she is one of the last of the fates, separated from her sisters——"

MacDhui snorted again. "Well, you're just the one then to reason with her. These psychotics will often hearken to a dominie where——"

Mr. Peddie sighed and shook his head sadly. "I hoped you would see," he said, "why I will not go. I will not interfere with Lori in any way or attempt to penetrate the sphere in which she lives. She strikes me as one who has looked upon our world and our way of life and has not liked it. Her contacts are other than ours; her devotion is to the service of helpless things that are ill or hurt. She is what the French would call 'une vraie religieuse.' There are not many left on earth."

MacDhui, whose patience was exhausted, said savagely, "All of whom were more than half mad, your religieuses—— Well, then, I trust you will have no objection if I go and deal with this woman personally and put an end to her interfering with my business and the business of the district."

Angus Peddie reflected, sitting on the edge of his chair, cuddling and scratching his dog, his mind awhirl with the problems set by MacDhui's proposal. And yet he thought that he saw, or rather felt, a possible pattern and considered it his duty to warn his friend. He rose to his feet, setting the dog on the floor, clamped his hat onto the back of his head while he regarded MacDhui earnestly. "No," he replied. "No, I have no objection whatsoever. But you know, Andrew, I should be careful if I were you. You may come into the greatest danger if you were to go!"

MacDhui exploded. "Danger! Danger? Are you mad yourself, Angus? Explain yourself, man——"

For the first time the minister looked embarrased. "I——" he began and then hesitated, leading MacDhui to say impatiently, "Well, well——"

"You must not be irritable with me when I bring in my God," Peddie replied. "God, you see, is my business and my vocation. It is in a way as if I were to fly off the handle every time you mentioned that you were going to vaccinate for blackleg, or inoculate lambs against dysentery."

MacDhui said nothing but waited for him to go on.

"Lori, I think is very close to God. Her life is the manner in which she worships and loves God—that is all. . . ."

"And what danger would I be running, might I ask?"

The little clergyman gathered up his dog and his medicine and replied, "Of coming to love God too." Then, tucking Fin beneath his arm, he pattered out. But no sooner had he closed the door than he popped his head back inside again. "Should you decide to risk it," he said, "it will not do to go to Lori's door, for she will not open to you or to anyone. But there is a bell with a rope attached to a covin-tree, a large oak that stands before her house. It is rung by humans and sometimes, I understand, even animals who have need of her. It is called the Mercy Bell."

MacDhui glared. "I'm damned if I do. What need have I——?"

The little man's eyes glittered curiously at this and he did not mince words this time. "If ever a man had need of mercy, it is you, Andrew MacDhui," he said, and went out, closing the door softly behind him.

14   I, Bast-Ra, cat goddess of Bubastis, now called Talitha, remember the day of the coming of the Man with the Red Beard.

I saw him first as in a vision, striding through a dream of prophecy with flaming hair, for I, Sekhmet-Bast-Ra, the lady of Sept, have first, second, and third sight.

And I cried out aloud in the night of the doom-dream, "Death! Death! Death and doom await the slayers of cats! He is Duamutef, son of Horus, brother of Anubis, the jackal of death. Red is the beard of his chin, the hair of his head, and the glare of his eyes; red is the blood that drips from his talons and fangs; red is the doom that envelops his ka, for he has transgressed and I, Bast-Ra, shall set the seal upon that doom. For it is writ in the Book of the Dead that whosoever causes the death of one of us shall not go unpunished."

And in the dream he came striding fiercely, with the sun blood red behind him, and in his hands he bore a red ax of copper and there was red stain upon the blade. He came, fearful and mighty as Sopdu and even I, Bast-Ra, was filled with fear and cried out so that I awoke.

I was at my fireside then in the cottage temple and the glow of the dying fire was as red as blood. In the next room I heard the sweet singing of Lori and the thumping of the loom as she finished her weaving. Even so she ceased her singing and called to me,

"Talitha! Poor puss! Have ye had a bad dream then? Och, but ye have nowt to fear——" and she came and lifted me up, cradled and stroked me.

Yet I knew that a doom had commenced—perhaps Lori herself had threaded it upon her loom—and must go on to its appointed end. The day when I would encounter the Man with the Red Beard was not far off, and in spite of myself and the sweet love of my priestess, I trembled and could not take comfort. It is not easy to be a goddess and know too much.

It all began next day hard by the covin-tree.

Other times, other customs. Had you heard of the covin or coglan tree? As Wullie, who explained it to me, said, "Och, any Scot, or even Scottish cat would know that. Ye cannot be a true Scot, Talitha." The covin-tree is the great oak or beech that stood in front of the manor house, or in the castle courtyard, where it spread its branches, offering shade from the sun or shelter from the rain. It is peaceful beneath its canopy.

Now, Wullie explained further, it is not that the Scot is in-hospitable; far from it. When he kens you he is the most hospitable man on earth. But first—and danger taught him this—before he welcomes you within he must know who you are and what your business. And thus it was under the covin-tree on a bench that the laird interviewed the stranger, the traveler, and the seeker, to have a word with them as to their purpose and their antecedents, before admitting them into the house.

We had such a one growing two gallops and a jump away from the front of the cottage temple, an oak that towered twice as high as any palm I knew in my ancient home and a hundred times as thick around. The branches towered over the roof of the cottage, their leaves scraping the slate in a wind, and the topmost crown was yet again as high, and from that vantage point one could see far down the glen and into the fields of the valley below and even the smoke rising from the chimneys of the town.

The Mercy Bell, of which I have already spoken, hung from the lowest branch. To its clapper was tied a rope which fell loosely to the ground, trailing there. Sometimes the rope was tugged by a human bringing some animal in distress for my priestess to heal, for Lori was a reincarnation of Renentutet the nurse goddess. And sometimes the bell was rung by the animal itself, for Lori to come forth from her weaving and help it.

Oh, you who are so clever and full of knowledge about the ways of your world and know and understand so little of that realm of gods and goddesses that is mine will ridicule and scoff at the idea of an injured animal somewhere deep in the forest determining to seek out Lori's help. You will not believe that it could drag itself for miles through woods and across icy burns to arrive at the covin-oak before the cottage, there to ring the Mercy Bell.

Yet in the days when I was God this would have surprised no one, for the beasts of the field and the birds of the air, the gods and the humans were as one brotherhood living with and for one another and sharing the knowledge of their magic and wisdom.

Man saw in the winged and four-footed creatures who shared the earth with him powers that were beyond him, and worshiped them. Magic and magical powers were the usual way of life. No one was surprised at anything that happened, for the gods were everywhere and dwelt in every object animate and inanimate. From what I have learned since my return, the gods no longer live and magic has gone out of style.

We were all about our business that pleasant summer's morning when the Mercy Bell was touched, shivered twice in the clear air, and was still. The jackdaw came a-screaming, "Danger! Great danger! Beware!" and we assembled, afluff with curiosity, I, and Mac, and Wullie, and Dorcas, with Peter the Scottie and Shep the sheep dog, to see what was toward, but with care because of the jackdaw's warning, for Jackie was a clever bird, and we came to the covin-oak warily, as Lori appeared at the cottage door, shading her eyes from the sun, and there we all saw the badger that had rung the bell.

The trap was clamped about his leg, with the length of chain where the badger had snapped it still attached to it. One end of this had crossed the rope trailing to the ground from the clapper of the bell, causing it to ring. There was no magic in that part of it. The magic lay in how the badger, more dead than alive, the white of the bone showing at the shoulder and foreleg where a dog had attacked and worried it while it was trapped, had known where to come and had dragged itself perhaps more than a mile to our temple and my priestess of healing.

We cats sat down at a respectful distance, for the beast was half mad with pain from its festered wounds; there was white slaver at its mouth and its yellow teeth snapped and bit in every direction. But the dogs were beginning to yield to that hysteria which is so characteristic of them and wanted to attack and kill the badger, which might have been all for the best, since it was more than half dead anyway.

But Lori ordered, "Sit. Leave him be," and they sat. She went to the animal and stood looking down at him for a moment, while the wicked teeth snicked and snacked, and in my eye of prophecy I could already see them sink into the flesh of Lori's hand, and as she knelt at the side of the beast, I quickly put a spell upon the badger and a blessing upon Lori.

Bending over, she freed the crushed hind leg from the trap and, gently lifting him up, cradled him in her arms and whispered something to him. And she was safe because of my spell and my blessing. From the first touch of her fingers, stroking his panting flank, the badger had become calm. His head was fallen to one side as she held him, but his eyes were rolling like a dog's, so that all of us could see the cream of their whites as he gazed up at Lori. She rose to her feet and carried him back to the stables where she tended her sick, with most of us following soberly after.

Old Wullie expressed the relief we all felt with, "Phew! Nasty moment that! It's a miracle Lori's hands and arms weren't torn to shreds." I held my peace. I had learned my lessons. As I said before; other times, other customs. There was no use in my telling them that it was my miracle, one which, when I was an acknowledged goddess in the temple of Khufu where the Nile divided about the isle of Bubastis, I used to work all the time, keeping rivermen who worshiped me properly unharmed from the tusks of enraged hippopotami or hungry crocodiles when they upset or fell into the river.

Instead, I put my tail up in a dignified manner and accompanied her to the stone building she used as her lazaret. I sat down in the doorway and watched as she gently laid the badger on the table of the room where she kept her bandages, salves, and medicines on shelves. Under it she then spread a clean white cloth, placing a basin and a sponge beside it, and then went to the kitchen in the cottage temple to fetch a kettle of hot water.

When she returned with it she put it on the floor for a moment, placed one of her hands beneath the badger's head and with the other stroked it gently, her eyes filled with love and pity.

From the badger issued the saddest sound I ever heard. It squeaked. There was no more growl or snarl left in it. It was partly a whimper too, but really more a squeak. Is it not strange how quickly hate and fear can be replaced by love? When something fierce and dangerous, of which you have reason to be afraid, is hurt so that it is rendered helpless and suddenly squeaks like a mouse, it breaks your heart.

I turned my head away for an instant and washed my back furiously. When I looked again, the tears were falling from Lori's eyes as she sponged the mangled leg and the awful festered wound at the shoulder where the white bone lay bare and the flesh of the forepaw was shredded. The shoulder was broken and the paw seemed to hang attached by no more than tatters. As for the crushed hindquarter—Lori said to me, "Do you see, Talitha? This poor beastie is sorely hurt, and me not knowing what to do for him. Look what has happened. A dog attacked him while he was caught in the trap and laid the bone bare. Yet he must have fought him and driven him off. One so brave and gallant must no' be allowed to die."

Carefully Lori laid out fur, skin, flesh, and bones and the claws of the badger on the white cloth and bathed them tenderly. Only one eye of the brute was to be seen, but it was rolled upward toward Lori and regarded her with trust and pleading.

Then Lori looked once more upon the fearful injuries and shook her head, saying so sadly, "I do not know what to do, Talitha; oh, not at all. I do not know even where to begin and he will die unless something is done. See how beautiful he is, how beautifully formed and marked. Surely God did not send him here to me to die."

Her hands fell to her sides for a moment in despair. But soon her head was lifted in resolve, and courage came into her eyes. She turned to me and said, "We will ask then for help, Talitha, you and I."

Ah, had she but asked help of me, recognized and acknowledged my godhead, I should have had the power; I would have made her a miracle.

She came over to where I was and sat down upon the threshold, and for a moment caressed my head and back and rubbed me softly underneath the chin. Then she folded her hands in her lap and raised her eyes to the sky. Her lips moved silently; her eyes were filled with confidence, and a smile of trust played about her mouth as she prayed.

I prayed then, too, as I had been taught in the long ago, to Ra, my father and Hathor my mother, to great Horus and Isis and Osiris, to Ptah and Mut and Nun, and even to dread Anubis to turn his face from the lintel of our door. I called upon the oldest of the gods, Khonsu and Amen-Ra the Creator of all.

After a time we heard the sound of the ringing of the Mercy Bell.

I gathered myself up and with two gallops, a leap, and the bound, I flew around the side of the cottage to see who or what it was had touched the silver bell for the second time that morning.

And I stopped in my tracks, frozen with horror and filled with fear. My fur stood up on end and a dark ridge crept up my back from tail to crown. My ears flattened back against the side of my head. A low, angry growl came into my throat, to be replaced by the long hiss of hate.

A man, a stranger, stood by the bell on the other side of the covin-tree. The sight of him filled me with loathing, disgust, and fear. For a moment I crouched there staring at this monster who was having such a terrible effect upon me. He was huge; huge and terrifying in aspect. He had fox-colored hair and a fox-colored beard covering his chin and wild and rolling eyes and he stood there pulling again and again upon the rope as though he would pull the Mercy Bell out of the tree.

And then I knew. I had never seen him in this life before, but it was he of my doom-dream, he the red monster, the slayer of cats, upon whom lay the curse of Bubastis. Doom lay across his brow, and yet it was I who was filled to the marrow of my bones with fear.

He had not yet seen me when I crossed the distance from the house to the tree with one bound and the next moment I was clawing my way up the tree, nor did I stop until I was lost in the very topmost branches, so high that I could no longer see or hear what transpired below. And there I remained until the setting of the sun and the drawing in of the night.

Yes, I, Bast-Ra, a goddess, succumbed to the fear of a mortal man and fled from him. Nor was I able to say why this had happened.

15 Now that he was there, Mr. MacDhui was beginning to feel something of a fool. During the long march up through the glen along the narrow track from the spot where he had had to park his jeep, there had been time to reflect upon what his friend Peddie had said about the figure he might cut in court. Thus the forthcoming spectacle of himself in the midst of a woods, bullying some creature who was touched in the head and hardly responsible for her actions, did not appear to him to be very attractive either.

Nevertheless there was his sense of duty toward his profession, and if farmers took to sending their sick cattle or sheep to this half-witted woman, there would be an end to the discipline he had installed in the valley.

But by the time MacDhui had reached sight of Lori's cottage and outbuildings and paused to reconnoiter, his anger managed to reassert itself, defensively in a sense, for he resented the eeriness of the feeling the place gave him.

He took in the silent cottage with the blinds and curtains drawn, sleeping in the cool and gloom of the forest of oak, pine, larches, and old smooth beeches, but which yet was surrounded by an intensity of wildlife, heard rather than seen, which was startling. The house slumbered at the heart of the rustle and whir of myriads of forest creatures.

He glimpsed the cottontails of a pair of hares disappearing from the open space in front of the house; a squirrel scolded, hidden somewhere above his head. Birds went into nervous wheelings and chirpings, in flashes of color about the chimney and eaves at his intrusion, and something large went flapping off through the forest aisles on the slapping beat of powerful wings, laughing to itself.

MacDhui paused now before the giant oak, from the lowest branch of which hung the silver bell with the pull rope tied to its clapper. And he was furious with himself that he did not march forthwith and stoutly to the door of the cottage and pound upon it with his knuckles, or yank at a bell pull if there were one, in the manner of custom and civilization. But neither the house nor its surroundings invited such brazen intrusion. Quietly and effectively it had cast its spell over him so that he did nothing but stand there, uncertain and fuming, his hands thrust deep into the pockets of his jacket.

A moment later he recalled that the Reverend Angus Peddie, who believed not in witches but in an unseen, all-powerful Creator and Director of the universe, had given him directions as to how to come to grips with the woman who was the center of this little forest mystery, and thrusting his head and shoulders forward with something of his former aggressive truculence, he pulled hard upon the bell rope.

The sweetness and brightness of the shivery note of the vibrating metal startled him, as well as causing the birds to whir and flutter more loudly. A roe deer appeared at the edge of the forest and for a moment her liquid eyes stared curiously into his before she turned and galloped away. But there was no other response.

Mr. MacDhui yanked again and again at the clapper rope, setting the bell to crashing and dancing. He felt, more than saw, a streak of something, some small animal that darted to the tree and for an instant, between peals of the bell, heard the dry scrabble of claws as it vanished up into the jungle of high foliage. And he was in no wise prepared for the sight of the plain-looking girl with red hair who appeared suddenly from behind the crofter's cottage and came toward him.

MacDhui had gathered from his talk with Mr. Peddie that Lori was no hook-nosed old crone in the tradition of witch and simple women, but he was not prepared for her youth and simplicity—at first glimpse he judged her to be twenty-six, perhaps twenty-seven at the most—but what startled him, for its contrast with the marks of blood upon her green smock, and upon her hands too, was her aspect of tenderness.

There was no other word for it, MacDhui decided, even at first glance, or rather this was the word he was aware of. She was not beautiful, she was not striking, but her bearing, her walk, the carriage of her head upon her shoulders, the flow of her limbs and the white arms, suggested gentleness and tenderness.

He was conscious of surprise even that so plain and ordinary a person should have impressed as hardheaded a community as Inveranoch to name her the Red Witch of Glen Ardrath and led children to fear and avoid her neighborhood.

And yet he was likewise aware that with her presence, all at once everything seemed to fall into perspective about the place, the feeling of many shy, inquisitive animals, unseen but present, the stirring and whirring of the many birds and even the thing that had flapped off laughing into the forest. If it was a piece from a fairy tale, it remained to be determined whether she was a good or bad fairy, was the strange thought pursued by Mr. MacDhui as she came striding toward him, accompanied by what, he reflected grimly to himself, might have been her familiars, two cats, one yellow, one black, an aged sheep dog and a rollicking black Scots terrier. The red squirrel ran down the bark of the tree, flirting his tail.

But he noted that the stains of blood upon her hands and smock were fresh, and the sight worked the needed disenchantment upon him, closing his mind to all else but the fact that if he needed any proof that she was practicing veterinary medicine without authority, here it was before him. She had apparently answered the summons of the silver bell straight from the operating table of her surgery.

It needed no more to evoke all the choler and indignation he had been storing for this visit, and as she drew near but without speaking, he cried out harshly, "Are you Lori?"

"Aye. I am Lori."

Tender. Tender and gentle. It surged through his mind again as the softness of her voice pierced him. But he had nursed and coddled his anger too long to have it thus put off by soft speaking and in voice no less harsh he rasped, "Do you know who I am?"

"No. That I do not."

He revealed it then with voice and demeanor that wanted only Jovian thunders and lightnings to accompany, and the trembling of the ground: "I am Mr. Andrew MacDhui, veterinary surgeon and sanitary officer for Inveranoch and district!"

If he expected her to be embarrassed, chagrined, or taken aback at this confrontation, another surprise awaited him. For she became suffused with a great joy, as one who can hardly believe her ears. A glow of relief and gratitude came into her expressive eyes, and for a moment all plainness vanished from her features as her face became illuminated from within.

"Och," she cried, with a smile of acknowledgment, "then you will have been sent in answer to my prayer. Oh, you are sair needed and very welcome, Mr. MacDhui. Only come quickly before it is too late——"

Mr. MacDhui suddenly found himself drained of all choler by the strangeness of this welcome. He, come to read the riot act to her, the answer to her prayers? What manner of talk and behavior was this? And then he thought he knew. For the moment he had forgotten that other name that she was called and what was said of her.

Daft, he thought to himself, *daft as a cat under a full moon, poor thing,* and never realized that he had characterized her to himself as "poor thing" instead of "wicked" or "scheming."

Yet he found himself following in her train as she glided ahead, as graceful as the red roe deer he had glimpsed, he walking soberly with the entourage of animals weaving about his ankles. They skirted the house and went on to the stone outbuilding, into which she led him, the outer door opening into a small room in which stood a table, covered with a white cloth, now blood and matter stained, on which reposed the still gasping form of a badger.

MacDhui's practiced eye at once took in the nature and extent of the damage, the crushed hindquarter, the cracked shoulder and shredded forepaw, while his nose acknowledged the sour odor of the infection.

He screwed up his face in distaste and said, "Faugh! Here's a mess." Then he asked briefly, "Trap?"

Lori replied, "Aye. And surely a dog must have been at him while he was fast. Then he broke the chain and came here. . . . I could do no more for him. I am not very skilled. That is why I asked for help."

Mr. MacDhui nodded absently, not quite having caught the point of WHO had been asked for help, or the immediate irony of his having come there to put the quietus on an unauthorized rival, only to be called in consultation. However there was obviously no use lingering over the matter and he came to the point quickly. "Have you a can of ether, or chloroform and a bit of rag so that we can have the beast out of his misery, for that is the best that can be done for him."

Lori said softly and confidingly, "God didna send him here to die, or you to be the instrument of his death, Mr. MacDhui."

He drew back somewhat and stared at her. "Eh? How do you

know?" And then he added curtly, "I do not believe in God."

Lori said, "It does not matter. God believes in you, else ye would not be here." She looked into his face with trust, and a soft, mysterious smile appeared at the corner's of Lori's mouth, a smile with almost a wisp of mischief in it, and which, for some reason he could not fathom, pierced straight to Mr. MacDhui's heart, touching him and moving him most unaccountably almost to tears, so that he drew back yet further, gazing at her with astonishment. . . . He was remembering then the sound her voice had given his name, a note he had almost forgotten. He became aware for the first time of the clarity of her gaze and the curiously endearing simplicity and containment of her features.

He was so shaken that he gestured rather too strongly and ridiculously toward the injuries of the animal on the table, saying loudly, as though addressing a particularly obtuse client in his own surgery, "But don't you see it is impossible, madame?" and then added, "Besides I have not my case with me—having come on a somewhat different errand."

Lori cried, "Oh no, no. It was because of your great skill you were sent."

Andrew MacDhui looked down upon the suffering badger again, noting the condition of the forepaw, the gashed flesh and torn tendons, the nasty three-day-old fracture at the clavicle, the mangled hindquarter further damaged by infection. And he experienced suddenly the most curiously young, almost boyish desire to show off before this strange creature, to shine in her eyes, to bring back that wisp of smile to the corners of her mouth. He stole a glance now at this country girl whose copper-red hair fell loosely to her shoulder, noting the line of the nose that emerged so straight from the base of the wide, calm brow and gave such an expression of gentle and intimate wisdom to her face, but a wisdom and knowledge of things other than mundane. He had quite forgotten that she was mad.

"Och," he said, "this is a very poor business—still, the major tendon is still attached—we must see now to what extent the nerves have been—you will have nothing to tie the beast down and no bit of chloroform either, I suspect——"

Lori said simply, "I will hold him. He trusts me." She slipped a hand beneath the head of the wounded badger, laid the other on his flank and, bending down, leaned her cheek to the beast's jowl close to his muzzle, while making sweet, soft sounds in her throat. The badger whimpered, sighed, and rolled his eyes.

Beads of moisture stood out upon the brow of the veterinary. "For God's sake, child," he cried, "that was a mad thing to do."

Lori lifted her head, the rueful expression had pre-empted her mouth. She regarded him with a stabbing simplicity and said, "They call me Mad Lori." Then she added, "I will keep him quiet. He will not stir——"

MacDhui did not reply but merely glanced at her again and thereafter, using what few primitive instruments and equipment she possessed, went to work, patching, sewing, building, and lecturing as he worked in the manner of a college professor to an audience of students:

"Hm—so. Now we have built an anchor for the muscle with a good blood supply—you see where I have attached it to the undamaged portion—of course we shall have to see how it takes—still these are hardy beasts with great vitality. Ah, ah! This nerve here; note how it has been crushed. But the nerve sheath has not been ruptured and so there is a chance if we can find a way to nourish it——" He stopped suddenly and asked a question of her. "What is this power you exert over the animal, Lori? It should be snarling and snapping."

"He trusts me." Lori replied, her eyes riveted fascinated upon the near miracles the skilled fingers of the surgeon were performing.

MacDhui improvised brilliantly with the broken shoulder,

punching two holes in a sixpence and using it in lieu of a silver plate to rivet it together. He said, "If this succeeds, here will be one badger who will never lack for bus fare." As he worked he questioned Lori again. "And where did you find this poor beast?"

"It came here."

"I see. And how did it know to come here?"

"The angels guided it."

"Have you ever seen an angel, Lori?"

"I have heard their voices and the rush of their wings."

Mr. MacDhui felt himself suddenly filled with an unaccountable sadness, the sadness that results sometimes from a forgotten dream, or some hidden hurt to the soul that is touched off by something accidental or ordinary in life. He bestowed a long and searching look upon the girl standing beside him, gazing with undisguised admiration upon his work, and his sadness did not diminish. He shrugged, completed the bandaging of the animal, and having finished, stepped back, and spreading his hands almost like a stage magician who has performed a trick, said, "There now. It is done!"

Lori's thanks caught him unprepared. She took one of his hands in both hers and bent her head over it. MacDhui felt the moisture of a teardrop and then the soft touch of her lips. The sadness welled up in him a hundred times intensified. He said gruffly, "I have done the best I could under the circumstances. The important thing is to keep the beast quiet. Tomorrow I will come and put a plaster cast on the shoulder and paw and then it will be safe. Have you some place to keep it?"

Lori replied, "Aye. Come."

She raised up the badger in her arms with infinite care and led Mr. MacDhui through a door opening to the other part of the building divided into stalls and a few cages partitioned off.

Here was indeed a small hospital, but if the animal doctor expected to find any of his ex-patients quartered here, he was mistaken; they were all wild creatures. He saw a fawn with a broken leg that had been well set and splinted, a red squirrel with one eye out, and a rolled-up ball of a hedgehog that seemed to have no visible wound. He encountered hares that had been victims of weasel bites, a fox cub that had become separated from its mother, and a family of field mice in a box.

A burden seemed momentarily lifted from MacDhui. He had a sudden humorous intuition. "I think the hedgehog is m-a-l-i-n-g-e-r-i-n-g," he spelled out.

He was rewarded. Lori's wonderful ruefully tender smile warmed him. "Shhhh. Of course," she replied, "but I let him. It makes him so happy."

"And this is your treatment?"

Beneath the eye of the huge man Lori was momentarily troubled. She replied, "I keep them warm and try to make them comfortable. I let them rest and give them food and drink"—her voice fell to a whisper—"and love——"

Mr. MacDhui smiled. The prescription was the old stand-by that he and other veterinarians had used for years—with the exception of the last, which he was sure in his case was supplied by Willie Bannock. MacDhui would have added only, "—and let nature take its course." He asked of Lori then, "Well, and when people bring their pets to you?"

"They have their own to care for them. It is the wild and lost, the lonely and hurt things of the forest that need me."

Mr. MacDhui suddenly remembered something. "And Farmer Kinkairlie's cow?"

Lori seemed neither surprised nor put out that the veterinary should be in possession of this piece of intelligence. The touch of mischief returned to her mouth. She said, "I sent her back with the message to be kinder to her and she would then yield milk again."

MacDhui threw back his head and roared with laughter. He had a vision of the expression on the face of Farmer Kinkairlie when this message reached him.

They went out. When they came back to the cottage Lori said, "Will ye no' come in for a moment?"

Curiosity led MacDhui to follow her inside, his eyes roving swiftly over the simple furnishings and the great loom that he could see through the door in another room. His attention was momentarily caught by a glass bowl that stood on a table. It contained some rocks, a miniature wooden ladder, water, and a small green frog. Something stirred in MacDhui's memory and he pressed his face close to the bowl, his gaze directed at the legs of the frog. The strong white teeth of the man showed through the red bristle of his beard in a delighted grin. Sure enough, there it was, the little lump and swelling indicating there had once been a fracture which had healed.

"He too?" he asked.

"Aye," Lori replied. "I found him one morning on my doorstep in a box. He had a broken leg."

MacDhui said, "I can describe the delivering angel. He was aged eight, with a bullet head, freckles, a runny nose, and was dressed in a scout uniform."

Lori looked troubled. "I didna see it," she said, "I only heard the bell——"

MacDhui wished he had not made the joke.

Lori said, "I have no' much siller to pay——"

"There is no need, Lori. I have been repaid."

On a sudden impulse she darted past him and ran into the room where she did her weaving. She returned carrying a scarf of natural-colored wool of incredible softness and lightness.

"Will ye take this?" she pleaded. "It—it will keep ye warm— when the winds blow."

"Yes, thank you, Lori. I will." He wondered whether she knew how moved he was. At the door he repeated, "Thank you,

Lori. I shall be glad of this—when the winds blow. I will come tomorrow or the next day and fix a proper cast."

He turned and went out, leaving her standing in the middle of the room, watching him go. But he had the curious last-minute impression that she no longer saw him, that the gentle eyes seemed to be turned inward, an expression of pain and sorrow was etched momentarily on her lips. He went down the path of the glen remembering the name by which she was known—Daft Lori.

Mr. MacDhui climbed into his parked jeep, placing the wool scarf beside him. On an impulse he picked it up and settled it about his neck. It was as soft and warm as a caress. The almost insupportable feeling of sadness returned to fill him once more, nor could he shake it off as he drove away in the direction of home.

16 Driving toward Inveranoch and all that awaited him there and which now took on the aspect of another world situated almost in another universe from the one where he had dwelt the last hours since he had come to the glen, Andrew MacDhui pondered Lori and Lori's God.

Was it a part of the God-madness that afflicted those whose religious devotion crossed the line of sanity to fail to question the cruelty and capriciousness of a God who would first condemn one of His creatures to the steel trap, there to be worried half to death by a savage dog, before relenting and guiding it to the home of the one human being in the vicinity capable of helping it?

Was it a gigantic Jovian puppet game, when the badger's case had proved too much for her, to arrange with dramatic timing the fortuitous arrival of an Edinburgh-trained veterinary to perform the necessary surgery at just the right moment, and God's little joke that said surgeon had gone there for the purpose of giving an interfering and meddling half-wit a piece of his mind? Lori in her simplicity had seen none of this. She had said only that he had been sent in answer to her prayer.

For a moment MacDhui entertained the notion to have at his friend Angus Peddie about this and then put it out of his head for an odd reason. He was genuinely and wholeheartedly fond of the little man. He enjoyed arguing with him, but he loved him sufficiently not to wish to triumph over him and leave him embarrassed and demolished.

Besides, he had a suspicion that when he found himself in sore straits Peddie simply retired behind the theologian's wall by holding that the ways of God were mysterious, that His all-over designs and purposes were not to be discerned in immediate events, and above all that He was unanswerable to man. If He chose to let a dozen million Chinese starve, or the Russians slaughter the patriots of a neighbor nation, or He put a wild thing of the forest to torture, it was for a purpose to be revealed later, or perhaps, God being God, never revealed at all. He reflected that there seemed to be an uncomfortable affinity between the long and often unpleasant arm of coincidence, God, and Moloch.

And yet there was—Lori.

She was touched—of that he had no doubt. Her way of living and her behavior were abnormal, and yet he knew that if there was one over-all characteristic, one key, one clue to her being, it was compassion. And here his thoughts turned again to that God whom, in her mild and sweet aberration, she served in such a strange and faithful manner. Was compassion the link between them?

Supposing God had made man, not in His own image, but in some reflection of His own love and spirit, and turned him loose on earth to work out his own destiny. Must not His heart, must not any great, creative, all-embracing heart be wrung with compassion for what His children had turned out to be? And perhaps bitterness too. For if earth was a cosmic test tube of the universe, a dead star on which the spores of life had been scattered to see how they would flourish, then it was already one of God's colossal failures. Yet, too, He must be riven with pity for the fate of the wicked and miserable victims of the experiment.

Were the faithful like Peddie and the half mad like Lori all that He could look upon as salvage? Surely there was no place in any theological catalogue for one of His more signal fiascos, Mr. Veterinary MacDhui. Well, as he was, so was he. At the outskirts of Inveranoch he pulled himself erect to show the town the old, well-known figure of bristle and defiance, shoulders back, chin out——

Yet now that he was there he did not drive at once to the houses in the lane, but cut around behind the street to the track that ran through the lush green strip of woods leading toward Stirling Manor. Here he parked and got out and sat beneath the branches of a beech tree and where he could see the salt-blue of the loch shining through, for he was not yet done with thinking.

But now that he had found a peaceful place and a peaceful moment, his thoughts, as so often happened, refused to be marshaled or submit to order. Instead they provided him with an uncomfortable kaleidoscope, flashes of past and present, presentiments of the future in jumbled array.

He produced his pipe from his pocket, packed and lit it. A lesser egotist might have suspected that the man who had returned from Glen Ardrath was no longer the same one who had driven up there, and in some ways would never be again. But he was not used to solving his difficulties, his turmoils and confusions, through sober reflection. Introspection was something new to him and he did not know how to begin. And as yet he could not foresee the fearful and apparently insoluble dilemma that was to face him, or the trials that were in store for him, the dogs that would bait and worry him before he could snap the chains of the trap that held him fast and drag his remains in search of succor.

From above his head came a familiar chittering and scolding and a red squirrel slanted down the tree trunk beside him in fits and starts with nervous pauses. But he was hungry, familiar with humans, and had been hand fed before. When he reached the ground he sat up prettily on his bushy tail, his black paws folded over the white blaze on his dark red breast.

Mr. MacDhui reached into his left-hand jacket pocket, where he was wont to carry tidbits to distract or win the confidence of nervous animals, and fished up a piece of carrot. The squirrel came close, accepted it with tentative daintiness, whisked off, a red streak, some five paces, and sat up nibbling it.

Mr. MacDhui puffed on his pipe and said, "Contented now, aren't you?" It was easier to watch and talk to the squirrel than to think. "Do not eat too quickly," he admonished, "or you will have indigestion, which may lead to worms or some other form of parasite to which you little chaps seem to be prone, and that wouldn't be very comfortable."

The squirrel turned the carrot over rapidly two or three times in its paws and munched on, but sat so that he could keep a wary eye upon this talking man.

"If I may introduce myself," Mr. MacDhui suggested, "my name is Andrew MacDhui, a veterinary surgeon by profession. That should interest you, since it is a doctor who treats animals belonging to people when they are ill. I am not very much liked hereabouts. Furthermore I do not believe in God or a higher power. And I have a daughter, a child of mine own flesh and blood, who will not speak to me because when her cat contracted a form of meningitic paralysis I had it killed to save its suffering."

The squirrel ceased munching for a moment and looked up, masticating what it had in its cheek pouches, the carrot nearly finished.

"Ah, but did I indeed, you ask?" commented Mr. MacDhui, "and the exception is well taken. It is a query I have put to myself often enough in the past days. Could I have saved the beast or did I destroy it because I was jealous of Mary Ruadh? Did I even diagnose its ailment correctly? Mary Ruadh is my daughter's name. She is called Ruadh because her hair is a shade between your coat and mine. She carried the wretched animal about with her wherever she went and slept with it at night. I would see her bury her face in its flank and hug it to her like a living doll and perhaps I could not bide that. The child is motherless, you know, and I have tried to be both to her. Now she cries and longs for her dead cat, but to me, her father, she will not speak."

The squirrel finished the carrot and got down on all fours, whisking its tail. The voice of the man was making him nervous and he was of a mind to move off.

"Wait," pleaded Mr.MacDhui. "Do not leave me yet. It is good to have someone to talk to. Look here; I will bribe you to stay a little longer." He produced another carrot and made clucking noises. "And we won't speak of my troubles any longer, but yours."

The squirrel reflected, accepted the carrot, and this time, soothed by familiarity coupled with generosity, sat up quite close by.

"What do you do when you are ill?" Mr. MacDhui asked, for it struck him that, strangely, he had never thought of this before. "To whom do you go? Is there a wise old squirrel who tells you what herbs or roots to eat, or does your instinct tell you? Or do you just crawl away under a bush and die, with no one to know or care? Angus Peddie, my neighbor and a minister, says of his God that not a sparrow falleth but that He is concerned. But what arrangements has He made? Strange, but I have never come upon a dead squirrel or hedgehog or deer. What happens to you? Are you all eaten by the birds or the carnivores? Where are your graveyards?"

MacDhui continued to catechize: "Do you have friends? Are you ever lonely? And what about your young? Do you under-stand and feel for them? Do they touch your heart so that when you look at them sometimes you think you cannot bear the grief caused by the gulf between you and the fact that you cannot communicate with them, that their little minds have already gone out from you? Do you, too, love them and lose them so quickly?"

And he asked finally, "Do you live out a whole life of your own, with love and happiness, or worry and heartbreak? Or is there nothing but food and flight, nesting, mating, and dying, and are you more fortunate to be born a little forest animal without a soul than I, a human being, with all my wonderful intelligence? Who is to answer me that?"

The squirrel, the carrot finished, prepared to pack up. "Well, I can see that you are not going to," Mr. MacDhui concluded, and arose. The squirrel ran off but stopped short a few yards away, sat up and winked an eye, and then vanished up the far side of a tree. Mr. MacDhui, sucking on his pipe, feeling curiously relieved, walked to his jeep, got in, and drove home. It was shortly before Mary Ruadh's bath and supper time.

Each night that he returned Mr. MacDhui hoped that his daughter would be waiting for him in the entryway; each time he suffered disappointment. His anger had long since given way to bewilderment and heartache.

On the advice of Mr. Peddie, he tried to take no notice of her silence. He talked to her even though she would not reply and behaved toward her as much as possible as though nothing had happened. He bathed her as usual, supped with her, and then put her to bed—but with one difference. She refused to say her prayers while he was in the room and he had had to defer, while Mrs. McKenzie came and heard them.

But he had made it a point to return to her room each night, bend over her cot, and kiss her good night. She suffered him to do so without protest, her eyes staring upward at the ceiling, her gaze and thoughts turned inward or far from him. She never kissed him back.

As he came in, the entry and hall were bare. MacDhui could hear Mrs. McKenzie at work in the kitchen. He went on into his daughter's room, which was on the ground floor on the opposite side of the hall from his. She was sitting on one of her play chairs. Her favorite dolls were in a corner. She was doing nothing.

He picked her up in his arms, saying, "Hi, chicken. Your daddy's home. Anything to say to him?"

No one who had seen them together could have denied father and daughter—red hair, blue eyes, and each with truculent, immovable, stubborn chin turned toward the other.

As he held her in his arms, silent and irreconcilable as ever, he noted that her skin was clammy. "Hello," he said, "I don't much like the feel of this. Perhaps we will have Dr. Strathsay stop by in the morning and have a look at you. Are you feeling ill, Mary Ruadh?"

When she maintained her accustomed silence, he said, "Right then. Let's have our bath and supper and early to bed, warm and snug. And while I am bathing you I'll tell you a story of a brave badger who lived in the woods above Glen Ardrath and how the Red Faery of the glen who dwells in a stone house with her friends of the forest, field, and stream, saved his life."

He saw then, as she sat naked at the bottom of the tub that she had grown thinner, that the color and tone of her skin was not good, and that she was no longer the little pink frog who used to splash her toys in the water, or squirt the cake of soap out of her hand, or make noises, and who did not even try to avert her face from the trial of washing.

Nevertheless he was aware that she was listening to his story.

He was surprised himself how it grew in the telling, and the strange affection he felt for the animal as he visualized it for his child.

In the story the badger became a person, heroic, noble, brave, possessed of feelings and a soul. It ranged the forest, loving life and the world in which it found itself. When it was caught in the trap he felt the pang at his own heart, and a cry was wrung from

Mary Ruadh, the first that he had heard from her lips. But it was for the unfortunate beast and not for him.

He waxed eloquent over the badger's gallant struggle to live even when attacked, and described the great effort it had made to snap the chain of the trap and drag himself to the cottage of the Red Faery. And when he told how Lori had cradled and cuddled and comforted the poor wounded beast, he saw tears flow from Mary Ruadh's eyes and these were the first he had seen, too, since she had cried to him to spare her cat.

That night when he came in to complete the ritual and give the unwanted good-night kiss, he leaned over the bed and said, "The brave badger will get well—and someday perhaps you shall see it——"

He picked her up and kissed her. Her arms seemed to fall naturally about his shoulders, and as he held her thus he whispered, "Mary Ruadh, I love you——"

Was there the faintest return pressure of those thin arms? Had there been? The surging of his heart within him told him that it was so. For an instant they had closed about him, clinging to him.

He laid her back upon the pillow, and though she did not speak to him yet, there was as a great singing inside him, for there were tears in her eyes again and he felt that the beginning had been made.

He kissed her again and went away, but that night he left her door open so that he would hear her, should she stir or call out. He himself went to his office and busied himself with district and county reports for a few hours before retiring to bed with a heart lighter than he could remember.

17 I, Bast-Ra, goddess, am about to do a godlike thing.

I shall invoke the power that lies within me bestowed by the great gods Ra, the sun, and Hathor, the moon.

I shall punish.

I shall doom.

It is not a simple matter to be God. I know this, for I have been and am one.

Men have envied the power of God. I envy man. To him has been given the power to choose between good and evil.

There is no good and there is no evil for God—only God's will.

This night it is my will to work a mischief and destroy the Man with the Red Beard.

And the doom I have foreseen for him shall be one that is worse even than death.

Not for nothing am I known as Sekhmet-Bast-Ra, the tearer and render.

18 Sometimes in the summer when the warm air from the south was rebuffed by the cold seas of the north, a hot, strong wind blew up the long corridor of the valley of Loch Fyne, as the pressures built up through the mazes of sea and land down by the Firth of Clyde and Kilbrannan Sound went whistling away to escape through any vent that offered itself.

Rarer, but not unlike the foehns of Switzerland and Austria or the mistrals of the South of France, it brought unease and discomfort during its brief stay, rattled doors and windows, made eerie sounds about the chimneys, not associated with honest winter gales, plucked at loose shutters, and ruffled the waters of the loch into unfamiliar splashings, gurglings, and suckings. Dogs whined during its blowing and were irritable, and people more so. Usually in twenty-four hours it blew itself out, funneling into the sky to form the alto-cumulus clouds which later would discharge themselves in the form of the rare but severe Highland thunderstorm.

Such a visitation announced itself that night already mentioned, when Mr. MacDhui certain that the Coventry his daughter had imposed upon him was about to end, was closing off his paper work in his study and preparing to retire.

It manifested itself with the violent crashing of an upstairs shutter and sent Mr. MacDhui dashing aloft to fasten it. As he leaned from the window, the wind tore at his sleeves, his hair, his eyelids and cheeks, disconcertingly and with a kind of evil glee, and he was glad to put his head inside and lock the window firmly.

He had experienced this Scotch mistral once before, and went about the house seeing to shutter and window fastenings, and making certain that the back door was firmly shut. He looked into the room of Mary Ruadh to see whether the banging of the loose shutter had disturbed her, but he noted that she was sleeping peacefully. He closed her window but for a crack, for later the wind would strengthen and try to enter houses. When he was satisfied that his home and his family were shipshape, he retired to his own room opposite, undressed, and went to bed.

It was half past ten when he looked at his watch before putting out the light and he lay there in the darkness, listening to the wind strumming the telephone and utility wires and the small crashes as the agitating loch began to burst its wavelets against the pebbly shore. His relief that the miserable, upsetting duel between his daughter and himself seemed about to end offset the disquiet of the night and a few minutes later he drifted off to sleep.

He was awakened, he knew not at what time, by the long-drawn-out mournful calling of the cat, somewhere close by, singing to the maddened night. The mistral was in full cry now, every tree branch bending to it, every leaf a-rustle, as the wind soughed through them relentlessly; the loch was roaring, answering the pressures that stirred its surface; loose things were flying down the street; a roof shingle was vibrating.

Mr. MacDhui awoke, chilled with the fear that grips humans suddenly returned to life with nature on the rampage. His nerves were twanging like the wires without and every sound and vibration seemed intensified and exaggerated.

The cat cried again. "Mrow—Mrow—MRRRRRRRROW." This time the call came from directly beneath his window, raising the hackles at the back of his head as he sat up in bed on one elbow to listen.

He would have been less than human had not the thought of a vindictive Thomasina, returned to haunt him, crossed his mind, and he shivered in the darkness, before angrily laughing off the notion. The neighborhood was alive with cats—there seemed to be one in the window or on the doorstep of every household in the lane.

Yet when he heard the thump and scratch at the sill Mr. MacDhui snapped on the light in time to catch a glimpse of the cobalt-glowing coals of the eyes, the pink muzzle and white teeth, and then it was gone.

Mr. MacDhui, unnerved by the vision and the whooping of the wind, remained leaning upon his elbow, waiting and listening, staring at the empty windowpane. A corner of his eye caught the time; a few minutes past midnight.

Then the cat yowled again, but this time there was an answering cry that rang through his head with fearful impact.

"Thomasina!"

It came from Mary Ruadh's room and sent a shudder down his spine. The next moment he heard the patter of her feet and saw the white flash of her pajamaed figure as it whipped past his bedroom, then heard the front door thrown wide, and the next moment the hounds of the summer mistral were within the house, raging through the corridor, upsetting the umbrella stand with a clatter, whirling papers, whisking a picture from the wall.

In the grip of fear and night panic, Mr. MacDhui leaped from his bed, pausing only to slip into his trousers and seize the electric torch from his night table. Switching on the beam, he ran from the house, filled with a thousand dreads and apprehensions.

He located the child immediately in the beam of the torch, a slim white figure with hair flying, bare feet whisking over the cobbles in pursuit of the cat. Immediately, too, the wind swooped upon him, buffeting, befuddling, pushing and pulling at him, further outraging his nerves.

"Mary Ruadh!" he shouted against the hundred noises of the night, "Mary Ruadh, come back!"

Either she did not or would not hear him, but the cat she was pursuing suddenly turned at right angles and ran across the street. With a great cry of rage, Mr. MacDhui drew back his arm and let fly the heavy torch at the animal.

It clattered and shattered against the cobbled pave, ringing as it turned over and over like a dislodged ninepin, missing the cat, which gave an agonized shriek and in a night-blurred streak vanished over a garden wall. Then it was that the child faced about and saw her father, his arm still rigid from the throw, his shirt flapping, his mane blowing wildly, his figure outlined against the light streaming from the cottage door.

She stood there, a slender trembling reed swaying in the grip of the wind, upon her face a look of such horror as Mr. MacDhui never hoped to see again. She opened her lips as though crying something, or wishing to cry out, but no sound emerged from them. Then her father reached her and gathered her trembling and shaking uncontrollably to his breast.

He enfolded her as though shielding her from all the furies, crying to her, "It's all right, Mary Ruadh. It's all right, I'm here. It was nothing but a bad dream." He punched his way through the wind back to the house and inside, shouldering the door closed, then knelt, still enfolding the shuddering child.

"There, Mary Ruadh. It was only a dream. There is nothing to be frightened of. Or was it that old cat of Mrs. Culross's that woke you? I didn't half send her over the fence in a hurry—frightening my little girl——"

It was the fearful silence of her that alarmed him. Not so much as a sob came from her, but there was no mistaking the renewed hatred and terror in her eyes. The little body trembled uncontrollably in his arms.

He said, "You've had a nasty fright, my girl, but there's nothing can harm you. Do you want to come in and sleep with Daddy?"

He held the miserable and shaking child away from him for a moment, looking for some sign. He wished she would cry; he wished that she would throw her two arms about his neck and cling to him and cry her eyes out against his cheek so that he could comfort her. But she did not.

"It wasn't Thomasina!" he said desperately.

He picked her up and took her into his room and laid her in his bed, smoothing the pillow under her head. "In the morning, we'll have Dr. Strathsay in for a look-see," he said. "Now cuddle to Daddy and we'll both get some sleep."

But for a long time, before sleep claimed them both, he could feel the awful, silent trembling of her body, as though she were racked by sobs that she would not or could not release.

Dr. Strathsay sat in the office of Mr. MacDhui and fumbled with the seal attached to his heavy-linked watch chain. He was a comfortably ponderous man with rough iron-gray hair and the jowls and sad eyes of a bloodhound. As years of the practice of medicine had deepened his wisdom, it had also softened his heart to the point where he was forced to conceal it beneath a dour manner and a kind of professional pessimism.

Now he spoke thoughtfully and unhappily, looking down at the fat carved stone seal in his fingers. "The child has lost the power of speech. Did you know this?"

MacDhui conquered the sickness at the pit of his stomach and said, "She has not addressed a word to me in almost a month, ever since the time she brought her pet cat Thomasina to me, suffering from a type of animal neuromeningitis. Its limbs were already paralyzed and I had it chloroformed. But she continued to speak with others."

Dr. Strathsay nodded. "I see. Now she is unable to speak at all."

MacDhui understood now the meaning of that last fearful silence the night before. He asked, "Did you find any physical——"

"I do not know—as yet," Dr. Strathsay confessed. "There seems to be nothing wrong in the region of the vocal chords. Of course there is always the further problem of—ahem"—and he coughed uncomfortably, for these were the kind of interviews he dreaded—"the speech areas of the brain, as well as, ah, other and perhaps less tangible factors. Has the child had a shock of some kind?"

"Yes," Mr. MacDhui admitted. "I think perhaps so. Last night during the wind, I was awakened by the caterwauling of a puss outside the window and the child's loud outcry of 'Thomasina!' She ran out of the house after it and I after her."

"And was it Thomasina?" Dr. Strathsay inquired gravely.

"Hardly. Thomasina is dead. From the glimpse I caught of it, it was a cat belonging to one of the neighbors. But in her sleep Mary Ruadh could have mistaken its cry for that of—of the one that had been her pet. When I reached her and brought her back she was trembling—I took her into my bed——"

The doctor nodded. "How long has she been ill?" he asked.

"Ill?" repeated Mr. MacDhui, and looked at the old practitioner anxiously, "But she has not been ill." Then he recollected, Mr. Peddie. He said, "Mr. Peddie did suggest—— And last night I found her skin somewhat clammy to the touch."

Dr. Strathsay said, "It is not unusual for the physician to fail to recognize sickness when it is near to him—— I should say the child was very ill."

Mr. MacDhui exhaled a long sigh. "Have you any idea as to the nature of the illness?"

"Not yet. Nor should I say there was as yet any real cause for alarm. I shall have to make a more detailed examination and the usual laboratory tests, blood and urine. Then we shall see. In the meantime I suggest she be kept in bed with rest and quiet and all the love and attention possible. She is badly frightened, as indeed you and I would be likewise if we were suddenly stricken dumb. What started out as a sort of a game, almost, has turned fearfully earnest. Ah—I don't suppose something such as another cat, or perhaps a puppy might——"

As Mr. MacDhui's nerves cracked again, he leaped from his chair, slamming the surface of the desk with his fist. The doctor placed a soothing hand upon the veterinary's arm. "Sorry! Of course you would have tried——" He arose heavily. "Well, we shall do our best. I have given her a sedative. Perhaps it is only a children's disease incubating and waiting to develop, coupled with hysteria, and we shall have to wait a time to see. I will look in again this evening."

Mr. MacDhui watched him go. Without putting it into so many words, the doctor had managed to convey that he considered the situation not to his liking. For the first time that he could remember, MacDhui did not envy the medical man his profession. Aye, family friend, healer, and humanitarian he might be, but what of the times when there was no cure and he must face the family and say to them, "Prepare yourselves. There is no hope?"

He shuddered and then pulled himself together strongly. Dr. Strathsay was known to tend toward the pessimistic side rather than raise false hopes by overoptimism. The first examination had indicated nothing organically wrong with the child——

But he could not maintain the pose. If he lost his daughter he would not be able to bear it. Again and again he cursed the miserable cat that had been the cause of it all and which, just as the struggle between himself and his daughter had appeared about to end, had seemed like a ghost to have returned from the nether world. The mere memory of it, the crying of its name, appeared to have been sufficient to destroy her and with her, himself too.

Mr. MacDhui arose, left his office, and went over to his dwelling and into Mary Ruadh's room. She was sleeping, and now that he stood there looking down, he noted what he knew he should have seen long ago, the bluish circles beneath her eyes, the pall and translucent texture of the skin, the bloodlessness of the young mouth.

Mrs. McKenzie was fecklessly and needlessly dusting things in a neighboring room that had been dusted ten times over; an eye and ear pitched toward Mary Ruadh's door.

MacDhui went to her and with more kindness than he had shown her in many a day, for he saw that she was looking wan and worried herself, said, "That's right, Mrs. McKenzie. Remain close in case she should wake up. Let the kitchen go for a while. She will want comfort and someone close by whom she trusts. She has had a shock and lost the power of speech temporarily. Should you notice anything alarming and I am not here, do not hesitate to send for Dr. Strathsay at once."

He was surprised at the hostility of the look the angular housekeeper turned upon him. "Shock indeed," she sniffed. "I wouldna doot that. The bairn's grievin' hersel' ower her Thomasina that ye pit tae daith wi' nae mair thocht nor heart fer yer ain kin an' bluid nor a stone. Like as not she'll end in a grave aside her beloved puss, and ye'll hae none but yersel' to blame, Mr. Veterinary MacDhui, an' it's time someone said so tae yer face, and ye may dae what ye like aboot it."

MacDhui merely nodded and said, "Stay nigh, Mrs. McKenzie. I gather we shall have some further news when Dr. Strathsay comes again this evening and it may not be all bad."

He went out and returned to his office and began packing his bag for his rounds. He could not get the cat out of his mind. Had he but been less impatient, treated it, caged it, let Willie Bannock look after it—— It might have died anyway, but the child would not have resented it so. The words of Mrs. McKenzie came back to him—"with no more thought to your own blood and kin than a stone——" Was this indeed what he was like? Was it true what they were saying of him in the town?

Tortured, his mind fled then into another and seemingly far-off world, one to be entered only through a magic door of glass perhaps. It was as lost, distant, and unreal as the realm of Queen Mab and all her faery train. Somewhere there was a stone cottage in a forest glade by a covin-tree from whence hung a silver bell, and where there dwelt a woman with red hair who was not all of this world, but who lived for the hurt and sick creatures of the wilderness. And in this dream he tugged the cord of the Mercy Bell and when she came forth and asked who or what it was needed her help he said, "I do, Lori."

He saw that without knowing he had taken a package of powdered plaster from the shelf and was holding it in his hand. He remembered then that he had promised to return to the glen and put a plaster cast upon the shoulder of the badger for the mad girl who lived there. He dropped the package into the bag and went out.

19 Ho, Ho, you should have seen me dance that morning! I leaped, I ran, I spun in mid-air. I jumped twisty-wise to the side, eight jumps all stiff-legged, then around and around I went and up the covin-tree and down.

I laid back my ears and ran. I ran and ran and when I came to where Lori was I put the brakes on and skidded across the grass, then leaped into the air across my own shadow and came down washing, so that Lori laughed. "Talitha! You funny, funny puss!"

Oh, I had never felt so gay and wonderful and godlike, for the night before, the power to interfere had come back to me on the wings of a wind like the ancient desert khamsin, and I had worked a perfectly stupendous mischief and was mightily pleased with myself.

I hugged my secret to my breast as I danced, for no one had seen me come or go. I slipped away under the noses of the foolish dogs and in the morning Lori found me sleeping in my basket, as usual. But, oh, I had been as the gods of old that night.

Wullie and McMurdock, and Dorcas and her kittens came out to watch as I ran and ran, first in ever-widening circles, and then straightaway in the cat gallop, pulling and kicking so that my paws hardly touched the ground and I fairly flew. Then around I went again with my fur and tail bushed and when I came to Lori I threw myself on my back at her feet and rolled from side to side while she laughed and leaned over and rubbed the underside of my belly and scratched under my chin and said, "Talitha, you're daft this morning."

And the dogs became infected with the gaiety of my dance and began to jump about and bark too, and the birds flew up. The magpie flapped its wings and croaked, "Talitha's mad!" The kittens commenced to chase their tails, the squirrel took to flying about in the branches of the covin-tree, and none of them knew I was celebrating the fact that I had visited a really prodigious punishment upon a mortal, as I was used to doing in the old days when I was all knowing and all powerful.

Yet, even as I danced and celebrated, I was not wholly happy or content, for no one believed that I was a goddess. I think that Lori suspected, for she was very wise, and her eyes were like the eyes of the priestesses I used to have in ancient Egypt. But when once you have been worshiped as I have, it is most disconcerting not to be.

That day Lori, too, was gayer than I had ever seen her before. She sang as she went about her feeding of the birds and animals; it was a song without words; the melody was one born in a human heart when the world was still young. The sweetness of it reminded me of the temple flutes of Khufu. And ever and anon she would stop and listen, or glance down the path that led from the glen to the cottage as though she were expecting someone.

Shortly after midmorning the Mercy Bell rang. I managed to get up a tree, one near the stables, just in time. It was the Man with the Red Beard.

God am I, warden of the heavens, spinner of the threads of destiny, yet this man I hate and fear.

To Lori I sent messages. "Beware! Beware! Send him forth from here. For I have placed a doom upon him and he is as one accursed. All who have to do with him will share his doom. Send him forth from here because of the evil he has done. Beware!"

But Lori did not hear me and I could not reach her. It was not thus in my temple in Bubastis. There I had but to think a thought, barely to feel a warning or a prophecy and my high priestess, Nefert-Amen, would arise and casting off her veil would cry, "Hear, oh hear—Bast-Ra has spoken." And the worshipers, without in the temple courtyard, would fall upon their faces and avert their eyes and groan and praise me for my wisdom.

Lori and the man went into the stables together.

He came not only that morning, but the next day and the next, and the next thereafter.

I spied upon them from the roof of the stables and learned his name and who he is. It is Andrew MacDhui and he is an animal doctor from the town below, where Lori goes sometimes to fetch supplies, and he healed Lori's wounded badger that came to her one day almost dead from its injuries. It is strange that I should fear him so. For I am Bast-Ra, the goddess, but before that I am a cat, the lord of the earth. Yet in the sight of this man my blood turns to water; I quake and tremble and run like the smallest, most timorous, most frightened of mice.

Why? Who is he? Except for the doom-dream I have never encountered him before. Yet my god-sense tells me that he is a slayer of cats and hence accursed and I have put my punishment upon him.

The MacDhui was worming his way into Lori's confidence by teaching her. I watched him show her how to make a plaster cast for the shoulder and paw of the badger, and they worked together side by side, and the man flattered her by marveling how skilled her fingers were and how a touch from them would soothe the wildest and most savage beast. When the plaster was set the MacDhui lifted the badger's head, pulled his ears, and rubbed his fur and said, "Old fellow, I think you're going to live to fight another battle. If anything you are going to strike even a stronger blow when this shoulder knits. But keep out of traps." The badger rolled his eyes at him like a worshipful dog and when I saw the smile that Lori gave him I nearly died with hatred and jealousy. Had I not been so afraid of him, I should have jumped down through the hole and scratched and bitten out his throat.

Another day I watched them as he taught her how to set and splint the broken wing of a crow, and I looked down with envy and disgust at the two red heads close together bent over the black bird and their fingers meeting as they worked to mend the broken bone.

But he could not seem to bear it when Lori spoke of her unseen friends with whom she often talked in the forest, or the little caves in the rocky parts of the glen. Once he went about the room, pushing out his bristly red beard at all the shelves and the jars of ointments Lori had got on them, and then there was nothing for it but he had to get into every one with his fingers, or his nose, smelling, tasting. Then he asked, "Where did you come by your knowledge of medicinal herbs, Lori? Your pharmacopoeia is quite creditable."

When she replied, "The Little People," he glared at her like an angry bull and cried, "What? What nonsense! I asked you for a sensible answer, Lori."

From my vantage spot, looking through the hole in the roof, I spit at him and cursed him again, for he brought a tear to Lori's eyes. She looked like a small child that has been scolded. She said, "They live under the bracken. You don't often get to see them, but sometimes if you go quietly you can hear them whispering——"

The MacDhui said, "I'm sorry, Lori—I didn't mean——" But he never said what it was he hadn't meant.

Another time he asked her, "Who are you, Lori?"

"I am—Lori. I am no one."

"Where do you come from, Lori?"

"From Sligachan in Skye by the hills of Cuchullin."

"That is a far piece from here."

"Aye."

"Have you any parents living, or relatives, Lori, no one to whom you belong?"

"No."

"How came you here?"

"The angels guided me."

And again he glared at her.

But all the time she was growing more skilled, more knowledgeable in the healing of hurt, more used to his ways so that now they worked more swiftly and silently, she understanding what he wished and having it at hand before he asked.

One day he brought a little dog in a basket. It was very sick. He placed it on the table, along with knives and instruments he had in a case. Then together, he and Lori worked for a long time over the dog, he explaining, she ever ready with what he needed.

When it was finished, he said, "May I leave it here with you, Lori? I have done what I can, but the beast needs now what only you can give it—— When you have made it well I will come for it."

When he went away Lori came out of the stables and stood looking after him until he disappeared around the bend in the path and his footsteps were no longer heard. I came down from the roof via the beech tree and twined about her ankles. I heard her whisper, "Who am I?" and then, "What am I?" and at the very last, "What is this singing in my heart?"

I rubbed harder against her ankles, but she did not seem to know that I was there.

20 Dr. Strathsay and Mr. Andrew MacDhui walked slowly together by the loch side, contemplating the gray waters, the walking gulls on the tide-bared sand and the heavy gray day. Across the long, narrow expanse of salt water a curtain of rain falling from fast-scudding clouds was traveling northward up the valley but along the opposite shore.

The grayness of the weather seemed even to drain the color out of MacDhui's hair and beard. It got into the folds of Dr. Strathsay's jowls and enveloped his battered hat and mackintosh. But his eyes were alive, intelligent and compassionate. His news seemed to be good, but he delivered it warily to the man who hung upon every word.

He said, "The reports have been returned from Edinburgh and they tally with what my examination indicated. There is nothing organically wrong with the child. There is not so much as the suspicion of a growth in the throat or the vicinity of the vocal chords. Scrapings were negative. The blood tests likewise. I do not mind telling you that at one time I suspected leukemia—separate and apart from the loss of speech. Well, we shall not have to worry about that any longer. The child is sound."

MacDhui breathed a long sigh: "Ahhhh! That is good."

"Yes," Dr. Strathsay agreed, "that is indeed good and I feel greatly relieved on that score. Kidneys, heart, and lungs are in excellent order. Later we may want an encephalograph. However I am certain the brain is not affected."

MacDhui exhaled again. "I am glad to have your opinion as to the brain. As long as there is nothing seriously——"

Dr. Strathsay nodded and poked at a cluster of beach pebbles with his steel-shod cane. "Nevertheless," he said, "the child is gravely ill."

The veterinary repeated the words "gravely ill" as though he wished to be sure that this was what the doctor said and, while MacDhui maintained outward composure, inwardly he felt close to panic again. It struck him as a fearful phrase to hear from the lips of a doctor. The adjective was rattling around inside his head and he was trying to seize it, to make it hold still long enough to place it beneath a kind of mental microscope to see what it was made up of, what it contained, what menace, what hope. A situation that was grave was bad, yet not irretrievable. People had extricated themselves from grave situations—but never from the grave itself—— He heard himself say, "Nevertheless since, as you say, she is suffering from no discernible cause——"

"Perhaps there is an indiscernible origin to be sought," Dr. Strathsay concluded. "In my grandfather's time people sickened from a number of causes not officially countenanced today. One read of a rejected suitor pining away, becoming hollow-eyed and gaunt; maidens suffering frustration in love became delicate and feeble and took to their beds. Betrayed wives, or aging women fearing betrayal became invalids or even paralytics, and all of these ailments were treated as genuine, which indeed they were. The sickness of a woman who cannot walk or suffers from fainting spells is just as real as—a child who suddenly cannot speak."

While Mr. MacDhui listened attentively he was thinking furiously all the while about the word "grave," and what it was exactly Dr. Strathsay was trying to say to him in words, both spoken as well as unspoken.

Oh, the hell of medicine and the human relationship! Was there any leaven of hope tucked away in that word "gravely"? He remembered suddenly and appallingly the hopes that he himself so frequently had denied and he had an instant of almost fierce relief that he did not believe in God, for in the God-regulated world transgression and punishment went hand in hand. It was something to cling to at the moment that the wicked and ungodly frequently were found sitting at the top of the heap. If he believed, it would have to be in a God who might take Mary Ruadh away from him, "call her to Him," as the preachers put it, because he was judged not fit to be her father—— He did not reply to what the doctor had said, and the latter, after prodding at some purple weed and sea slime carried in by the tide, continued.

"Were my late grandfather, Dr. Alexander Strathsay, to return to this earth and visit Mary Ruadh, he would enter, sniff the air of the sickroom, half his diagnosis completed as he crossed to the bed, take the chin of the patient in his hand and look long and piercingly into her eyes. He would satisfy himself that there was no organic malfunctioning, and thereafter, closing the door of the room behind him, would announce without further equivocation to the nearest relative, 'That child is dying of a broken heart.'"

Mr. MacDhui still did not speak, but it was from numbing shock now. So there was punishment after all, punishment not arranged by any magistrates or judges, read out from codes of law, but sentences nevertheless to be lived, worked or suffered out. Yet by whom and where from were they ordained? Was there somewhere in the universe a scales that worked out weight for weight and measure for measure and for how long you had to pay? And whose justice and what kind was it to impose a lifetime of guilt, misery, and regret as quittance for the expunged life of a sick cat? Was this a planned vindictiveness from behind the stars, or just the luck of a spinning globe wandering in its orbit, unhampered, with chance, as in the turning roulette wheel, the arbiter into which slot or morass the little pellet of your life should sink?

"If I were not a reasonably modern practitioner, familiar with modern methods which read the pulsations of the heart by electricity, I might be tempted to say with my grandfather, 'That child is ill of and suffering from a broken heart.' And for this, the finest mechanical heart built and prepared to beat during repairs in Edinburgh hospital is no substitute, and no electrocardiograph will show why it is slowly failing——"

They came to a boundary fence where the public path ended at private property and the two reversed their steps as the gray curtain of rain shrouding the hills opposite began to edge across the narrow arm of the loch.

"I think we shall have a taste of that," Dr. Strathsay remarked of the threatening weather, and then added, "Had you ever thought of remarrying, Andrew?"

Mr. MacDhui stopped still upon the path and stared at his companion. A month ago he would have replied unequivocally, "No, nor do I ever intend to." But in that same moment in which, with the simple inspiration of the great doctor, Strathsay had reached to the heart of the matter of his daughter's illness, so had he with similar accuracy probed the dilemma on which MacDhui had been impaled ever since for the first time he had laid eyes on Lori.

"No, no," the old man assured MacDhui, "I am not meaning to pry into your affairs as it may have sounded. What I am trying to say is that the child needs love."

"As if I did not love her—to despair," groaned Mr. Veterinary MacDhui, and for that instant could not have said whether he was speaking of Mary Ruadh or Lori. He knew only that he loved them both and one was slipping away from him and the other was unattainable.

"Yes, yes," conceded the doctor, his sad bloodhounds' eyes

looking sympathetically upon his colleague, "that is indeed true of all us fathers. We love them to despair, or to distraction, or to the limit of our abilities insofar as they reflect our own images. And we give them their first experience of the power of the love of man, but it is not the same as the softer, more protective, more secure and sweeter love of a woman or a mother."

"I have tried——" MacDhui began, when Strathsay interrupted him.

"I am not saying, Andrew, that you would not have succeeded had not a serious crisis arisen in the life of the child, the details of which I do not yet know. But it must have begun before the cry in the night that was like that of her dead pet."

"It began the day I had the cat chloroformed."

"I suspected as much. It is just during such times of exaggerated grief or crisis that parents of both sexes are most sorely needed to tide them over. Each makes a necessary contribution, he of strength, she of tenderness and feminine understanding and when these two are beautifully combined a bulwark is reared, a dike against which the storms lash in vain."

"Is this your prescription then?" Mr. MacDhui asked bleakly, and with such an expression of despair upon his otherwise lively and aggressive countenance that Dr. Strathsay could not forego a gentle laugh.

"Come on, man," he said. "You aren't being led to the block yet. Don't look as though the executioner were beckoning."

"Still if Mary Ruadh is—grave——" MacDhui hesitated over the hateful phrase and Dr. Strathsay completed it for him.

"Gravely ill. Yes, I used the word 'gravely' advisedly, for there is a process working that must be reversed. She is proceeding downward along a path that—well, she must be turned from it. But I would say that she was in no immediate danger, for she has always been a healthy child with vitality and resistance. We will try to keep that resistance high."

They were approaching the outskirts of the town and the lane close to the shore where MacDhui lived. The doctor gave him a clap on the arm and said, "Come, man, don't look so glum. Let's see some bristle back in that great, red bush of yours. All is far from lost and we will do everything that is possible to—bring her back. Love, love, love! Give her love in great, huge, heaping over-doses. Had I a warehouse as big as Ben Lomond, or The Cobbler, filled with love, I should soon empty it with prescriptions, for there is no better cure in the world for the ailments of man, woman, or child—and for beasts as well, as you no doubt have discovered for yourself in your profession. Well, I'll be off," and he went stumping down the street.

MacDhui watched him out of sight with reluctance. For the first time he was experiencing that dependency upon the man of healing that humans come to feel when sickness strikes and death threatens, and that sense of loneliness when the doctor leaves. For MacDhui there was nothing or no one else to whom to turn.

He entered the house and, shedding his hat and mackintosh, went into Mary's room. He was used now to the silence reigning in a house that had once rung cheerfully with the noisy presence of a young child.

Mary Ruadh lay half propped up by pillows, her red hair and the extreme pallor of her face contrasting with the green comforter thrown about her to keep her warm. She lay staring up at the ceiling. Mrs. McKenzie had been sitting at her bedside, sewing, but she now, with an instinctive feeling of tact, arose, mumbling about looking after something on the stove, and went off to her kitchen.

Mr. MacDhui knelt and gathered his daughter to his heart, her head tucked beneath his chin. He held her strongly close to him, yet tenderly so that the love he felt for her would flow from him to her and to that heart of hers, which he could feel now slowly beating against his and which, according to the old doctor, had become broken and needed mending.

He sent the current of his love to heal her, but found that he was unable to speak to her. The love words would not rise to his lips, for he was a man and now for the first time he understood what Dr. Strathsay had meant. From a woman would have come those sweet and loving words of comfort, "My darling, my precious, my poppet, my bonnie; my little girl, my dearest; I am here. Do not fear; see, I am here with you; I hold you enfolded close to my heart where nothing can harm you, my bonnie, my dear——"

Why was it these speeches came so hard to a man and so easily to a woman? He groaned with the inward burden of what he could not express to his daughter and after a time put her away from him, leaning her gently against the pillow, stroking her head and hand. Her eyes remained fixed upon his face. He could not fathom the expression in them, but he felt his inadequacy.

In his mind Mr. MacDhui replaced himself now with the figure of Lori, and at once he saw the gentle inclination of her head as she bent over the bed of the child. It was almost as though she were standing there beside him, so vividly did he remember that half-rueful, half-tender expression at the corners of her mouth. He saw how the copper-red hair would fall upon either side of her shoulders to mingle with the red-gold of Mary Ruadh's, and he was remembering how she had cradled the injured badger in her arms. He saw his child held there instead and heard the love words that this gentle woman would speak to her.

Mr. MacDhui sat down by the bedside with a sigh, as the bitterness of his dilemma drove him to the point of despair. For the hundredth time he saw the dream destroyed by the cruelty of reality.

For Lori was fey, Lori was mad, Lori lived an unnatural life; her eyes looked within rather than without. There were names in the scientific and clever world for the sickness that beset her mind.

Lori heard voices from heaven and communed with the unseen. Lori had abandoned actuality to live within a myth. Lori had taken the veil. She served not humankind but the animal kingdom. It was the supreme irony that Lori could never be the woman that Dr. Strathsay had prescribed to bring love and affection to a motherless child and fill the heart of a wicked, lonely man who loved her. Mr. MacDhui buried his face in his hands, pressing his fingers into his brow as though to force some solution to come into his brain. When he removed them he saw that Mary Ruadh had gone quietly to sleep.

He observed now all that Dr. Strathsay had mentioned, the translucence and the pallor, the shadows and hollows, but what wrung his heart most grievously was that most beautiful of all features in the sleeping of children, the mouth. It seemed to him that it had formed into the shape of surrender.

Mr. MacDhui arose heavily and went out of the room. He thought that he would seek out and have a talk with his friend, Mr. Angus Peddie, minister of the Reformed Presbyterian Church of Inveranoch, the inside of which he, MacDhui, had yet to see, or any other. He wished to ask him a question.

21 The study of the rectory attached to the Presbyterian church was unfamiliar to Andrew MacDhui, and he felt as ill at ease there as a schoolboy.

Ordinarily nothing would have been simpler than for the veterinary to have dropped in upon the Reverend Angus Peddie at his home next door, as he did frequently for an evening of smoking or arguing and over a pipeful of shag and a glass of beer or two, and to have unburdened himself.

It was significant of the emotional state in which MacDhui found himself that he was unable to do this and place his dilemma before Peddie on an easygoing, man-to-man basis. Instead he paid his friend a formal afternoon call at his place of business, so to speak, and found himself constrained as any back-country parishioner in unfamiliar clothes and unfamiliar surroundings sitting, bowler hat in hand, on the edge of his chair, waiting for a word with the dominie.

True, Mr. MacDhui was dressed no differently than ever, in his old tweed jacket with the leather elbow patches; his flaming, unruly hair was hatless, but his spirit was subdued and he did favor the edge of the chair. From there he contemplated the minister sitting behind his desk, on which were piled books and papers, looking somewhat like a Mr. Pickwick in a literary mood, the potted plant standing on its mahogany pedestal in the corner, the tall bookcase, the electric fire beneath the brown mantelpiece, the chessboard with pieces on a small table, the etchings on the walls, and the dark paneling of the walls themselves.

Peddie, masking his surprise well at seeing him there, had said, "Come in, come in, Andrew, and sit down. No, you do not disturb in the least. The break is welcome and will save my congregation a sermon fifteen minutes too long, for I shall bring it to a close here and now."

But when MacDhui had settled himself uneasily on a straight-backed chair a silence fell between them which was not relieved until Fin, the minister's dyspeptic pug dog, got up out of his basket next to his master's desk, puffing and wheezing, came over to the veterinary and sat up before him, begging with little paddling movements of his paws.

There was a dish of bonbons at MacDhui's elbow and he reached absently for one, popping it into the dog's mouth. The animal bugged out his eyes with pleasure and fell to enjoying it.

The Reverend Peddie regarded his friend with a triumphant smile. "There, you see?" he said.

Even MacDhui had to laugh and, the ice somewhat broken, he made a great show of loading his pipe to enable him to get a grip upon himself and somehow make a beginning. When he had got it drawing he said, "I wanted a few words with you, Angus."

Anxious to help him, Peddie tried to read what was on his mind. "Is it that the child is no better? I shall continue to pray for her."

Mr. MacDhui said, "Thank you. That is kind of you," with a kind of stiff formality that the minister was not slow to note and he wished now he had not said it, or that he had waited for MacDhui to speak.

The veterinary, who had no conception of the meaning of the prayer that arises from the sincere and believing heart, felt a kind of odd resentment at the dominie's words and at what he considered the implication that the most precious life on earth to him could be turned on or off, or regulated through mumbled words of supplication, incantation, or bribery-through-praise. It seemed to him a kind of presumption on the part of the minister that he had connections on high that MacDhui did not and that he was willing to contact them for him. He wished that his friend had not reverted to his profession even though he had come to consult him professionally, and he wished too, now, that he had not come at all, that he had had the strength to persist and try to find within himself the answer to his dilemma.

Yet, he felt, after a moment, since he was there he might as well make a beginning and so he said, "The diagnosis is still the same. Nothing is wrong and yet—everything is wrong. But that is not why I am here. It is about Lori."

This time Mr. Peddie kept his face impassive and roundly placid as he said, "Ah yes. Lori. You said you might be going to pay her a visit. I gather you have done so."

Into Mr. MacDhui's mind came suddenly the recollection of Mr. Peddie's warning to him. "You may find yourself in the greatest danger—the danger of coming to love God." He wondered what his friend would say when he learned that it was not God that he, MacDhui, had come to love, but Lori. Aloud he replied, "Yes. I have been there a number of times, as a matter of fact."

Mr. Peddie was feeling his way carefully. "And did you accomplish what you set out to do?"

"It was not necessary. Her—what she was doing had been—misrepresented to me. She is an innocent person and in no way can be said to fall foul of the law."

The Reverend Peddie smiled engagingly. "Splendid. I was sure you would see this for yourself."

"I was wrong," MacDhui admitted. "I own it. I—I"—and here he fumbled for words—"I felt that I wished to help her."

At the word "help" a gleam of understanding came into the eyes of the minister behind their gold-rimmed spectacles and he leaned forward on his desk, regarding his friend with renewed interest behind which lay just the faintest hint of amusement inspired by an appreciation of the little ironies of life and sympathy for one caught in their toils. He said, "That was good of you," and did not add as the mischief in him might have prompted him to do, "For 'help,' read 'love.' "

"She is innocent and good," MacDhui repeated, "but quite mad —obsessed, I might almost say. Yes, that is the word, I think, obsessed rather than possessed. She believes that she can communicate with animals. It is true that she wields an extraordinary power over them, but this can be explained naturalistically. She professes likewise to speak with angels and hear their wings and voices."

Mr. Peddie reflected and then said, "You know, there once was a man by the name of Francis who paused by the roadside in the vicinity of Assisi and preached an entire sermon to the birds, asking them first to still their chatter, which they did, and no one thought it odd, either then or since. Francis considered the beasts of field, stream, and air his brothers and sisters, an opinion since concurred with by a great many men of science, the structural similarities being unavoidable——"

Mr. MacDhui exploded, much to Peddie's relief, for this calm, repressed MacDhui was unnatural. "Damn it, Angus, one can never pin you fellows down. You are slipperier than conger eels. You know very well that Lori lives an unnatural life, that, for whatever reason, she has abandoned reality to live in a world of her own creating, that——"

"Oh yes, Andrew," Peddie interrupted his friend. "You chaps have a convenient label for everything that doesn't coincide with your definition of normal—neurasthenia, schizophrenia, psychosis, manic depression—and every one must fit into one or the other categories, including those who do genuinely hear the voice of God. You leave us believers little choice but to register at the nearest asylum."

The outburst unsettled MacDhui still further. "Then you are trying to tell me that you consider Lori sane?" he said with a touch of his old truculence, which Peddie welcomed.

The minister arose and went to the window which looked out upon the neat, whitewashed church and the graveyard behind it, through whose sprouting of graying tombstones the blue of the loch could be glimpsed, and he thought carefully before replying. Then turning to his friend, he said, "If to love and communicate, or attempt to communicate with a supreme being, in any one of a hundred different ways, is mad, then nine tenths of the people inhabiting this globe are insane. Or let me put it this way: the great appeal of Jesus was his compassion. Two thousand years ago He introduced love, pity, and gentleness into a brutal and demented world. Yet that world has been steadily moving away from His kind of sanity ever since. Five hundred years ago Lori would have been considered a saint."

"Or a witch," MacDhui added grimly, "as some call her even today." The veterinary pursued his point again. "But if she were mad—or even only slightly deranged, a psychotic taking refuge in phantasy and escape from reality? There are some such, you know, for madness is not an invention, but an affliction——"

Peddie said, "Yes, if she were indeed, then——?"

"Well," said MacDhui with a kind of desperation, "if she were —touched, or even as you say, a saint, dedicated and devoted, would it be a sin——"

He broke off here, for he could not bring himself to confess to Peddie that he was so deeply in love with Lori that he could see no way out of his dilemma. One did not wed a madwoman——

The stout little minister came away from his window, pointed a round, chubby finger at MacDhui's breastbone and asked severely,

"What have you to do with sin, Andrew MacDhui, and why should you who do not believe be concerned with it? Do you not know that sin is the peculiar privilege of the religious and one of the penalties connected with the life of an agnostic is that he can never enjoy it?"

MacDhui asked uncertainly, "Are you joking with me Angus?"

"Never less so! Don't you see, my friend, that you are involving yourself in an unresolvable paradox? You are asking me whether it would be a sin to love and wish to espouse and have children by a woman you consider out of her mind. Do you not see that if you believed in God, you would not think Lori mad but only good, gentle and kind, a most dear and praiseworthy anachronism in a harsh and insensitive era?"

MacDhui's reply was a bellow. "God! God! Always God! Is there no escape from God?"

Peddie replied ringingly, "There never has been, Andrew!" Then in milder tone he continued, "Do not be surprised that I mention Him. If you visit a psychiatrist you will hear of neuroses and libidos; a doctor will speak to you of glands and organs; a plumber hold forth about plungers and washers. Why should you be exercised when a minister speaks to you of God?"

MacDhui said heavily and without choler, "You set me an impossible task, Angus."

"Do I? I have not that feeling. You and Lori each inhabit the extreme and far outer edges of your separate worlds. If both you and she were to move even slightly in the direction of the other——"

"I tell you it is impossible. Did you know that she hears—voices?" MacDhui could not bring himself to say "heavenly voices," but he could not keep his glance from turning momentarily aloft as he finished the query.

Mr. Peddie looked the picture of innocence behind his gold-rimmed spectacles. "So did the Maid of Domremy!"

MacDhui glared at him. The minister ignored the look and said, "Had it ever occurred to you that there might be voices to hear?"

MacDhui arose and wandered over to the chessboard, where he idly lifted a few pieces. "Someone who manipulates us like these at His whim, or in accordance with some undisclosed rules of the game? No, no, Angus. I cannot. I cannot. I cannot." He turned toward the door, but before departing, said with genuine sadness and disappointment, "You have not helped me, Angus."

At his desk the little clergyman considered his friend's accusation, searching his heart. Was there more he could have done or said? Was this the time? To Peddie there was no comfort to which humans could turn in time of travail but that of religion. What else was there in this world, into which he had looked so deeply, but darkness and despair? The dismal clank of the chains carried about by the agnostics had been ringing in his ears for years. A logical and philosophical man, some five thousand years of history and record of God's manifestation of Himself and His Spirit to man appeared irrefutable. Yet he did not cite this to his friend. Instead he said, "I am sorry, Andrew. In the end you will help yourself. You will not find, you will be found, for that is the way it has always been. That which you will someday experience is not so much a faith or a belief in a myth or a series of myths, as a deep-seated feeling, a conviction that fills every corner of one's being until there is no longer so much as an atom's area of room for doubt. And to this conviction you can only help yourself. No one as yet has been able to explain a revelation or foresee the moment thereof."

MacDhui said, "I do not understand you."

Mr. Peddie sighed and said gently, "Well, then, do not try, Andrew. But let us each to our methods. You were upset before when I said that I would pray for Mary Ruadh, but you would not be were Dr. Strathsay to tell you that he meant to try out the effects of a new antibiotic on her. Yet in both cases conviction as to results have been obtained through experience and successful experiment."

MacDhui nodded slightly, but said no more and went out, closing the door softly enough behind him. Long after he had departed, the Reverend Mr. Peddie sat motionless at his desk, a small, silent, thoughtful figure, as he reflected whether he had done right or wrong and how difficult it was to know.

For, while he was well aware of his Church's attitude towards proselyting and the desirability of acquiring converts, he had his own concept of respect for his deity and His ability to look after His own affairs. While he kept his opinions to himself, he did not, in this modern world, hold with belaboring and persecuting agnostics into unwilling belief.

And besides he was well aware, not only of the wellsprings of MacDhui's atheism, but also of the fact that he had already abandoned it but could not yet bring himself to acknowledge it. He saw in MacDhui that same violent, childish nature exhibited by the Italian peasants of the Romagna, who, when crops failed or storms damaged their harvest, punished their saints by removing them from their niches in the churches and banishing them to the cellar, awaiting a tangible demonstration of better behavior before restoring them.

Knowing the vet's background and early problems, he felt sure that at some time as a young man he had prayed, "Oh God, help me! Please let me be a doctor." Well, God's will had crossed his will and a MacDhui was not one to take this lying down. However much he might be longing for the comfort that address and communion might bring him, he was too stubborn, willful, aggressive, and bitter to acknowledge it.

Sitting there, pulling at his lip, his short legs barely touching the ground, the little man felt almost certain that this was the key to MacDhui's character. It was not so much that Peddie was afraid of losing MacDhui to God as to himself. The big man was in deep trouble. If the child never recovered her power of speech, if she were to die, he must inevitably face and bear the burden of his own guilt and be destroyed, unless help were forthcoming.

Miserably Peddie reflected upon his own inadequacy. He did not doubt but that God would dispose of the matter as He saw fit. It was his own role in the curious drama that was sorely troubling him.

22 The three boys were sitting uneasily, straight-backed in a row in the waiting room, where there were several other clients with pets to be attended that morning. MacDhui recognized them the first time he thrust his head in through the door, a gesture which these days carried with it far less truculence than before. There was Wolf Cub Geordie McNabb squirming and fidgeting, lean Jamie Braid, the pipe sergeant's son, looking both nervous and mournful, and the cool, handsome, quite self-contained Hughie Stirling, the only one of the three who seemed to be enjoying himself.

There was obviously some sort of conspiracy afoot, for upon the appearance of the animal doctor, little Geordie and tall Jamie at once rolled their eyes nervously in the direction of Hughie Stirling to discover any signs of panic or inclination to fly in their leader. There was none. The handsome boy remained calm and steadfast.

MacDhui himself was curious as to the nature of this delegation and the reason for it and when he had disposed of the last client he set Willie Bannock some work in the hospital section, opened the door to the waiting room, and called, "All right, lads. You may come in now."

They filed in behind Hughie Stirling solemnly and filled with so much import that it was threatening to spill over before

MacDhui, seated at his old-fashioned roll-top desk in the corner by the window said, "Right. Now, out with it. What is it I can do for you?"

The three ranged themselves in step-down row according to sizes like three organ pipes, and spokesman Hughie Stirling asked forthwith, "How is Mary Ruadh, sir? Is she better? And may we go and visit her, sir?"

MacDhui suddenly felt his heart go out to the three. It was strange how one could come to regard people in an entirely different light within a few moments. He had seen the boys around town, knew vaguely who they were, but they had never pierced below the outer skin of his consciousness. Yet now they stood there suddenly as three friends.

"Mary Ruadh is very ill," he replied gravely. "Yes, you may go to pay her a visit. Perhaps it will cheer her up. It is good of you to think of her and to come here first to ask permission."

"We didna ken she was sae sick," Jamie Braid intoned mournfully. "I have na' laid eyes on her since the day o' the burial——" He gulped and clamped his lips shut at a fierce nudge from Hughie.

"Has she got another puss Baldrin?" Geordie asked.

Gentler with the younger boy, Hughie merely laid a hand upon his shoulder and said, "Hush, Geordie. You'll soon enough see." Then to Mr. MacDhui he said, "It is said that she cannot speak any longer—even to—well, to us. Is this true, sir?"

The veterinary felt the current of sympathy flowing strongly between himself and this boy and wondered whether this was a measure of his desperate longing to be one with and comprehend childhood, now that it was too late. There was something direct about the approach of the young to problems that he had never understood, a cutting of corners and the dismissal of the unessential.

And yet, withal, he appreciated that the lad was showing a regard for his feelings and sensibilities he would not have credited to one of his age. It seemed somehow the first glimpse he had been permitted of the pity of the young for their more backward elders. A window had been opened onto a world where adults were discussed, plots were laid, plans hatched to get on with them in spite of their queer and often unjust behavior, or schemes thought out to circumvent their baser natures without hurting their feelings if possible, or getting into trouble.

"Mary Ruadh has lost the power of speech," he replied, "we hope only temporarily and that it will return. By all means go to see her and tell her what you have been doing, or things that might interest her. If—if by any chance Mary were to reply or speak to you, I wish that one of you would come here and notify me at once. I should be most grateful."

"Yes, sir," Hughie Stirling said, "that we will. I've been sailing with Dad and we tipped over. I'll tell her about that. Perhaps it will make her laugh."

Yet they made no move to leave and Mr. MacDhui was now convinced of something he had been suspecting, namely that there was yet another reason for the delegation.

The vet felt a moment of resentment at such subterfuge and was seized with the impulse to bark angrily at them to come out with it. Nevertheless he restrained himself. There was that in the doleful countenance of Jamie Braid with which one could not be angry. Besides he was sure that at the first sign of his old choler all three, or certainly Jamie and Geordie would take to their heels. Curbing himself, he loaded a pipe in the interim and concentrated upon the handsome head and trim figure of the ringleader.

"Sir," Hughie Stirling asked, "may we speak to you about another matter?"

With careful deliberation, MacDhui got his pipe glowing before replying through clouds of smoke, "Yes, yes."

"Sir," Hughie Stirling began. "We've all done something that was wrong. But it was my fault," he added quickly, with a side glance at his now uncomfortable companions. "I led them on. And besides, I had the money too."

"Ah," said MacDhui. "I thought there was something else had you standing first on one leg and then the other. Been up to mischief, eh? I suppose you've damaged something. Well, then, make a clean breast of it——"

"Oh no, sir, it wasn't anything like that," Hughie explained. "It's something quite different. We—we went to see the gypsies last night."

Jamie Braid swallowed his Adam's apple and said, "It was nae only Hughie's fault. We were a' keen to go."

"They *beat* the bear," Geordie McNabb announced, and unaccountably tears gathered in his eyes and began to roll unchecked down his cheeks.

"Ah," commented Mr. MacDhui, to keep the ball moving, "so that's it." Though he did not yet understand at all.

"You see," Hughie explained, "it was forbidden. We had asked, but none of us were allowed to go. We'll catch it at home if they ever find out."

MacDhui said, "And quite right too. That's no place for youngsters," and smoked on.

"But you see, there was a performance. They give a performance, though it's not official or the police would interfere. It's almost like a circus. And they ride up and down bareback and pick up handkerchiefs off the ground and stand up on the backs of their horses and they have some dogs and monkeys that can do tricks, and a bear. Of course I've seen plenty of bears in zoos and I've been to the real circus in Edinburgh, but Jamie and Geordie had never seen a real live bear."

The story was developing, but the purpose behind this confession still defied MacDhui. When he remained silent, Hughie continued, "So then when my great-aunt Stuart came to visit and gave me a half crown, we had the money because you see I already *had* sixpence, and tickets were a shilling each. And so we went."

"It was awfu' sir," Jamie Braid said. "I wished sair I hadna gone."

"They beat the poor bear," Geordie wailed, "and its nose was a' bluggy and it lay down on the ground and cried." The child commenced to weep in earnest until Hughie produced a pocket handkerchief, said, "Oh, come on, Geordie, be a man. It's all over now and we're doing something about it," wiped the round face and got the nose blown. He turned then to the veterinary.

"That was it, sir! That's why we've come to you. They were horrid cruel. They beat the bear and the horses and the dogs and monkey too. There were only a few other people there to see the performance and they weren't from the town. Perhaps that's what made the gypsies angry. The bear isn't much of a bear, sir, and when it wouldn't dance they beat it with a chain."

MacDhui removed his pipe from his mouth. "They usually do, you know," he said.

Hughie nodded. "I've heard. But that wasn't all, sir. There were other animals in cages in the dark. They were supposed to show them to us for our shilling, but they didn't, because they were so angry that no more than a dozen people came to see their show. But afterward we sneaked around behind in the dark and snooped. Because we *had* paid our shilling each, and were entitled to, weren't we?"

MacDhui did not reply.

"We couldn't quite see what all of them were, but some of them were lying there in the dark just moaning and whimpering. And the smell was awful."

"I wouldna doot that yin skelpies practiced some kind of abominations upon the puir beasties," Jamie Braid said, his long face set in folds of sadness.

"The gypsies came and chased us away with sticks," Hughie

Stirling concluded, "so we ran and came home. That was last night. So this morning we got together and held a meeting. . . ."

Mr. MacDhui puffed at his pipe, producing a vast smoke screen. "I see. And what did you decide at your meeting?"

"That we wanted the police to go there and make them stop beating their animals and punish them."

"That is a laudable resolution," the veterinary admitted, "but why don't you go to Constable MacQuarrie with it? That's his business."

The three exchanged glances. THE question, the one they had known all along must be answered, had been asked. Even Hughie Stirling was embarrassed. Finally he replied, "Sir, when the gypsies first came, the police said they might stay as long as they behaved themselves——"

"But I gather from what you say that they are not behaving themselves now——"

"Yes sir. But at the same time, Constable MacQuarrie said that if he caught any of us boys going anywhere near the gypsy encampment, he would skin us alive——"

"Oho!" MacDhui grunted.

"So you see if we complained to Constable MacQuarrie, we would first have to admit that we had been——"

"There would, nae doot, be official forms to be made out," Jamie Braid filled in, "and oor signatures to be put to them and the constable nosing about oor hames——"

"And what is it then you wish me to do?"

The uncomfortable hurdle taken, Hughie breathed a sigh of relief and launched into the plan: "We thought, sir, that if you were to go, on account of who you were, and knowing everything about animals, you could either make them stop, for they would be afraid of you, or if you went to the police and complained, they would listen to you, and——"

"Losh!" grunted Mr. MacDhui. "Thank you for nothing. I

have no mind to be pulling police chestnuts out of the fire. Gypsies and complaints of cruelty to animals are their jurisdiction, and——"

"Oh sir," pleaded Hughie Stirling, and MacDhui felt himself oddly wrung by the young voice, "It wouldn't be the police chestnuts—they're our chestnuts!"

MacDhui sat up, sucking on his pipe and gazing at the three now with keen interest. "Well, at least you're honest," he growled. "I don't know that I have the time, what with Mary Ruadh so ill and——"

"Oh, one of us would stay with Mary Ruadh. And there's Mrs. McKenzie. You see, even if we sent an anomous letter to the police, by the time they got it and did anything Geordie's bear might be dead."

Geordie commenced to cry again at being identified with the bear, which clever Hughie had done on purpose, and wailed, "He hit the bear with a chain and the blug squoorted out!"

Mr. MacDhui tamped down the ashes of his pipe with a fore-finger long fireproofed by this habit, and sighed, as Geordie suddenly dug hard with his fists into his eyes and made a fierce effort to control himself. He succeeded and said, "I think the bear was lame. That's why it couldn't dance. It had a sore on its hind leg."

Jamie Braid testified, "There was a horse struck wi' a loaded crop, sor. It went to its knees——"

Mr. MacDhui sighed again. "It is not a pretty picture you draw," he said.

Hughie Stirling was at him eagerly. "Then you *will* go, sir?"

The vet was surprised that he so much as entertained the idea, for he had enough on his plate without becoming embroiled with gypsies who in the end would merely be told by the police to move on and would then go elsewhere and continue to practice their cruelties unless witnesses could be produced to corroborate specific charges.

Besides, the boys could have been exaggerating. In the dim light of smoky gasoline flares, or lanterns, things might have looked worse than they were. True, the Ursari, the gypsy bear trainers, were not notably kindly men, but often they were savaged and mauled by their beasts.

But small Geordie McNabb and lank Jamie Braid, with their laconic sentences, had seared a vivid picture into the brain of the animal doctor, of helpless creatures brutally maltreated. And he was remembering, too, that it was Geordie who had brought him a small frog once with a broken leg and had been turned out of his office. That frog he had later encountered healed and living contentedly in an out-of-the-world house in an out-of-the-world glen. Perhaps this was one he owed both to Lori and Geordie. He said finally, "I will think about it."

Translated by the code of the young used to dealing with adults, it meant to Hughie a firm "yes," though actually the vet had not yet decided and meant what he had said.

The three now prepared to file out, saying their thank-yous. Only Hughie Stirling hung back for a moment after the other two had made their escape. He said, "We'll try very hard with Mary Ruadh, sir. It was really to see her that we came, sir. I just thought we might be able to combine—as long as we were here, because of Geordie—he's taken it very hard."

Mr. MacDhui put his hand on the boy's shoulder with surprising gentleness and said, "Thank you, Hughie, for telling me. Now run along."

After the boy had gone he sat quietly smoking and thinking, and feeling, and wondering what it was that had come over him.

And if the veterinary was thinking and feeling, so was Wolf Cub Geordie McNabb. For in his code of grownups "I'll think about it" meant forgotten. His active little mind turned to the last time he had visited Mr. MacDhui for a favor and had been refused. And so the veterinary was not the only one that morning who thought upon a green frog with a broken leg and that other place where mercy could be found for animals that were sick or injured——

23 Things are changed hereabouts. No one pays much attention to ME any longer, not even Lori my priestess.

Am I not then Sekhmet-Bast-Ra, cat goddess of the night, defender of the sun, devourer of the moon, who laps the milk of the stars from the bowl of the sky?

Yet here they do me no honors and say me no prayers; bring me no gifts or libations, nor bow down in my presence.

I am sad, who was once gay and proud and omnipotent. I do not prance and leap about, or run up and down the covin-tree. For sometimes I am not sure that I am God any more, or even who or what I am. I have had strange and disturbing dreams of yet another life about which I have spoken to no one, not even Wullie or McMurdock. Yet must I have lived a thousand or more lives since first my divine ka descended from the heavens to preside over the destinies of men. Who then am I now? And where? And why?

How is it to be borne—to have been God once and then be God no longer?

Could I but once more hear, "Bast, thou divine, thou ruler of the night, thou goddess of love, thou infinite, thou all, thou wise and knowing, thou god, come to my aid!" What wonders would I not work for such a supplicant.

Yet am I called only Talitha, a name the meaning of which I do not understand, but which seemed to cause Lori some secret amusement and bring the tender smile to the corners of her mouth each time she summoned me.

"Talitha Tabby, my pussie baudrons," she would cry to me, "come here to me whilst I see if ye have picked up any ticks this day," and she would run her fingers through my fur while I shivered with delight.

But that was not being God.

And Lori was different too. She listened less to those voices of the infinite that used to speak to her, the same, no doubt, that used to reach me in my most secret recess in my ancient temple in Bubastis. Her attention was more taken with gazing in the direction of the pathway leading from the glen to the covin-tree, and when she listened, it was for the sound of the Mercy Bell.

I well knew for whom she looked and listened and it made me the more determined to destroy the Man with the Red Beard.

Yet the doom was not so easily contrived as in the old days beneath the Egyptian sun when it seemed as though I was able to gather all the threads of human destiny in my sacred claws, hold them and shake them like the reins of the charioteers guiding their wild Nubian steeds, and drive foolish mankind whither and to what ends I would.

I worked upon his doom, mostly when Lori sat at her weaving and I lay by the hearth, my paws tucked up under me, and watched her through the doorway, for the two things are not dissimilar.

Her loom was in a bare chamber with whitewashed walls. The deep window opened to the rear of the temple looking out onto the woods and the brook, and once when she was weaving I saw a red deer come forth from the forest and thrust its head in through the window. Lori ceased her swift movements for a moment and they looked at one another with such tenderness that I was wildly jealous. I could not bear it for Lori to love or serve anyone but me.

In the daytime, when it was bright, the sunlight poured into the room and sometimes the hanks of dyed yarn the crofters had sent to her to make them shawls and cloaks to keep them warm in the winter were reflected on the walls.

The colors shimmered and danced upon them, and in the middle, her own hair aflame, her face rapt with concentration, sat my Lori weaving, weaving, weaving the colored strands, making her fingers fly in and about and through the bed of the loom and all the while, inch by inch, the dappled cloth waxed and grew, and in like manner, I lay on the hearth, spinning and weaving the threads that would furnish the shroud of my red-bearded enemy.

For the fashioning of a proper doom is in the manner of weaving. Through the long warp of character, ambition, greed, habit, intolerance, yearning, faith, love and hatreds of the humans, the loom bed from which they cannot escape, we interlace the strands of chance, threads borrowed momentarily from the lives of others, the stranger, the friend, the innocent, the guilty, the young, the old, a chance phrase overheard, a corner turned just an instant too soon, a word spoken in anger, later regretted, a letter delayed, an article forgotten or left behind, some trifling matter overlooked, the ill-temper of another.

It was not easy. It had been four thousand years or more since I had made a doom. And there were strange influences working against me. I did not know what they were, but they seemed to be centered in the room where Lori sat. Was she weaving counter-threads to my pattern?

Her hands and fingers flew, the loom thumped rhythmically as she trod the foot pedal each time she completed the threading of the weft across the warp. I could not take my gaze from her. Sometimes it seemed as if strands I wished to use had become mingled with her colored yarns and had become a part of her design.

Once the thumping of the loom stopped. Lori, her hands gripping the frame on either side, was looking up with pain and bewilderment and she cried aloud, "What am I then? What has happened to me? What is this singing in my heart?"

I was filled then with the blackest jealousy, so violent that I lost the strand and forgot my spell. I went into the weaving room and rubbed against Lori. She let her hand fall carelessly and touched my head and back, but her look was far off and away and she did not know that I was there. I returned to the hearth and squatted there with my back to her. I was filled with rage and hatred. Beware, beware the anger of a jealous god.

The birds were stilled. Peter the Scots terrier was shivering and whining. Wullie and McMurdock went about with their tails fluffed up; Dorcas would not leave her kittens and cuffed them impatiently when they tried to wander from her side. The jackdaw sat mournfully on a branch of the covin-tree, its feathers drooping, looking down with a beady eye. The air was oppressive and the sky was heavily clouded over. Darkness would come early that night.

I walked about, proud and pleased, with my tail stiff and erect and quivering with delight. For this was MY doing, I, Bast-Ra, the Great Cat, lord of the heavens . . . This was the beginning. The air was hot and heavy, like a weight, and was filled with the foreboding of the doom that I had unleashed. Henceforth and when this black night was done, Lori would be mine, and mine alone.

At that moment in the growing gloom of cloud-laden dusk, the Mercy Bell shivered and rang once, loudly and clearly so that the echoes went shattering away endlessly up through the mountain pass above the glen, long after the metal had ceased to vibrate.

The jackdaw shrieked once, horribly, and then flew off, his wings slapping together hollowly in his panic. Peter barked hysterically and then subsided to a whine. Then in the silence that followed there was no sound but the swift drumming of Lori's feet upon the path as she ran from the stables to the place where the bell was hung.

I, Bast-Ra, the goddess, was again filled with misgivings. For the ringing of the bell was an interference. It was no strand that I had woven. Should it be the Man with the Red Beard——

Cautiously I peered around the corner. There was no one there. As Lori stood there looking about her I came forth as did the others. There was no single, solitary soul to be seen. Then Peter began to yap and shrill and bark and make short rushes at something almost beneath Lori's feet. We all saw it then. It was a stone and beneath it was a small piece of paper with some writing on it.

Lori sank to her knees and seized it eagerly, as eagerly as she had run thither. I saw it. The writing was a kind of scrawl on a not very clean piece of paper. In the descending gloom it was difficult for Lori to make out, and so she read it aloud, carefully as she deciphered each word.

"Dear Ma'm, Please go to the gypsy camp and make them stop. They are being cruel to all the animals. They beat the poor bear who is sick. If you do not go the bear will die. Oh please do go. Yours faithfully, Geordie."

"P.S. I am a Wolf Cub."

"P.S.S. I am the one who brought the frog."

For a long while, it seemed, Lori knelt there, smoothing out the sheet of paper and studying it, reading it again and again. When she arose she stood looking down the glen in the direction of the distant valley and I could see the resolve that was filling her.

My tail bushed; my fur stood erect, crackling with rage and electricity; I was stiff with fear and horror. For this was not of my spinning and weaving. A spell gone wrong? A cantrip forgotten?

Wrong demons invoked, wrong strands threaded through the pattern? Or was it that had I been shuttling my warp with the weft of hatred, while Lori was weaving with love?

"Come," Lori cried to us. "Come all. We'll sup now, for it is a long way I have to go after."

I cried, "Don't go, Lori! You will only find misery, destruction, and death there. I have pronounced and fabricated a doom. Remain here. There is nothing you can do."

In the old days MY priestesses would have understood. The knowledge of my thoughts and commands would have penetrated to their marrows; they would have bowed and obeyed.

"Oh, miaow, miaow," Lori said. "Are ye singing for your supper then, my Talitha puss? Come then quickly, for I must go where I am needed."

She set us out our suppers, and as usual the dogs gobbled like pigs, but I had no appetite for mine, nor did Wullie or McMurdock, though Dorcas, of course, had the feeding of her kittens to look to.

Wullie, who would not admit I was a god but knew that I had ways of understanding Lori that he did not, asked, "What's toward, Talitha? By my fur and whiskers, whatever it is, I'm no' liking it."

I explained. They listened until I was finished. Wullie said, "That's nae good. My skin is a-crawl with the feeling of trouble."

McMurdock asked me, "Can ye no' stop her from going, Talitha?"

"No."

The yellow cat sneered, "Ye're nae much of a god then, are ye?"

I could have wept then with rage and exasperation. My glory trampled underfoot by a common yellow tomcat who would hardly have rated scraps in the outer temple court of Khufu at Bubastis where I sat upon the gold and emerald throne.

"You'll see. You'll see yet all of you," was all that I could say, and both McMurdock and Wullie snorted. Wullie said, "We'll keep watch until Lori returns."

McMurdock said, "Aye. I'll take the top of the covin-tree. I ken my way up in the dark."

Wullie remarked, "I don't mind going up onto the roof, mysel'."

I said, "I'll follow the path 'til I come to the Great Rock. There'll be a view into the valley from there."

Lori came forth from my temple. She was wrapped in a dark cloak of cloth of her own making. She carried an oil lantern that drained the color from her face and some of the redness from her hair. She saw us all assembled there like a court. The dogs were whimpering. The hedgehog had arrived and unrolled himself and was sitting up wrinkling his nose. We cats sat in dignity with our tails wrapped about us, but you could tell our unease by the set of our whiskers.

"Do not fear," Lori said. "There is nothing to fear. Bide you here. When I have done what must needs I will come back." Then she added once more, "Have no fear," and made off down the path.

The heavy cloud made it quite dark. The lantern threw a flickering yellow light at her feet. Silently I trotted after her until we came to the bend and the Great Rock, upon which I sprang and squatted in the shadows. I watched her yellow light descend until it disappeared. Far below I could see the twinkling of the town. I lay there quivering, not only for Lori, but for my beautiful doom I had placed upon the Man with the Red Beard. What would become of it now? What would become of us all if it fell upon Lori instead? How would it all end?

An owl hooted in the trees. A wind sprang up momentarily, swaying the branches, rustling the leaves and bringing snatches of music from the gypsy camp in the valley, the gypsies, the strands of whose lives I had woven into the death of the Man with the Red Beard.

When the wind dropped, the sound of the music died away too. With all my god-power I willed and commanded her to return. Yet she did not.

Total darkness set in. Far below I could see the lights of the distant town that I had never visited winking like the little stars.

A strange thing happened to me then. For a moment I was Sekhmet-Bast-Ra no longer, but who or what I was I did not know, only that I was a lost and bodiless ka in the darkness between heaven and earth. And in that ka, or soul, there was such a yearning for something or someplace below in that distant valley as was not to be endured. Had there been a body to this strayed ka, it would have been drowned in misery, lamentation, and tears.

Something caught in the mirrors of my staring eyes and the moment passed. I was Bast-Ra again, the goddess.

It began at first no more than a gleam of light where there had been darkness before in the valley, distant from those of the town, then a flicker, followed by an orange tongue of flame such as sometimes shoots from a piece of smoking coal in the fireplace. It died away and flickered anew. A moment later an orange glow was reflected from the sky in the distance.

Fire! Fire! Fire!

Far off in the distance something was burning. I was cold to the bottom of my stomach with fear. What did it portend? Where was Lori? What was burning? Fire was no part of the doom I had sent forth that day. I had not called upon Ra, my father the sun, lord of flame, to scorch and devour.

The glow increased. Fire, fire, burning burning! My god's eye seemed to see Lori and the Man with the Red Beard. They were surrounded by flames. Something had gone wrong with my doom. Some thread spun by another had enmeshed Lori.

I lay there, trembling and weeping in the darkness while the orange glow flickered on the low clouds.

24 It was close on to nine o'clock that evening before veterinarian MacDhui did what he had promised the three boys; namely, to think about the matter of paying a visit to the gypsy encampment. Now that he was doing so, the more he considered it, the less he found himself liking the idea. Andrew MacDhui did not hold with the poking of noses into other people's business. In the morning he might drop a judicious hint to Constable MacQuarrie and let the matter pass from his mind.

He pulled down the lid of his roll-top desk for the night, swung his revolving chair away from it, and came face to face with the place on his carpet where the three boys had been standing, stepdown, according to sizes that morning, and they came vividly to his mind, but most clear was his memory of the soiled and tearstreaked countenance of Geordie McNabb, as Hughie Stirling worked over it with his pocket handkerchief, and the child's cry: "They *beat* the poor bear and its nose was a' bluggy and it lay down on the ground and cried." The picture then that had formed in his mind that morning, during the recital of the boys, returned to plague him, but with still another added to it.

He was seeing then, not only Geordie's bear with the "blug squoorting from its nose," but the agony of Lori's badger, the expression in those tortured eyes rolling trustingly toward Lori and the courage and gallantry of the beast.

Calm and trusting, it had lain in Lori's arms, for there was healing there. He thought of the bear, too, and how Lori would cherish it. He thought of the tenderness and the love of Lori's arms.

He closed and locked his office and went next door to his house and Mary Ruadh's room. Mrs. McKenzie was there reading to the child, who was regarding her with lackluster eyes.

"I came in and saw she was awake," Mrs. McKenzie explained. "I thocht if I read tae her, she micht grow sleepy."

It was now Mary Ruadh that Mr. MacDhui was seeing in Lori's arms, cushioned to her breast, red hair mingled with red hair, and perhaps a smile on the face of the child. His own heart felt as heavy as though it would fall out of his body. "Aye," he said. "Bide here with her. There is somewhere I must go." At the door he turned to the housekeeper and said, "I shall be at the gypsy encampment—there is some mischief afoot there—should I be needed."

"I'll nae stir," said Mrs. McKenzie. She wished there were some way to comfort him and help him in his distress, for she felt sorry for him now.

Though darkness came late in the summertime in the northlands, MacDhui needed the headlights of his jeep to thread his way through the murk caused by the heavy low-hanging cloud that shrouded the mountains and filled the valley. The hot wind that had soughed up the loch the week past had promised the relief of a rare Highland thunderstorm, but heavy and oppressive though it was, the animal doctor did not think that it would break that night.

It was fully dark by the time he reached the encampment, signaled by the horseshoe of wagons set about in the field from whence issued the stench of frying oil and garlic and the pungent, squalor reek of a primitive people. The wagons were of wood with crooked iron stovepipe chimneys emerging from the roof, or canvas-covered.

MacDhui drove slowly. At the end of the horseshoe and opposite from the road he noted two smaller vehicles divided into narrow cages, and marked their position. His headlights picked up some horses grazing, rib-thin, with dark patches on flank and hindquarters that could have been sores.

Booths had been set up for palm reading and fortunetelling and the sale of articles of gypsy handicraft as well as dubious cakes and sweetmeats. These were illumined by petrol torches that gave off a flickering yellow light and much black smoke. A kind of course had been set out on the turf, marked by such torches set into the ground, at the end of this were a few rows of makeshift seats, planks set across some boxes and barrels. A dozen or so visitors were seated in this section.

MacDhui heard a sound like a pistol shot, followed by the scream of a horse. He stopped his jeep in time to see a horse rear, and in the smoky yellow light a tall, booted fellow in a black shirt and broad, nail-studded black leather belt raise his arm and beat the animal. The veterinary gazed somberly for a moment until the rearing beast was brought under control. Then he parked his vehicle near the entrance and got out. His palms were sweating and he was damp beneath the eyes. His skin was prickling and in his mouth was the bitter taste of antagonism.

Andrew MacDhui was not the man for intuitions, or atmospheres, but for the first time he found himself regretting that he had not brought so much as a walking stick or whip or any kind of weapon. For no sooner had he approached and entered the enclosure than he felt himself almost overwhelmed by the malevolence, cynicism, and hostility that pervaded the place.

A crone, a bundle of old and dirty clothes with a greasy black leather purse hanging from her waist, sat at a rickety table by the entrance. A placard read "Admission one shilling." MacDhui dropped a ten shilling note onto the table. The crone dipped a claw into the purse and spread out change in shillings and sixpences, and waved him in impatiently, croaking, "Hurry, hurry, the performance has already begun."

MacDhui left the change lying on the table and snarled down at her, "Come along, mother. Put up the other shilling. That is too old a game——"

She became shrill and voluble at once, cursing him and crying out. A man came striding menacingly out of the darkness, a strapping black-haired fellow. MacDhui saw it was he of the boots and wide, nail-studded black leather belt. He carried a horsewhip with a heavily loaded stock.

"What are you trying to do?" he shouted. "Rob this poor old woman? We are poor people here."

The veterinary thrust his beard within an inch of the gypsy's face and said, "Try a new one, Romany! I gave her a ten-shilling note. Count the change yourself."

The man did not even bother but made a sign to the woman, who produced another shilling. MacDhui pocketed the change and went inside through a lane of rope. The man with the whip walked alongside him a few paces, grinning at him impudently, then laughed and swaggered away.

Not far from the seats was a square wooden platform on which sat three musicians, two men and a woman, the former playing fiddle and accordion, while the latter thumped and rattled a tambourine. An exhibition of horsemanship was on, gypsy lads riding down the lane of torches. MacDhui watched for a moment and spat at the contemptuous cynicism of the display. There was nothing that any Highland farm boy of ten could not do.

He waited until a rider who had just performed returned to the starting point. Again he heard the scream of a horse and noted that the gypsy band played up to cover the noise, the woman jangling her tambour and shouting. No one was paying any attention to him. He slipped around the rows of seats out of the light, crossed the field quickly, and made his way through the darkness by memory to the place where he had noted the wagons with the cages from the road.

The stench was appalling. Out of the shadows came faint rustlings, moans and whimperings, and the sound of a woman sobbing, yet he could see no one. MacDhui listened for another moment, then drawing in his breath sharply, extracted his pipe lighter and flicked on the flame, shielding it with his hand.

"Lori!"

"Andrew!"

He was too disturbed at finding her there to note that for the first time she had used his Christian name. He had not seen her for the darkness of her cloak and the cowl that hid her bright hair, and for the fact that she was kneeling before a cage, the door to which she had opened. She was holding a wizened, half-dead monkey in her arms. The monkey was sucking at her finger and weeping.

MacDhui whispered, "Be very quiet, Lori." He did not question how she came to be kneeling in the midst of this pit of horror. It was enough that she was there..He was not even surprised.

Carefully guarding the lighter flame with his hand so that it could not be seen from the other wagons, he passed down the row of cages. There was not a beast on its feet. They lay gasping and panting on their sides or miserably huddled together. There was a stoat, a pair of foxes, a squirrel and a polecat or pine marten. Another cage housed a disheveled eagle drooping in a corner, an unhappy mass of feathers, and, adjoining, three more miserable monkeys. The cages were small and in a state of unspeakable filth. A brown hare lay stretched in a corner. From its attitude and the smell MacDhui judged that no one had been near it for days and that it was dead.

He extinguished his light. When his eyes had become accustomed to the shadow and he could see again by the rays of the farthest torches, he returned to the woman huddled on the ground.

He could see her pale face now and the liquid eyes. She whispered, "Andrew—what is it? They're dying——"

Curtly he replied, "Starvation." He reached into the pocket that was his larder, produced a piece of carrot, and offered it to the monkey Lori was holding. It snatched at it and devoured it hysterically. The tears it shed were now tears of joy. Above them, three pairs of spidery, black arms stretched through the bars pleadingly. MacDhui emptied his pockets of every shred of food.

From the far end of the field came a burst of music, shouts, and a pattering of applause. "Come," MacDhui said, bending down and raising Lori up, "there is nothing more for us here."

She whispered, "What shall I do with him?" The monkey was huddled to her, both arms wrapped about her neck.

"Put it back." He disengaged it gently and replaced it in its cage, where it chittered frantically. "There'll be no more of this when I'm done with them. Come."

They walked close pressed together through the evil night. The air was thick with cruelty and beastliness. MacDhui was grateful for the presence of the woman at his side and breathed in the fragrance of her hair and skin as an antidote.

They came to where the spectators were located, but themselves remained withdrawn in the shadows on the far side, unnoticed. The musicians had left the platform but remained close by. Four men headed by an obese, swarthy gypsy wearing a red-frogged uniform coat and battered kepi appeared, dragging a cage into the torchlight. It was no bigger than a doghouse and barred. The sneering boy with the black belt reappeared and after a chord of music, introduced the uniformed one as the great Darvas Urgchin, the world's greatest wild-animal trainer. The door to the cage was opened and a small black bear dragged out at the end of a chain.

Lori sighed, "The bear. The poor wee bear he wrote about——"

MacDhui looked at her in amazement. "Who wrote about?"

Lori replied, "A note was left. It was signed 'Geordie.' He once brought me a frog."

"Ah, ah!" breathed Mr. MacDhui, "the little devil," and understood Lori's presence now.

"What will they do to it?" Lori whispered.

"We must wait and see."

The fat trainer, who was drunk, was keeping the bear turned so that his left side remained hidden from the sparse audience, but MacDhui's quick diagnostic eye had already caught sight of the huge open sore on the hindquarter and the fact that the bear dragged the leg painfully as he was pulled onto the platform.

He saw, too, the incrustations on the sensitive nose of the animal, hardly healed of the last brutality. Andrew MacDhui, who was used to surgery and blood and animal suffering, thought that if so much as a single drop of blood oozed from that poor nose, he would not be able to endure it.

Shivering, Lori whispered, "Andrew—Andrew——" and pressed even closer to his side, holding tightly to his arm.

The musicians struck up a czardas as the fat, drunken trainer jerked the bear onto its hind legs by means of the chain. At the side hovered the powerful, belted gypsy with the whip, prodding and flicking the animal.

The trainer began to shout, "Hui" and "Hop," jerking on the chain and dancing himself. The bear, which could hardly walk on four legs, much less two, kept falling to the platform on all fours. In the torchlight its eyes gleamed miserable and fear-stricken and once it huddled and bared its lips from blunted broken teeth. It could not have bitten a child.

Quivering, MacDhui stood there watching. A climax was approaching, but what shape it would take or where it would lead he could not foresee. He knew only that he was looking upon this suffering not only through his own eyes, but through those of Lori, and the tears of a small boy as well. Emaciated as the bear was, his hindquarters had the baggy shapelessness of a tramp clown and MacDhui thought he had never before seen anything so sad——

Then all was violence!

As the animal collapsed once more and was jerked to its feet, the gypsy with the loaded whip struck the bear upon the nose with the heavy stock and something which, in the flickering half-light of the smoking torches, looked black, spurted forth.

MacDhui heard Lori's sob. He did not remember freeing himself from her grip and moving to the wooden platform, but he could recall the power and satisfaction behind the blow he struck at the face of the big gypsy. It might have killed him had it struck his temple. Instead it smashed his nose flat and sent him tumbling backward off the platform.

The animal doctor thereupon tore the heavy whip from the hands of the prone man and, turning upon the trainer, whipped his fat buttocks, bellowing, "Dance, you fat swine! Dance now!"

There was turmoil in the rows of spectators, cries of "Bravo! Well done! He had it coming to him!" to more timorous reactions —"We'd best be out of here!" Their ranks began to thin as shouts were heard from the encampment at the far end and a half dozen or so men came galloping down on their horses. The belted gypsy still lay half stunned on the ground, fingering his smashed face. The drunken trainer had fled. The bear lay grotesquely flat on its belly and tried to lick its injured nose.

MacDhui held the platform as the gypsies advanced. "Where is your leader?" he cried. "I mean to take him to the police and charge him."

The man on the ground, the surprise and the cold rage of the red-bearded man upon the platform, confused the gypsies momentarily and kept them from the attack. One of them replied, "King Targu is back there in his wagon. If you want him, go and get him."

MacDhui shouted to the few remaining spectators: "Go home.

There will be no further performance tonight." He went to Lori, who had knelt on the platform, taken the bear's head in her lap, and was trying to staunch the bleeding with a kerchief. Bending over her he said, "Go home, Lori. It is all over. But there may be—some trouble. I beg of you go home."

She stood up at his side but made no move to leave. MacDhui said, "Where is this Targu? I wish to see him at once."

The spokesman nodded in the direction of the wagons. "Back there—if you think you are brave enough."

MacDhui shifted the whip in his hands so that the loaded stock came uppermost. "Open up!" he commanded, and strode forward. The men yielded a narrow path between them, so close that he brushed against them with his shoulders and smelled their rancor. Lori followed behind him. When they had passed through, the path closed. The gypsies came crowding after.

In his anger and indignation Mr. MacDhui forgot fear. He was so filled with truculence against these people that he felt capable of beating them singlehanded. He found himself wishing that this King Targu were a giant twelve feet tall, so that he might enjoy the satisfaction of bringing him to earth as he had the fellow with the belt.

But Targu was not. Quite the opposite; he was a wizened little fellow with a mahogany-colored face and small, piggy eyes. He was clad in ordinary trousers and wore a shirt without a collar, an unbuttoned waistcoat and a bowler hat. His only distinguishing feature was one large gold earring hanging from the lobe of his left ear. He came walking forward, followed by the rest of the men and women of the band, with a ragtag of children trailing them.

MacDhui asked, "Are you Targu, in charge of this band?"

In a curiously dry and wispy voice the little man in the bowler hat replied, "I am Targu. What is it you wish of me? And why have you struck down one of my young men and beaten Urgchin, my trainer, with a whip? What do you seek here with this red-haired witchwoman who is casting the evil eye upon our children?"

The gypsies had closed about them, hemming them in. MacDhui had a momentary realization of his folly. The innocence of the appearance of the little fellow in the bowler hat, like any Argyllshire farmer on a Sunday afternoon, had deceived him. He knew now that he and the woman beside him had left behind them their world of law and reason and in a second had passed backward through six or seven centuries, Ghazi interlopers in the Medieval kingdom of the dangerous and superstition-ridden Romany world.

Yet there was now no turning back and MacDhui, his brush thrust forward aggressively, said, "Targu; you will accompany me to the police station where I mean to charge you with inhuman cruelty to——"

Whether or not the gypsy chieftain was prepared to countenance murder was never to be known, for at that moment a wild cry rang from the outskirts of the crowd; some word in a foreign language. It was repeated. The gypsies turned and opened a path. It was the booted fellow with the black belt and the smashed nose. His face was a mask of blood. In his hands was a length of chain. Swinging it, he ran at MacDhui with intent to brain him.

It was the press of men about them that saved them first, for the gypsy's aim was deflected and the chain came down upon the shoulders of another, felling him, but the action triggered the tensions that had been building; clubs and knives appeared, and the next moment MacDhui was fighting for the lives of Lori and himself.

Bellowing like a bull, an arm about Lori, the other wielding the heavy whipstock, he half cleared a way for them before Lori was torn from his grasp and he was staggered by a blow on the head. The whipstock broke as he got his back up against a wagon, but he wrenched an iron bar from an attacker and flailed with it. Yet he knew that his moments were numbered, for the killing lust had seized the mob and they were getting to him like dogs about a beast brought to bay from the side and even above, where some boy climbed the canvas roof of the wagon and rained blows of a stick upon his head, while another sought to stab at his legs from between the wheels.

Winded and gasping, his chest afire from his exertions, his strength draining from him, MacDhui's sight began to dim, when a new cry, wild and eerie, rose up out of the hurly-burly of shouts, grunts, and the whistling of battle-drawn breath.

"A MacDhui! A MacDhui!"

It was Lori. Somehow she had freed herself and from the nearest of the wagons had plucked a flaming petrol torch with which she advanced, bringing the attack upon the veterinary momentarily to a halt.

The flame revealed her cloak, half rent, spilling from her shoulders, her dark red hair a loose, disheveled aureole about her face. But it was the expression and the light in her eyes that MacDhui was never to forget to the end of his days. Gone was the gentleness. Mouth twisted, eyes ablaze, she was as battle-drunk as any Celtic queen of old, pressing to the side of her beleaguered chieftain.

"A MacDhui! A MacDhui!" She came on, flailing her torch, scattering blazing petrol, opening a path to where the spent man stood wavering and near to collapse. She held him erect with an arm about his waist, keeping his attackers at bay. But as they rallied and again closed in, she shouted her battle cry once more, "A MacDhui!" and then adding, "This for ye," plunged the torch into the side of the canvas wagon.

In an instant the creeping orange flames were eating into cloth and wooden hoop—the dry material went up like tinder erupting into floating bits of burning material that fired the next wagon and yet another——

The fight was over. The quarry was forgotten in the fire panic. Screaming, cursing, some tried to pull the burning wagons from the circle, others scrambled to withdraw possessions from the flaming caravans, a few formed a bucket brigade from the river.

Unnoticed, MacDhui and Lori moved off behind the wagons until they came to the cages, where the weary man sank to his knees for a moment and the woman knelt beside him.

"Andrew," she cried, "are ye all richt?" She herself was smudged and smoke-grimed and there was a bruise on her cheek.

"Aye," he said, "I am but spent." He knew that he had a nasty crack on the top of his head, which was buzzing as though filled with bees, as well as bruises and welts on arms, legs and body, but nought more serious. "Thanks to you, Lori, or I would not be here."

She did not see the blood matting the top of his head, for she was looking deeply into his eyes, and the wildness had not yet all gone from hers. "Andrew!" she cried and yet again, "Andrew!" Then she seized his battered face in her hands and kissed his mouth. Thereafter she arose and, turning, ran off like a young deer in the direction of the glen.

He called after her, "Lori! Lori! Come back to me!"

But she was gone, leaving him on his hands and knees, shaking his head to loose the dizziness from it. Behind him the orange glow and the crackling diminished, as the gypsies began to bring the flames under control—— MacDhui wondered whether he was dead or alive or dreaming. But as his breath returned, his head cleared somewhat and he grinned foolishly to himself. "Time to be getting out of here," he said half aloud.

But first there was something to be done. Terrified by the fire, the caged beasts were barking, whimpering, chittering, scolding. Methodically MacDhui removed the staples from the hasps of the cages, opened the doors, and freed them. If they perished, it would at least be in freedom. Then he staggered off in the direction of his jeep.

At the wooden platform at the end of the field where the tragedy had begun, he came upon a small, dark heap. It was the bear and it was dead. He looked down upon the deflated heap of fur and thought how sorry Geordie would be to hear that his bear had lain down for the last time and would bleed no more. He thought, too, that the tears that Geordie had let fall for this poor beast whose plight had touched his heart had been well shed. He wondered whether Lori had passed this way, too, in her flight and had paused to weep. He found himself wishing that he himself could cry. After a moment he turned away and got into his jeep.

At any rate, he thought, as he passed the gypsies still pouring buckets upon the smoking ruins of three of their caravans, the bear had been avenged. A mile down he stopped by the river and bathed his face and bruises and washed the blood from his face and head, noting that it was not a serious scalp wound. Then wearily he climbed back into his jeep and drove toward the town.

Just before he reached the saddlebacked bridge, a car coming in the opposite direction blinked its lights at him and MacDhui noted the third light atop the roof, indicative of the police car. He pulled to the side of the road, as did the other, and Constable MacQuarrie came over to him, swinging a torch. He said, "Ah good. It's you, sir!"

MacDhui said, "The fire's out. But I shall have a charge for you against a man named King Targu, and a fat, greasy bear trainer—inhuman cruelty to animals——"

"Och aye," said the constable. "In good time. But it is upon another errand we have come. 'Tis you we were sent to fetch."

"Ah, ah——" MacDhui breathed, and felt the dreadful grip of a different kind of fear upon his heart, squeezing that organ as though trying to halt its beat.

The constable looked down and shuffled his feet. "You're

wanted at home at once, sir. Dr. Strathsay— Well, he said to find you and bring you as quickly as ever."

"Ah——" breathed MacDhui again and then asked the question that took more courage than he had displayed all through the wild night. "Is the child alive or dead?"

The constable could look up again. "Alive, sor! But Dr. Strathsay said we were to find you——"

"Lead me——" MacDhui begged. "Lead me—and in mercy's name, drive quickly."

The police car roared about and drove off, wailing its siren. Mr. MacDhui followed, concentrating with all the strength that was left him upon the red eye of the taillight that was leading him to sorrow.

25 Ah! What have I done? Have I then played God who am not one? Are all of the old gods dead and magic no more? Is Sekhmet-Bast-Ra but a dream? Am I then no more than Talitha, a stray found in the forest by a red-haired weaver woman who lives by herself and ministers to small things that are sick or helpless?

And who is Talitha, and whence came I? In which world am I to live?

The doom I prepared has failed. Long after the fire in the valley died down that night Lori returned and passed by the rock where I lay watching. She walked unseeing. By the light of the lantern she carried, I saw that her clothes were torn and stained with blood and burned by fire and that her face was wet with tears.

When she had passed I crept down from my rock and trotted softly in her footsteps until we reached the clearing. It seemed as though a spell was on the others. Peter did not bark, but crept on his belly, whining and moaning. Wullie and McMurdock were back on the ground, but as nervous as witches, and spat at me when I appeared out of the darkness until they saw who it was.

Wullie said, "What has happened? Is Lori injured? I saw blood!"

McMurdock, who in spite of his denials always had a lingering suspicion that I was perhaps a god, growled at me, "Is this some of your doing? You've been acting very strangely lately, my girl. If you've been trying any of your so-called Egyptian tricks, you'll have me to deal with."

I did not deign to reply, but went inside.

Lori sat on a bench by the hearth, as she was, smoke-grimed, disheveled, her clothing bloodstained, a bruise mark upon her face, and wept. Her face was buried in her hands and she wept quietly and endlessly. I wished to comfort her, if this might be. I rose to my hind legs beside her and, with the pad of my paw, twice touched the hand that covered her face.

She looked then and gathered me into her arms and held me. Did ever any woman weep so? She did not sob or cry out, but only let fall the warm and ceaseless tears from her eyes.

Once she spoke to me, holding me hard, pressed to herself, her wet cheek next to mine. "Talitha! Talitha! What shall I do? What is to become of me now?"

Ah, had she but prayed to Sekhmet-Bast-Ra, lady of Sept and of the star Sothis, fertile Isis, chaste Artemis, in all of whom I am embodied, I would have emptied the skies to join her tears and importuned my father Ra to dry them—the blessings of heaven and earth would I have showered upon her——

After a time she let me go, arose, took off her torn and soiled garments and washed herself, and never once did the tears leave off from her eyes. Then she did a strange thing. She took from the hearth mantel an oil lamp and with it went to her mirror and there regarding herself long and with a kind of bewilderment, as though the image of herself was one that she had never seen before.

She fingered the bruise upon her cheek again and again, almost as though it were something she cherished. And she looked long and deeply into her own eyes, from which the tears were still falling, then touched her hair and her mouth as though she were not quite sure they were hers. Then she spoke to the image in the mirror as she had spoken to me. "What am I now? What has become of Lori? What am I to do? What am I to do?" Then she prepared for bed, and I, as usual, retired to the hearth.

But that night she called to me from the head of the half flight of stairs that led to the loft where she lived and slept, "Talitha—Talitha—don't leave me. Come, puss, bide with me tonight——"

I had never been allowed abovestairs before. I went to the foot of the steps and called up to her to make sure that she really meant it.

"Ah yes, puss," she said, "come to me. I would not be alone."

I gave the happiness croon and ran up the stairs and jumped into her arms and purred and she rubbed her cheek against my flank.

A bed, a chair, and a chest of drawers stood in the plain, white-washed room, and a lamp by the bedside. Lori held me in her lap for a moment and looked long and deep into my eyes. She no longer wept. She said, "Tell me, Talitha; you who were once dead. What is it like? Is there peace?"

I did not understand what she meant, for I have been dead a thousand times and a thousand times more and will die yet more thousands, and still my ka will sail in its bark along the River of Darkness between heaven and earth through eternity.

She let me go and I curled up at the foot of her bed. Lori said, "Thank you for staying, my puss. Good night to ye," and blew out the lamp.

From somewhere in the darkened room there came the most delicious fragrance, and then was gone. What was it? Whence had I known it before? In what age; in what incarnation? What was it that it reminded me of, to set me purring? Was it a memory of temple incense, or some wild herb encountered in a bygone forest hunt?

I raised my head and sniffed. Again I caught it—a faint hint and it was gone again. But it loosed such a turmoil of dreams and longing in me. In the darkness, with the now quiet breathing of

Lori deep in sleep, my lost ka seemed suddenly very near to me, almost as though I could grasp and hold it and, holding it, be lost no more.

Once more this sweet scent came to me out of the night, just as I was dropping off to sleep. They would be good dreams that night at the foot of Lori's bed and I hurried on to sleep to meet them.

But I remember, just before, making up my mind that now that I had become Lori's upstairs cat I would make it my business to investigate the source of this wonderful and exciting odor at the very earliest opportunity.

26 The house was ablaze with light as Mr. MacDhui hurried up the footpath, and Mrs. McKenzie stood behind the open front doorway, peering out. As he entered she said, "Och, 'tis me that is glad ye have come. I sent for the doctor, sir. When I went to make her comfortable for the night after reading tae her I saw that she was failing—her eyes seem tae have sunk in so——"

He nodded impatiently. "Yes, yes. You did quite right," and went in and hurried to Mary Ruadh's room, where he came upon the doctor by her cot looking down upon her, his face grave with concern. And it struck him as odd that in that moment of panic and crisis, he should notice how beautiful and compassionate was the face of the old man.

Dr. Strathsay looked up as MacDhui came into the room, saying, "Ah, good. I am glad they found you."

"Is she dying?" MacDhui asked.

The sad-eyed general practitioner considered for a moment. "She has lost the will to live," he replied. "She is no longer fighting. Unless this process can be reversed——"

MacDhui asked then, "How long, Doctor?" He felt almost an avidity to hear the worst, to hear the full extent of this catastrophe, to see it at its darkest.

Strathsay shrugged. "I cannot say——" He had his opinion—the morrow, a few days at the most, but he would not deny a man hope while there was yet the breath of life. "The child had great vitality, but it is burning low. She has all but succeeded in extinguishing it."

MacDhui nodded, went to the cot, and looked down at his daughter. He noted the bluish tinge of the skin, the lusterless eyes, and the all too faint rising of the bedclothes at her breast.

"Man!" Dr. Strathsay burst out with a sudden explosion of energy and drive akin to exasperation, "You must do something! You must arouse her interest; restore her desire to live. You are her father. You should know your child. You love her and surely she must love you. Wake up! A life is hanging in the balance. Surely you can think of something, some way of awakening her to fight."

MacDhui looked at Dr. Strathsay heavily and his reply led the doctor to fear for a moment that fear, grief, and worry had momentarily driven the veterinary out of his mind, for his bitter reply was, "Aye. If a dead cat could be brought to life again and placed in her arms, she would smile again and will to live."

"I do not understand you," the doctor said.

"Medicine——" MacDhui began, but Dr. Strathsay shook his head. For the first time he noted the disheveled condition of the veterinary, his torn coat and slit sleeve and the bruises on his face. "Man," he cried, "have you been brawling in a tavern at a time like this? When medicine fails there is only one appeal left—to a higher power."

MacDhui turned upon the doctor, filling his huge chest with breath, his face purpling with choler and outrage. "You! You! YOU!" he shouted, unheeding of others present. "How can YOU believe in a God who permits so much suffering, injustice, and misery as you encounter daily on your rounds? What does your God want with the life of this child here when—it is everything to me?"

The room was silent after his tirade. He had not done yet. "I would crawl upon my hands and knees, begging for her life, if I thought there was any mercy, justice, or design to any of it," he cried, glaring at Strathsay.

In his loneliness, in his isolation, the memory returned to the animal doctor of a cry he had heard that night, when all seemed lost, including life itself. "A MacDhui! A MacDhui!" And for the first time he lifted himself from the depths of despair. "Ah, wait," he said, "I have thought of something. If she lives until tomorrow, there is hope——"

Dr. Strathsay sighed and picked up his bag. "There is always hope. I will look in in the morning," he said, and went out.

MacDhui remained standing in the center of the room, lost in thought. There was Lori—Lori—Lori no longer daft—Lori who could fight like the very devil of a Scotswoman at the side of her man—Lori would pull Mary Ruadh back from the brink of the grave, and perhaps himself too. His spirits began to lift. His whole being sang with the name of Lori. In the morning he would go to her——

Dr. Strathsay came the next day, looked at the child, gave the verdict that there had been little change during the night, and left. Mr. MacDhui made his dispositions at his own surgery with Willie Bannock, left Mrs. McKenzie in charge again with instructions, climbed into his jeep and departed.

He had not gone to bed that night, but had remained awake with Mary Ruadh, sitting at her bedside as she slept, holding her hand, stroking her forehead when she stirred, trying to communicate his love to her, feeling himself almost a battery stored with love, a life-giving charge to flow from him to her. Thus he kept vigil until the dawn broke and the new day showed her to be still living. He then made ready to go upon the errand he hoped would bring Lori to his aid.

On his way to the foot of the glen he passed the scene of the battleground of the night before and paused there for a moment in astonishment. Except for trampled grass and wheel ruts, some ashes and bits of burned wood and canvas, the field was as deserted as though the gypsies had never been. They had decamped, bag and baggage, during the night, taking their burned wagons with them. There was no sign of the carcass of the bear, nor any indication of what had become of the animals MacDhui had liberated. They had undoubtedly taken to the hills. He smiled suddenly at a picture that came to him: the monkeys eventually turning up at the cottage, tugging upon the rope of the Mercy Bell, and Lori coming forth to take in these lost children from the fauna of a distant land.

The urgency of his own need set him upon the road again quickly. He drove up to the entrance to Glen Shira, parked the vehicle, and hurried on foot up the now familiar path that led to the place where Lori lived.

He climbed so quickly that his heart was pounding violently when he reached the covin-tree and he had to pause for breath as well as to collect the words he would speak when Lori appeared. "Help me, Lori. Come to me. My child is dying. Only you can save her."

Yet now that he was there he found himself experiencing a strange reluctance to tug upon the rope and set the echoes clanging with the ringing of the bell. The clearing was unusually quiet that morning, there seemed to be no animals about and the stillness weighed upon him. The bell, once rung, would start a chain of events beyond recall.

His great chest still heaving, MacDhui stood gazing at the stone cottage. The green door was shut. As always, the blinds were drawn at the windows fronting the clearing and the covin oak. There was no discernible change in the physical aspect of its mass and yet in some way the house seemed to have averted its sleeping face from him and sealed its lips. Was it only his imagination, heated by the urgency of his quest and his sleepless night, or was there no longer a welcome there?

To his surprise he heard the sweet, silvery tone of the Mercy Bell in gentle vibration, and looking up, startled, saw that he had brushed the rope with his shoulder and that the clapper had touched the side. The accident decided him. He seized the cord and rang it, setting the echoes afire, raising the wind of a hundred wings about the house. From the barn behind, that was Lori's hospital, furious barking arose, but no dogs appeared. The echoes died away; the birds subsided. The dogs were stilled. Lori did not appear.

He rang again, crying, "Lori—Lori—— It is I, Andrew Mac-Dhui."

The dogs barked again, but the birds this time refused to take wing. . . .

MacDhui had a moment of panic. Supposing Lori had been seriously injured or burned in his defense the night before and was unable to answer the summons. It should have sent him shouldering through her door, yet the sleeping, evasive, unwelcoming house forbade this. And the picture of her returned to his mind, the clasp of her hands to his face when she had kissed him, the softness and passion of her mouth, and the sound of her flying footsteps as she fled from the scene.

He tugged at the bell rope hard and harshly to shatter the dreadful oppressive silence that clung to the place that day and shouted again. "Lori! Lori! Dinna ye hear me? 'Tis I, Andrew." And he was growing angry.

He was growing angry because of the love he felt for her, to which he could not give expression, things he wished to say to her, the confessions, the promises, the pleas and the sweetnesses.

"Lori!" he bellowed then at the top of his lungs, "Come forth! I love you!"

The confession shouted to the winds, the trees, and the rushing burn in the background inflamed him further, and he tugged upon the clapper of the Mercy Bell as though to tear it from the tree. His rage and despair drove even his daughter's need from his head. "Woman, can ye no' take heed for a man who's sick with love for ye?"

The clearing was a-quiver with the endless clangor of the bell as MacDhui, near the end of his senses, pulled it wildly and endlessly; the birds now rose again in panic; the dogs and other animals in the rear matched the hysteria with shrill cries and barks. His bellow arose over the shattering clangor. "Lori! Did ye no' hear me tell I love you? Here I am. Will ye no' have me? Will ye no' listen to my offer of marriage?"

Later it was said that the clamor of his proposal was heard all the way to the edge of Inveranoch.

Within the cottage, kneeling by her bedroom window, peering through a crack in the lowered blinds, Lori looked down with panic upon the great, bristling, love-enraged man summoning her, and could not move a muscle or stir a limb.

Within her she was crying silently, "Oh, my dear dear man, my dear love, cannot ye wait? Och, it is too soon, too soon——"

His fury and his violence confused and frightened her. He had led her at first so gently out of the tranquil world in which she had lived for so long, that wonderful world of dreams and phantasies and the love of gentle creatures. She had discovered it when she was very young and had chosen to live in it until the Red MacDhui had come storming into her citadel as man, as healer, and a little, in a way, as God. It never dawned upon her that she had likewise led him part way from his world into hers——

He had taken her far, but the echoes of her lonely, dedicated life were still heard. She wanted more time—and gentleness.

His bellows and bell ringing rattled the shutters outside her window. "Aye, ye were no' so proud last night. Ye cried 'Mac-

Dhui!' kissed me, and were my woman. Will ye then no' have me now?"

The memory of the fight and the battle-passioned kiss she had bestowed returned to fill her with confusion and she no longer looked upon the man courting her in such strange fashion, but hid her face in her hands and wept hot tears of shame.

"As ye are—I want ye to wife, Lori!"

She cowered, remembering how fiercely she had clutched the great, bleeding head in her hands and pulled his mouth to hers.

He struck the bell a tremendous clang and shouted, " 'Tis the last time. I'll no' be asking ye again, Lori."

She shivered as she remembered her fierce pride in the victory they had won and yet was in vain, for the little bear had died. She lived over the fiery night when another Lori seemed to have come forth from the flames.

Then she became aware that the unruly clamor of the Mercy Bell was stilled and that the glen echoed no more to the untamed bellowings of MacDhui. Lori removed her hands from her face and peered through the crack. He was gone. A different kind of panic beset her now, and she ran down the stairs, unlocked her door and fled through it to the covin oak. "Andrew!" she called, "Och, Andrew——my Andrew."

She waited a long time beneath the covin-tree, should he perhaps return. But he did not do so.

MacDhui was stumbling, a beaten, insensate man, his ears closed, his eyes half blinded, down the path, nor heeded where he went or where the way lay and so he came into the woods below the clearing, tripping over roots, falling upon rocks, cursing, thrusting his way bull-like through the shoulder-high bracken, tearing himself on brambles.

For he was at the end of all his high hopes, to the end of all hope. His temper and frenzy of rage mounted as he crashed his way through the undergrowth as though by charging blindly ahead he could come to grips with the fates that had tricked him and robbed him at every turn of everything he held dear.

Thus in the course of his descent through the woods he emerged into a small glade bare of trees but ringed round with beech and oak and dappled birch. The floor was carpeted with leaves and moss and small strands of fern and low shrubs that bore red berries. In the center of this glade was a small grave mound over which new grass had crept and weeds and broad-leaved plants had grown up around it. Sun and rain had faded the lettering upon the wooden marker headboard of the grave and the winds had somewhat shifted it so that it now stood not quite straight.

Astonishment at finding a burial place in this wild and deserted spot halted MacDhui in his flight and momentarily restored him to his senses, so that he paused to look about him.

It was such a grave as a small child might have occupied and MacDhui was swept by a new wave of bitterness as he reflected that the once gay and happy Mary Ruadh was to be confined beneath the sod in a crowded dour churchyard, less sweet and peaceful than this lonely forest retreat.

The reminder was all the more poignant and painful in that the child still lived, but must die. There was still a spark that glowed in the almost extinguished twin coals of her eyes and he thought how he had looked upon her all through the night, trembling lest the faint movement of her breathing should cease and the beginning of the days and nights must be faced when he would never see her again.

The grave in the glade held him as one caught in a spell. Before, he had been prey to fear and anxiety and kindred emotions as it became more and more apparent that his daughter's life was hanging in the balance, but this sight filled him with a welling and inexpressible grief.

At last he went over to the mound and knelt at its side, half fearing in his heart that he would read, "HERE LIES MARY

RUADH MACDHUI, AGED 7, BELOVED DAUGHTER
OF ANDREW MACDHUI——"

He tilted his big, burning, aggressive head to read the legend
inscribed on the board, bending low to make out the faded,
washed-out lettering and, in this manner, came into possession
of the knowledge as to who and what lay buried there, for he
could make out, "H re lies T omasina born Jan. 18, 1952,
FOUL Y MURDERED Jul 26 1957 Sleep Sweetly Sain ed
Freind."

The true horror of the place to which he had come grew upon
him only gradually. Kneeling there, a massive, self-sufficient man,
red beard as always outjutted in defiance of the world, he was
not at first even aware that his head, twisted to read the accusing
letters, was shaking from side to side in negation.

Foully murdered! Foully murdered! Foully murdered!

It was untrue! It was a lie! There had been no time. The cat
was already half dead. It would have died anyway. Who had
written those words that forced themselves like hard, cold stones
into the pit of his stomach and turned his bowels to ice? Who
had dared to pass this verdict upon his judgment and write it
for anyone to read?

Now the picture of Hughie Stirling of the handsome head, the
clear blue eyes, and the level gaze came into the mind of Andrew
MacDhui, and with it the forms and faces of his two companions.
And it was as though he heard three young voices speak and they
cried out, "Mr. Veterinary Surgeon Andrew MacDhui to the Bar.
You are to be judged by childhood. The verdict will be rendered
out of our way of seeing things and the sentence will be the
contempt you have earned in our eyes."

He saw them again, his judges, lined up in his study; long-
necked, long-faced Jamie Braid, Hughie Stirling of the open countenance, crop-headed tear-smudged Geordie McNabb, making
their accusations against the gypsies for cruelty and inhumanity

toward something helpless that had set off the spark of love in their breasts and touched their hearts.

"They beat the poor bear! They were awfu' cruel! They struck a horse wi' a loaded crop!"

And behind them the silent shadowy figure of Mary Ruadh. "He killed my cat!" How long had it been since he had heard the sound of her voice, or seen her eyes light in a smile at his presence? "Murder!" had been the verdict of the three stern unbiased judges. Here they had interred the victim, to the drone of the pipes of Jamie Braid; here had stood Mary Ruadh in her sham widow's weeds and laid her living child's heart alongside her dead.

"Foully murdered," the judges had added, and Mary Ruadh had passed upon him the sentence of silent contempt.

The cold, congealing portent of the full circle he had come crept to his heart. Would they write "Foully murdered!" too, upon the gravestone of his child? A groan, "No! No!" burst from him, and he struck his forehead with the heels of his hands savagely to drive away the fearful thoughts storming in upon him. But it was too late. . . . The breach in the dam of his arrogance and self-sufficiency had been made and through it overwhelmingly poured the floodwaters of his guilt and failure as a human being.

His arsenal had been the stony heart and stubborn will and monumental selfishness. Even in his wooing of Lori he had forgotten his child and had bawled like a madman for her to come to him. This fearful grave with its contents and inscription had in one blinding flash succeeded in showing him to himself and the enormity of shouldering through life without pity, compassion, and human sympathy. He had loved neither man nor beast, but only himself. He had failed on every count as father, husband, lover, doctor, and man. The mocking grave laid his daughter's death at his door.

This then was the way that Andrew MacDhui, veterinary of

Inveranoch, was brought to his knees, the shivering wreck of a once proud and self-sufficient man whose tears of revulsion burst the restraint of his manhood and coursed unheeded down his face as at last he brought himself to cry aloud words he never thought would pass his lips.

"God forgive me my sins! God help me!! Help me, God!"

Then he staggered to his feet and fled the glade, the grave, and its marker, leaving behind him, undiscovered, the sole spectator to these events, the small, ginger cat with pointed ears who lay above his head upon the branch of a giant beech growing at the edge of the glade that stretched almost to the little mound. She had been there from beginning to end, her paws tucked up under her and a smug, pleased, and interested expression on her long, narrow face as she gazed down through the leaves at the strange and disturbing spectacle below.

27

I AM the Pasht, the holy, the dedicated, the sacred! Glory to Amen-Ra, creator of all!

I am truly Sekhmet-Bast-Ra, mistress of the skies, before whom man and beast tremble. The sun is my father, the stars are my playthings. When I stretch I span the universe; my growl is the thunder; the lightnings flash from my eyes; the earth shakes when my whiskers quiver; my tail is the ladder from earth to heaven.

I am God!

I have been worshiped once more. I have been acknowledged. I have been prayed to.

I said that if but one walked this earth who knew me for who and what I was in this incarnation of my sacred ka, my divine power would return to me and I would be as once I was before, all wise, all seeing, all knowing, all terrible, all merciful.

Such a one there has been and I am God again. Bow low ye foolish ones in the presence of all cats, persecute or slay them not, for Bast sits once more upon her throne and fearful is her vengeance.

It came about the day after the night of the fire in the valley and the change in Lori, when I had despaired of who I was, or what I was.

I had gone to a quiet glade in the forest where I liked to be when I wished to be peaceful and think upon things. There was a grave there of one of us who in her life had been known as Thomasina. The branch of a great beech tree stretched over it and I was accustomed to climbing out and lying upon it.

The quiet and my thoughts were disturbed when raving and cursing, mine enemy, the Man with the Red Beard came crashing from the forest and into the circle of the glade, where he paused, staring about him like a mad bull.

Then he went to the grave of the one who had been known as Thomasina and a great change came over him. For he wept for one of us. He groaned, and rolled his eyes, and tore at his flaming beard and hair. He knelt there crying great tears in an agony of remorse.

And then he looked aloft and worshiped me. He confessed his sin and begged my forgiveness. He prayed to me to help him in his need. I have granted him his prayer.

It matters not that he was mine enemy upon whom I had placed a doom and whom I had hated to this day.

I hate him no longer.

I am a merciful and forgiving god to those who acknowledge me.

"God help me! Help me God!" he cried to me.

By Isis and Osiris, Horus, Hathor and my father god, the sun, now you shall become acquainted with the power and mercy of Sekhmet-Bast-Ra, queen of the night and cat goddess of Bubastis on the Nile!

28 When at last Andrew MacDhui returned to the house in Argyll Lane he found a knot of the curious gathered outside the door, including Constable MacQuarrie and the three boys, Hughie, Jamie, and Geordie, and was prepared for the worst. It was midday.

But the constable touched his checker-band cap and said, "About whatever happened last night, sir——"

"Aye——"

"I only came to tell you, sor, there'll be no trouble. The gypsies have moved clean away." He hesitated and then added, "And thank you, sir. We should have kept a better eye on them——"

MacDhui said, "Yes, I know——"

The constable then said, "Aboot the wee one——"

MacDhui was surprised to find how numb he was with resignation. "Aye——"

The constable looked embarrassed. "I'll be prayin' that she pulls through, sor."

"Thank you, constable. Do."

The boys were at his side, wishing to speak. MacDhui faced his judges. Hughie Stirling asked, "May we go inside, sir?"

"I think not right now——"

Geordie McNabb asked, "Is Mary Ruadh dying?"

Hughie Stirling lost his head and shook the boy roughly. "Shut up, you little beast!"

MacDhui held Hughie's arm. "Let him be," he said and then added, "Yes. I am afraid Mary Ruadh is dying." He faced them squarely.

Jamie Braid said, "Och, 'tis grieved we are. 'Tis I will play the Lament for her."

MacDhui marveled. Could they then so young, like the wisest of the bench, judge, sentence, and hold no rancor?

The irrepressible Geordie asked, "What happened to the bear?"

MacDhui understood that the death of the bear would mean more to this boy than the death of his daughter, but it did not make him angry. He felt only the necessity to keep the news of the bear's end from the child. He said gravely, "The bear has gone away, Geordie, and I promise you it will not be hurt or suffer again." He was rewarded by the look of relief and gratitude in Hughie Stirling's eyes.

Hughie said, "Sir! We heard about what you did last night. You were"—he groped for the word that would convey their admiration and finally found it—"super, sir. Thank you."

MacDhui said absently, "Yes, yes——" and then to those gathered at his door, "Please go. When it happens, you shall know." He went inside.

Dr. Strathsay, Mr. Peddie, Mrs. McKenzie, and Willie Bannock were there. The pendulous folds of the doctor's face were deeper and sadder than ever. But he looked up from his attendance at the bedside and asked with some asperity, "Where the devil have you been?"

MacDhui replied curtly, "Seeking help."

Mr. Peddie, the eyes in the round face behind their spectacles filled with concern, exhaled softly. He thought he knew where MacDhui sought it. "Did you find it?" he asked.

"No." MacDhui went over to the bed, picked the child up and

held her in his arms, her head tucked beneath the red bristles of his chin. He noted that she seemed to have almost no weight. Pressing her close to his heart, he faced them all with a trace of his old truculence. "I will not let her die," he said.

"Man," said Dr. Strathsay almost angrily, "Have you prayed?"

MacDhui replied more quietly, "Aye. I have."

An involuntary sigh escaped from Mr. Peddie. The veterinary looked his friend in the eye. "I did not attempt bribery," he said.

The anger was drained out of Dr. Strathsay, as MacDhui tenderly laid the child back in the bed and accompanied him to the door. The doctor said, "If you think there is something more I can do, call me—at any hour—and we will try."

Oddly, MacDhui found himself wishing he could reassure and comfort the old practitioner, and wondered where from himself this new emotion of compassion welled. What repeated anguish and agony was the share of those who dealt with sickness and health, life and death! And he knew the deep lines of the face to have been etched by the lifetime of sentences pronounced upon so many, greatly loved by others who could not bear to see them go.

He appreciated that Strathsay would not speak those words to him that banished all hope, but in his way was telling him that the child would not live out the night.

When the doctor had departed MacDhui returned to the room and said, "It will not happen yet," to Mrs. McKenzie and Willie Bannock. "I will call you." They left. Mr. Peddie lingered a moment, preparing to leave himself when the animal doctor nodded to him and said, "Stay, Angus—if you like——"

The minister asked, "You went to the glen?"

"Aye. I had hoped—if Lori could come—If Lori would but once hold her to her heart——"

"Yes. I see. And she would not?"

"I rang the Mercy Bell. She would not come forth. She must

have known it was I. Then—then I lost my head, and made off. She will not come. It is all over now."

Peddie shook his head decisively. "No," he said, and then repeated it. "No. It is not too late. Perhaps——" He studied his friend. "You said you had prayed, Andrew."

"Aye."

"Were you helped?"

"I don't know," said MacDhui.

"Will you try again, Andrew, and I will join you?"

The look that MacDhui threw his friend bore a trace of the old, truculent, unbeaten agnostic, but it was compounded more of the shame and embarrassment of a man who has just come to the discovery that self-sufficiency was not enough, whose old, hard crusts of disbelief had been penetrated but not yet sloughed off.

The Reverend Peddie had one of those rare and inspired flashes of insight that made him what he was. He read the thought behind MacDhui's brow, now flushed fiery red, knew the words that were forming at his lips—"I will not bend the knee, Angus"—and himself spoke swiftly to prevent their being said, lest by the tenets of his creed and Church he be forced to insist upon what would lose him this sorely tried man.

He spoke from a heart filled with divine and human pity. "You need not abase yourself, Andrew. You will be heard upon your feet as well as upon your knees. You need not even join your hands. Mercy and love are not dependent upon gestures or attitudes."

MacDhui felt a sudden warmth of both gratitude and love toward this man and he thought he understood for the first time what his God meant to the Reverend Peddie and the manner in which he tried to serve Him on earth. He felt at ease with his friend. As for himself, ever since he had stumbled upon the grave in the glade he had been possessed by that conviction of which Peddie had once spoken and which he knew had been present within him in spite of himself for more years than he could tell. Yet the old habits were hard to break. He said, "It is hard for me, Angus. I do not know how to pray. What shall I say?"

Strange, MacDhui thought, how the small, rotund figure of the minister suddenly seemed to grow and fill the room as he said, "Say? Keep silent. But feel. Feel what is in your heart and let it go out from you. I will do the same." Then Peddie, with infinite tact, turned his back upon his friend and went to the window and looked out upon the now empty street and the dark, heavy cloud lowering in the west.

MacDhui crossed to the bed of the child, who seemed to have slipped off into a doze, and looked down upon the pale, transparent countenance. Even the hair appeared to have lost some of its color. Within himself he thought silently, Sir—might she perhaps be spared? Punish me as I deserve, but I beg of you to let her live her life——

The two men turned and regarded one another. MacDhui said, "Yet what if it is already written. Strathsay said——"

"You will be prepared to accept that verdict too. Yet nothing is written that cannot be erased; there is no process that cannot be reversed——"

"Tell me, Angus; do you truly believe in the possibility of miracles?"

"Yes," replied Peddie with finality.

MacDhui said, "You have given me hope."

"That is what Strathsay had in mind when he asked whether you had prayed, for you had none before."

After Peddie had departed, MacDhui went about his duties eased in spirit somewhat, but dreading the coming of nightfall and in particular those early hours of the morning when the hold of the body upon the animating spirit is the weakest and the weary heart gives up its beat.

All through the afternoon it became increasingly oppressive

and thundery. Pre-storm stillness, charged and nervous, settled over the town and the loch. At six, when MacDhui closed up his office and walked the short path to his dwelling, the path where it seemed years since a redheaded sprite in pinafore and holding a limp ginger cat draped over her forearm had stood at the door to welcome him, the first distant mutter of thunder in the darkening west was heard.

The sound filled MacDhui with renewed uneasiness; he felt his scalp prickle and a fluttering at his stomach and he wondered whether the forces of nature were to be arrayed against him as well, with flare of lightning and crash of thunder to accompany the ghost of his child from one world to the next.

Mrs. McKenzie appeared to greet him. Her vigils had rendered her thinner and more gaunt and MacDhui saw that she had grown older in the past weeks. He seemed to see her with different eyes now. She had been there all of the time, prepared to give a woman's love and comfort to this child and his jealousy had not permitted it. He said, "You badly need a rest, Mrs. McKenzie. Lie down for a while. I will watch."

" 'Tis you that needs the rest," she cried. " Mon, when were ye last in yer bed?"

He said, "It doesn't matter."

"At least," she said, "let me bring you a tray." She suddenly gripped his arm and looked into his face, crying, "The guid Lord willna' take the bairn away from us—wi' her as innocent as the Lord was himsel'." Then she turned and fled into the kitchen.

MacDhui went into his study, whence he could look across the hall into Mary Ruadh's room, and pondered all the Gods he had encountered that day—Dr. Strathsay's, the Doctor of Last Resort, who stepped in where medicine failed; Mrs. McKenzie's guid Lord, who liked hymns sung at him through the nose and was a kind of policeman, Santa Claus, Lost and Found Bureau, and Pardoner all rolled into one; and the gentle Friend and Employer of Mr. Peddie.

As to the One who without warning had sprung into being in his own heart, the animal doctor did not know, and he was content not to look further for the moment, but he thought there must be something of Lori's in Him, and of Mr. Peddie's too. He felt the same warm rush of affection as he reflected upon the fat little minister with his jolly face and deeply concerned eyes. But when he thought of Lori and his own folly that day he was filled with such deep sadness that it was all he could do to master it.

Mrs. McKenzie came in with a tray. "Wud ye no' gie yersel' a few hours sleep after yer dinner?" she said. "I'll bide wi' the wean."

The mutter of thunder came closer and then receded again as though the storm were visiting about the neighborhood, first calling in upon other valleys before releasing its long-pent-up summer fury upon Inveranoch.

MacDhui replied, "I would have you get some rest. When the storm breaks there'll be no sleep for anyone—we'll all be needed."

He heard her retire to the kitchen, next to which were her quarters. He ate a little, then lit his pipe and sat sucking on it in the gathering darkness, nor did he make any light when the advancing storm blotted out the late northland glow.

The stillness seemed more oppressive than ever. Not a gull was a-wing or mewing, and the chimes from the church tower striking the hour of nine, a quarter of a mile away, sounded as though from next door. He could hear the wireless crackling and playing in some neighbor's house. The loch was motionless and glassy.

MacDhui went into Mary Ruadh's room. Earlier, Mrs. McKenzie had been unable to tempt her with food. He placed his hand on hers and said, "Don't leave me, Mary Ruadh." He thought to see a momentary flicker in the sunken eyes. "Ah, Mary, Mary, my Mary!" he cried. And then it was gone as though she no longer had the strength to maintain even so much and the eyes went dull once more.

The fearful stillness that followed as he stood there in the dusk with the small, cold hand inside his was broken by the jangling of the doorbell. MacDhui went into the hallway and switched on the light. He called, "I'll go, Mrs. McKenzie," for he was certain it would be the Reverend Peddie come by once more. But it was not. When he went to the door and opened it he saw that it was Lori.

At first he thought that his eyes had been deceived by the queer light beneath the lowering gloom and that it was surely a neighbor's woman come to call. Then all in a rush, he recognized the cloak as the one she had worn the night before, with cape thrown back from the copper hair, the glowing eyes and the peculiar tenderness of the mouth.

"Lori!" he cried.

Her usually pale face was flushed—perhaps from the long walk from the glen. She said, "I came as quickly as ever I could, Andrew. I had to feed the animals and lock them up."

"Lori!" he repeated hoarsely. "Come in—oh come in, Lori, quickly, before you vanish like a dream——"

She did not think what he said odd, but passed inside before him while he shut the outer door. When he followed her she turned to him and said, "Ah, Andrew—why did ye not tell me that ye had a bairn that was so ill?"

Now that she was there he stared at her, not quite believing. "Lori," he cried, "was it God who sent you to me?"

"No," Lori replied truthfully. "It was Mr. Peddie, the minister. He came to see me and told me."

Now that the miracle of her presence was so simply explained, a strange kind of peace seemed to fall upon the house and upon MacDhui as well, as of things suddenly finding themselves sensibly in order, and a smile came to his lips as he thought of the practical side to the religion his friend pursued and the bustling, cheerful man who set out to do what he could from his end, asking no more of his God than that He should be an ally and a consolation rather than a Mr. Fixit and general last-resort extricator from impossible situations of lives that had gone agley. And for an instant MacDhui felt himself warmly in communication with such a One.

She was watching him now, the ruefully tender expression returned to her face as she regarded him. She said, "Ye made a great noise outside my house this morning, Andrew. Are ye then always so impatient? Had ye not gone away, I should have come forth in the end——"

He neither knew what to do nor say in the face of such utter simplicity, nor even did he understand the meaning of it wholly then. In the next room his daughter stirred faintly and drove all else from his mind. "Come Lori——" he said and took her by the hand and led her inside.

Lori slipped from her cape. She was clad in some soft stuff the color of old moss, and against it her hair and eyes gleamed. She went to the bedside and knelt, but at first she did not attempt either to speak or touch the child who lay there and whose tired eyes now turned to her. It seemed minutes to MacDhui that they thus regarded one another and that Lori was holding her and speaking to her with and through her eyes. Finally she asked softly, "What is her name?"

"Mary. Mary Ruadh."

In her soft, gentle voice, Lori called down to the child, "Mary Ruadh—wee Red Mary—— Do you hear me?"

MacDhui said, "She cannot answer you. She has been stricken du—she has lost the power of speech through shock. It was of my doing——"

"Oh, Andrew." The look that Lori turned upon him was filled with pity. Then she asked, "May I take her?"

His voice hoarse again with his great desire to see his child pillowed against Lori's healing breast, he cried, "Ah yes. Take her. Take her Lori. Do not let her go."

Andrew MacDhui thought that his heart would break from the grace and tenderness and the sweet inclination of Lori's head as she bent and gently lifted the girl out of the bed. She sat curled upon the floor and held her to her, laying her cheek upon her hair, just as MacDhui had seen it in his mind's eye, though he had not by a hundredth imagined the sweetness or the beauty of it, or the love names that Lori would murmur, the little rocking movements, the caresses, the little cries in the throat, the love that poured forth in unstinted measure, the things that happened to her mouth as she touched the hair and cheek of the ailing child with her lips and then the ancient, haunting, lullaby that she sang to her in a voice of piercing sweetness as she rocked:

> "Hush-a-ba, babby, lie still, lie still;
>   Yer mammie's awa tae the mill, the mill;
>   Babby is greetin' for want o guid keepin';
>   Hush-a-ba, babby, lie still, lie still——"

She was in the middle of the second strophe when she broke off suddenly, the child held still more closely to her, and turned an anguished face to the father. "Andrew!" she cried, and to MacDhui her voice seemed full of tears, "Andrew! There is so little of her left——"

Cold panic gripped at MacDhui's vitals and the sweat broke out upon his brow. Then the last battle was not yet joined. Perhaps Mary Ruadh had already slipped away from them too far. Perhaps it was too late and not even Lori could hold her or bring her back.

The room was filled by a blinding glare followed by an appalling peal of thunder and rush of wind. Then the heavy drops of rain began to patter down, to turn into a steady roar as the storm at last broke in earnest over the valley.

263

29 Ha ha! How do you like my storm?

Shall I make you a confession? I don't. I hate it. I am frightening myself to death. I loathe storms. They make every hair on my back stand up; I can't think properly and I crackle with electricity from nose tip to tail.

I promised you that when I was God again I would show you something of what I can do. Mine is the power to loose the rain, the thunders, and the lightnings. But I didn't mean quite to invoke SUCH a storm.

This is not the first time I have been terrified by the god-things I can do. Do you find it strange that the gods should know fear? YOU created us in your image and in the image of the birds of the air and the beasts of the field. What did you expect?

God I have been—God I am. But quite frankly, sometimes it is all just a little too much for one small cat. The *demands* made upon me!

Ofttimes, in the old days in my own holy temple of Khufu in the jeweled city of Bubastis, I used to get sick to death of the whole business, the crowds thronging the temple courtyards, the foolish men and women prostrating themselves and forcing gifts upon me, all the shouting and singing and the incense and the clamor.

Do you know what I used to do sometimes when it was all

going on with the most frightful hullabaloo in the temple fore-court, with tambours, flutes, cymbals and sistra and my priestesses singing and dancing and waving palm fronds? I'd just sit on my gold and emerald throne in my inner shrine and wash and forget about the whole business. And when they came and asked me to work miracles for them I wouldn't.

I wish I could forget my own storm now. Lori has gone away. She fed us and locked us in—ME in the house of course and the others in the barn. The lightning is flashing in at the windows and the thunder deafens my sensitive ears. I started this storm to help the Man with the Red Beard, but it is terrifying me. I suppose I was so pleased to have my god power back again I used too much of it. And like all magic, it isn't reversible. We can turn it on but not off. If I were not a god, I should go upstairs and hide under Lori's bed. Whatever I have said, or whatever you may think, gods do NOT hide under beds.

Oh! that awful flash of lightning. I think I will just go up the stairs and look——

Do you know what I have found?

I have located the source of that sweet, the wonderful, that ineffable, that nostalgic fragrance that gave me those sad and dear dreams that night when first I was allowed abovestairs into Lori's bedroom. And at the same time I have found the perfect hiding place from my dreadful thunderstorm—one where I need not sacrifice my dignity—our kind of a hiding place.

It is in Lori's chest. She must have hurried when she dressed to go away this evening, for she left one of the drawers open—just enough for me to get inside.

And there was the fragrance. I do not know what it is, for I never smelled anything like it in Egypt. But it comes from some kind of herb and is contained in a little bag. I smelled it and smelled it and it filled me with the most intense rapture and satisfaction.

There are some soft clothes in the drawer to lie upon; the lightning cannot get in here, and the thunder does not boom and crash so loudly.

Am I or am I not a clever God?

I shall sleep, for I want once more to dream those dreams that come with this wonderful scent. I am comfortable. I am warm. I am no longer frightened, but getting drowsy. My nose is right up against the bag of fragrance and I am purring all through my body. Rage on, then, O my storm, for all that Sekhmet-Bast-Ra cares——

30 A purple flare of lightning was followed by a shattering of thunder, as though a great brass gong in the sky had been struck with an iron hammer. The echo went booming and pounding away through the hills, descending to even deeper notes of concussion until the final one rattled all the doors and windowpanes.

The four people in the room with the sinking child stirred uneasily. Such a storm had not been known in Inveranoch in the memory of the oldest inhabitant. Trapped in the long valley of Loch Fyne, it had receded once, only to return with renewed fury.

Mrs. McKenzie sat on the edge of a chair, pale and frightened, in some formless kind of wrapper, her wispy graying hair a mass of pins and curlers. MacDhui had summoned Willie Bannock over from his quarters in the building next door, for such was the quality of the night and the tempest that it was good for no man to be alone and the animal doctor wished all those connected with him to be under one roof.

He and Lori were by the bedside of Mary Ruadh, whence they had not stirred since the storm began. A moment before, the child had been sleeping in a kind of stupor, but the horrid brassy reverberation awakened her and terror showed in her eyes. She opened her lips slightly, moving them, but no sound emerged from them. MacDhui thought how a thousand times more heartbreaking was a child who could not cry than one who could.

Another glare illuminated the room as well as the landscape without, through the rain-sluiced windows—the outline of a tortured tree and the dark shape of a mountain rising from the other side of the wind-whipped loch. The thunderclap following was deafening. Willie Bannock, fully dressed, sat immovable upon a chair in a corner, clasping his cap in his hands, his sad, benign gaze never wavering from the struggle at the bedside.

Lori whispered, "Dinna ye fear, Mary Ruadh. In the morning it will be all gone and forgotten and the sun will shine again."

Yet all felt the presence of death in the room and that the cannonading of the thunder hurtled from mountain to mountain to end in earth-shaking thuds might be the last horror that would cause Mary Ruadh to turn her face to the wall and relinquish her hold. MacDhui glanced at his watch. It was waxing upon four in the morning, that hour of weakness when spirit and body are easiest parted. By the time the sun promised by Lori reappeared, the presence would have departed from the room and taken with it the child.

Mrs. McKenzie asked, "Shall I be sending Wullie for Dr. Strathsay?"

"No," replied MacDhui. "He can do no more. His last prescription was—to pray."

He saw Mrs. McKenzie move her lips and Willie Bannock lower his head and mumble, but he did not do so himself and he felt an extraordinary surge of love, warmth, and kinship toward Lori. For she who heard and listened to the voices of the angels now was ceaselessly engaged in the expending of herself by the side of the sick child, wiping the sweat from her brow with a kerchief, gently caressing the cheeks or hair; holding to the blue-veined semi-translucent hands—pouring forth love—trying to replenish the little girl's emptying well of vitality with strength of her own.

It was no return of his old intransigence that kept MacDhui

from joining in the supplications. On the contrary, it was a humbleness such as he had never experienced before. "God," Mr. Peddie had once said to him, "is not so much a faith as a conviction." And Mr. Peddie might have explained further that to each man the conviction occurred in a different manner, nor were any two concepts resulting therefrom exactly alike.

It seemed to MacDhui that further to call attention to himself and his single tragedy in a world so filled with pain and misery would be an arrogance far beyond any he had ever practiced. One could deny God, or curse Him, or trust Him, but not, in MacDhui's concept, ceaselessly importune and send the loser's whine endlessly aloft. His guilt sat upon him horribly. He was comforted nevertheless by the prayers of Mrs. McKenzie and Willie Bannock, for these were the simple, the innocent, and the unstained. A, THE Divinity, whatever, wherever It was, or however It made Itself felt in the hearts of man might find it not difficult to love such as these.

The housekeeper spoke aloud now and MacDhui listened to her argue with her God. She said: "Guid Lord, ye have so many bairns already; leave this one to us. Guid Lord, hearken to the plea of a lonely old woman," and almost unconsciously found himself nodding his head, for it seemed reasonable.

He had been staring at the window and another bolt of lightning half blinded him. Electricity and telephones had long since been put out of order by the storm, and the little room was lit by two paraffin lamps and several candles. MacDhui groped his way back to the bed and knelt beside Lori and felt the pressure of her shoulder against his, a pressure that remained hard and firm, transmitting its message of human needs. Sleeves and clothes intervened, yet the comfort remained supreme as the current flowed between them. All the words that needed to be said could or would be spoken at another time, or perhaps never. He felt the answer to his loneliness in the huddle of Lori's body against his—

replying to his own. He did not even place an arm about her. Whoever or whatever she was could not ever make a difference, for the touch had made them one, and in it, understood by both, lay the depth of their need for one another.

The child suddenly began to move and strain in the bed. Lori and MacDhui glanced at one another. The gentleness and pity still filled her face, but there was something else there, too, that MacDhui saw with a thrill of recognition. The softness was gone from the tender mouth. In its place was the defiance of the Scotswoman who had fought to his side with her burning brand, crying his name as her battle slogan.

She half took the straining child to her breast again as though to shield her from the summons of the angel of death. MacDhui could neither help nor repress the cry that burst from his lips, "Ah God! Sir! Please——" The final struggle was at hand.

31 I said to myself upon waking up, "Thomasina, old girl, you'd better nip out of here before Mrs. McKenzie catches you."

Mrs. McKenzie always was cross when she caught me lying in one of Mary Ruadh's chests of drawers on her things. I did it to annoy her and smell the lavender. I simply *loved* the smell of lavender.

There was a bag of it right by my nose that very moment and I had been smelling it all the time in my sleep. Bliss. Still there was no point in pushing a good thing.

There was a flash of light followed by a deep rumble. At once my hair stood up and I felt uneasy and uncomfortable. I knew what that was. I had been through one once before. It was a thunderstorm. I thought, "I'd better get into Mary Ruadh's bed. She'll be frightened in the storm and will want to hold me. And I'll feel better there myself——"

I jumped out of the drawer and onto the bed. A long glare of lightning lit up the room. I stared! My tail and hair stood up stiff! I arched my back with horror! Mary Ruadh wasn't in the bed! It wasn't Mary Ruadh's bed. It wasn't Mary Ruadh's room! It was no room I had ever been in before that I could remember. I was in some strange house.

I gave way to panic for the first time in my life, I, Thomasina, born of an aristocratic family that was always noted for its calm and poise.

Where was I? How had I got there? What had happened?

I raced about the room like one possessed, leaping from bed to floor, to chair, to chest. Another lightning flash showed me a stairs. I went down them five at a time, to find myself in another unfamiliar room filled with different objects, a fireplace, a table, a basket by the hearth obviously for some cat, some chairs. I found a kitchen—not MY kitchen—with dishes tumbled about and strange smells and fled from there into another room in which there was some kind of monstrous machine which looked as though it was lurking there waiting to pounce upon me.

My fright and panic grew as I raced about the place. It was small —not half as large as our house and I was locked in. A half a dozen frantic rushes to doors and windows showed me that everything was closed, bolted, or locked from without. There was not a handle to be budged, or a loose board to be squeezed through; the floors and walls were of stone and the doors of oak. There was not so much as a hole a mouse could have got through anywhere.

I stopped still in the middle of the room, my heart beating, trying to think, trying to remember what could have happened to me, Thomasina. I said to myself, "For heaven's sakes, keep calm. You may just be in the midst of *dream*. Dreams are often like this where things chase you or you can't get out of places." To make sure, I gave myself a couple of washes. Then it wasn't a dream because you *never* wash in dreams.

There was the most fearful, crackling, blinding glare of lightning and simultaneously an appalling ear-splitting explosion of thunder, followed by a tearing and crashing, and from somewhere nearby came yelps and barks and the wails and shrieks of animals.

It was too much for my nerves. I went up the chimney.

It was horrible! I was blinded and choked with wet soot and half-way up I got stuck. The rain falling down the chimney had made the sides greasy and slippery so that I could not get a grip with my paws. My shoulder was wedged against a corner of brick sticking out in the narrow space, my legs hanging down kicking. I felt my strength oozing from me. What an awful place and way to die for a decent cat. I didn't want to die. I wanted to go home.

Home! Home! Home! Hanging there in the darkness I was filled with the thoughts of home and Mary Ruadh. It seemed that I could see every familiar corner of my house in Argyll Lane, the bedroom, the kitchen, the place where my saucer was kept, my favorite chair, the color of the blankets and quilt on Mary Ruadh's bed, and above all, that plain-looking, snub-nosed, red-haired child in her pinafore, holding me dangling over one arm.

And do you know, there in the dark and slime and soot of that fearful chimney flue there came to me the memory of the smell of Mary Ruadh. It was as though she were there, hugging me to her. It was all her own, and was compounded of the odor of freshly ironed cotton or flannel, silken ribbons, soap, bread and butter and jam, mouthwash, warm skin and hair. It was her night smell.

How I HATED to be held and dragged about by her like a stuffed doll, and yet at that moment when I thought I was about to be suffocated and die in a strange chimney and the memory scent filled my nostrils I became filled with such love and desire to be carried by her but once more that I thought my heart would burst from sadness, and I gathered myself for one last despairing effort.

Another lightning flash showed me the opening at the top of the chimney, so near and yet so far, and the booming of the thunder shook it so that more soot and pieces of brick and mortar came tumbling down upon my head.

But my frantically kicking legs caught something solid for an instant and pushed. Above, where a piece of brick had been shaken loose, was a rough, dry surface. I reached with my claws, caught it, and pulled hard.

Kick and pull! And then I was free!

Free, free! I was out of the narrow and fearful chimney and onto the roof in the wind and the rain, clinging to the slates for dear life.

The purple lightning showed me that a tree nearby had been struck and split in two and one of its branches had come to rest upon the roof, like a stairway. Instantly I leaped upon it and the next moment was safe upon the ground.

My first thought was to find some shelter from the howling wind, and the pouring rain, the thunder and the lightning. Some cats don't mind rain, but I do. My second was to get cleaned up, for the chimney must have left me filthy and above all I am a clean cat and always have been.

The thick-piled branches of the fallen tree made almost a kind of a cave. I crept beneath them where it was nearly dry. I did not know where I was, but no matter. I was no longer locked in, and THAT was what mattered. When we are locked in and want to get out it makes us frantic. When daylight came it would soon enough show me where I was and then I could think of the next thing to do.

I set about washing. Paws first; then backs of paws; then head and face and behind the ears.

"Go home, Thomasina!"

Did someone speak? It seemed as though I heard someone say something to me. Now flank and shoulders, followed by——

"Go home, Thomasina!"

"Who, me? In this weather? I don't even know which way home is!"

"What do you care about the weather, Thomasina? You're wet through already anyway. Have you so soon forgotten the Mary Ruadh scent that came to you in the chimney? Go home, silly cat."

"Ah, no—I haven't forgotten. And the warm saucers of milk, the sweet porridge in the morning, the watchings by the mouse-holes, and the taste of the salt tears when I licked Mary Ruadh's cheeks when she cried in the night. I seem to have been lost for a long time—— Indeed I want to go home. I——"

Why, it was me that had been speaking all of the time. There weren't any voices. It all came from inside of me. I ceased my washing and listened. A peal of thunder died away.

"Go home! Go home, Thomasina!"

"But I'm afraid of the storm."

"Go home!"

I came out from underneath the branches. The rain dashed into my face. "Well," I said, "it will finish the washing job any-way." We were always philosophical in our family. I raised the antennae of my whiskers to see whether I could pick up direction. The next lightning flash came close to singeing them. But it also showed me a path, and when the thunder had quieted again I heard, for the first time over the beating of the rain, the roar of a swollen burn somewhere nearby. Burns flow down into rivers that flow into the sea. It was by a sea loch that my home lay. I trotted off.

Had I known how long, how far, how hard the road, how cold and wet the rain, how wicked the wind, how terrifying the storm, I should not have gone; I should not have continued.

My pads were worn and sore, my very bones chilled, my senses stunned by the thunder, and I was filled with fear and often despair. A hundred times I gave up and found shelter for my soaked and aching body, and a hundred times the voice from within me drove me on; "Go home, Thomasina."

Sometimes I trotted, sometimes I ran, sometimes I dragged myself. And there came a time when I reached a road, and crossed a river by a bridge and came to the edge of a town where there were houses, that I was so weary I could not move myself another foot and I lay for a moment beneath a hedge, not knowing any more the difference between waking or dreaming, between life and death.

Yet I must have slept then for a moment in sheer exhaustion, and I DID dream, for at that instant I was not Thomasina, but another. I sat upon a golden throne, it seemed, and set in the gold of the throne were cats' eyes of emeralds. About my neck there was a golden collar likewise set with emeralds, and the cushion beneath my body was of purest linen, stuffed with down.

On either side of my golden throne stood two golden braziers and from them rose the smoke and fragrance of incense that was pleasing to my nostrils. Then a great light shone and there came a clangor as of brass gongs and two great doors of bronze at the far end of the sanctuary in which my throne was set swung open, admitting many lovely maidens in white robes, carrying leaves of palms which they waved as they sang sweetly, while others set up a quivering and shivering of sound with some strange musical instrument which they shook, which filled my whole being with delight.

And when they reached the forefoot of my throne they bowed down before me and remained prostrate. And there came striding through the bronze doors the figure of a man. He was clad in a brown tunic and the hair of his head and beard were the color of flame and his eyes were hard and cruel.

But when he came before my throne, he knelt, and the cruelty and hardness melted from his glance and he laid before my throne the offering of a golden mouse with ruby eyes. Then he prostrated himself, too, and groaned, "Wondrous one! Great Queen of Sept! Daughter of the sun and moon, destroyer of the serpent Apophet; devourer of the stars—oh, sacred and holy Bast, help me—help me——"

Again the great gong boomed, but this time it was the roll of the thunder and the dream was no more, for I was Thomasina, drenched, exhausted, miserable and shivering beneath a hedge while the purple lightnings filled the skies and the rains seethed down and roared through the gutters and the voice within me that would not give me rest spoke to me again.

"Go home, Thomasina. Go home to your Mary Ruadh—home —home!"

32 Lori whispered, "Will you take her?"

The struggle was pitiful, the duel between the will to live and the resignation to die. Lori's tears mingled with the beads of sweat forming upon the child's brow and cheeks.

MacDhui leaned over and wiped dry the pinched and agonized face. "No," he replied. "It were better in your arms. It is thus that I would go."

Mrs. McKenzie covered her face with her hands and commenced to sob quietly. Willie Bannock, too, had bowed his head in his hands and turned his face to the wall.

The storm was spewing forth its farewell venom in a crescendo of glare and concussion. Between the thunderclaps there were even more frightful minutes of silence except for the sluicing of the rain and the churning of the wind-lashed waves upon the foreshore. In one of these they heard the clock in the church tower strike four. Across the figure of the child, held cradled in Lori's arms, she and MacDhui exchanged despairing glances.

A lightning bolt struck into the nearby loch, simultaneous with a stunning clap of thunder and a wild, wind-driven sluicing of rain against the windowpanes. The last shuddering boom of the echoing reverberations through the granite hills seemed to them all like the crack of doom.

Mary Ruadh opened her eyes. They looked for a long time into those of Lori, as though for the first and last time she was gazing upon the person from whom such currents of womanly love and tenderness had been flowing. Then the eyes of the child, dying embers in her small, wasted face—it seemed no bigger in size than one of her dolls—sought those of her father. For an instant a false flush of color came to the pale cheeks and momentarily expression returned, and for that instant she looked almost well and pretty.

At that moment they all heard the cry of the cat against the rush of wind and sea and rain and the departing mutter of thunder in the hills.

Startled, they all looked up, Lori and MacDhui, the tear-stained Mrs. McKenzie and Willie Bannock, whose long, limp mustache hung from a miserable and swollen countenance.

They heard it again, the long, wailing, plaintive meow, a chilling cry to accompany a small girl to dissolution.

Someone in the room said, "Thomasina!" It was hardly a voice at all, so long had the vocal chords been unused.

Mr. Andrew MacDhui, from a shocked and tortured heart, cried, "Who spoke?"

Willie Bannock replied, his mustache suddenly alive and bristling, his soft, kind eyes popping, "The bairn! I'll swear it was the *bairn!*"

A long protracted, purplish glare of sheet lightning dulled the lamps and candles in the room to red pinpoints but illuminated the window and the miserable, anguished, waterlogged ginger cat poised on the outside sill thereof, begging to be let inside.

Mary Ruadh's second cry of recognition and Mrs. McKenzie's shriek were almost simultaneous.

"Thomasina! Thomasina!" The little girl was pointing to the window, now black and blank again.

"Maircy on us all!" It was Mrs. McKenzie. " 'Tis Mary Ruadh's Thomasina come back to us frae the grave!"

Andrew MacDhui started to his feet, his eyes half mad, crying, "Ah, no, no! Am I out of my mind? The ghost of Thomasina come for Mary Ruadh——"

The window leaped to life again, framing the head and body of the cat, with its expression of outrage at the stupidity of those within the warm, dry room. It was the good, solid Willie Bannock whose wits returned the first. " 'Tis nae a ghaistie!" he cried. " 'Tis Thomasina real as life. Will ye not let her in to the wee bairn——?"

MacDhui grasped at the miracle now. "Mrs. McKenzie"—he whispered hoarsely, lest the animal hear him and take fright— "Mrs. McKenzie. She knows you. Do you open the window. But gently—oh, in God's name, gently."

The old housekeeper arose trembling and in the dim light of the lamps and flickering candles, one hand clutching her wrapper closed, went to the window, which again was dark and empty.

The room seemed filled with unbearable tension, but only Lori heard the hard, dry beating of the pinions of the angel of death in retreat.

Mrs. McKenzie slowly and carefully, as she had been bidden, raised the window. Gusts of storm-driven rain swept in and nothing else.

"Come, puss," croaked Mrs. McKenzie. "Come Thomasina! Come and get your porridge!"

And Lori's melodious voice rang out, too, above the soughing of the wind, "Talitha! Come, my puss. Come, Talitha!"

There was a soft plop and a soaked and bedraggled cat landed upon the floor of the room, looked about at them all, and opened her mouth in a silent "meow" of greeting; then she shook herself to send the drops of muddy water flying in all directions and thereafter raised first one paw and then the other, fore and aft in rotation, shaking it in a kind of drying-off dance. Willie Bannock, the practical, had slipped up behind her and jammed the window shut. They all then stared as though they could not get enough of staring. But there was no doubt of it. Thomasina had come home.

It was impossible, but it was so. Andrew MacDhui went over to the animal with the fearful feeling that should he touch her she would vanish in a puff of smoke, or that his hands would grasp nothing, that it was a mirage or an apparition that had bemused them all. . . . Yet when he lifted her gently she spat at him realistically enough. She was solid, wet, and indignant. For an instant he held her aloft as though she were the Holy Grail. "Sir! SIR!" he cried from a full heart, "Thank you!"

Then MacDhui carried the cat over to Mary Ruadh in Lori's lap and placed it in her arms. The child, leaving off with dying, embraced it and covered it with kisses. Thomasina began to purr. Mary Ruadh cried out in her small, cracked, newly returned voice that was hardly a voice at all, "Daddy—Daddy! You've brought Thomasina back to me! Really live Thomasina, and all well!" There would be a long and careful convalescence, but in that instant the child's world had slipped back into place. The big, wonderful, smelly man was God again.

MacDhui looked upon the scene from the depths of bewilderment, relief, and gratitude. "Do you understand it?" he said to Lori.

The old, enchanted, rueful, and tender expression had returned to the corners of Lori's mouth and her eyes were filled with wisdom. "Yes," she replied simply. She arose and placed the child, with Thomasina clutched to her, in her bed. When the girl relinquished her hold, the cat at once went to work washing herself. There was much work to be done there, including cracked and bleeding pads and a paw where several claws had been torn almost loose. But she had time occasionally, as of old, to bestow a side lick or two with the rough tongue upon the neck and cheek of Mary Ruadh and to look up with undiminished hostility into the face of the big man with the red hair and red beard and the strangely wet cheeks as he stood looking down upon them.

The storm abated at last and withdrew muttering into the distance. The child gathered the unprotesting cat into her arms again. A few moments later both were asleep.

Willie Bannock and Mrs. McKenzie were sent off to bed. The rain had stopped and the wind had died down. . . . There came a knock upon the front door. MacDhui opened it to the Reverend Angus Peddie, owlish after a sleepless night and clad in old clothes. He, too, had been up with his family. He said, "I saw your light, Andrew."

The veterinary stood regarding his friend for a moment. There was something about his expression, a calmness and peace. The deep concern and anxiety no longer filled the eyes behind the gold-rimmed spectacles. "Ah," he said, "then you know."

Peddie would have wished his friend the joy of telling him the news, but could not deny the truth of the revelation that had come to him during the night, the wonderful certainty that his prayers and MacDhui's had been answered.

"Ah—yes," he replied, "I do. The child is well and will live——"

"She can speak again."

Peddie nodded. MacDhui then said more slowly, "Thomasina has returned to her," and waited to see the effect upon his friend, but Peddie merely nodded again and said, "Ah, that too. Well——"

They went in and tiptoed into the room where Lori was watching by the bedside of the sleeping child and cat. Mr. Peddie's cheerful smile lit up his round face and inside his breast there was a singing happiness. "Aye," he said. "A lovely sight——"

MacDhui suddenly remembered something that had puzzled him and when they had all three repaired to his study across the hall he said, "Lori——"

"Aye, Andrew——"

"When Mrs. McKenzie opened the window and called to

Thomasina you called her too, but it was another name. What was it?"

"Talitha."

"Talitha?" MacDhui looked bewildered.

But the Reverend Peddie could not repress a chuckle as the veterinary stared at him. "Mark, Chapter V; Verse 35, *et sequitur*," he said.

Lori smiled, but MacDhui continued to look baffled.

"If I can quote from memory," the dominie said, "or at least the pertinent part——" and looking up and within himself he launched into it: " 'There came from the ruler of the synagogue's house certain which said, Thy daughter is dead: why troublest thou the Master further? As soon as Jesus heard the word that was spoken, he saith unto the ruler of the synagogue, Be not afraid, only believe. And he cometh to the house of the ruler of the synagogue and when he was come in he saith unto them: Why make ye this ado and weep? The damsel is not dead but sleepeth——"

Lori was still smiling her slow, mysterious smile, but MacDhui now was regarding them both sharply.

Mr. Peddie continued, "——And he took the damsel by the hand and saith unto her, *Talitha cumi*; which is, being interpreted, Damsel, I say unto thee, arise. And straightway the damsel arose, and walked. And they were astonished with a great astonishment——' "

MacDhui said hoarsely, "I do not understand." But he had a glimmering.

Lori said, "She was not dead, but only asleep. I watched the children at their burial play from the woods. When they had gone I went and opened the grave, for fear of some mischief——"

"Ahhhhh." A long sigh escaped from Mr. MacDhui.

Lori looked inward and backward to that day. "My tears fell upon her, for she was a sweet, sad sight, curled up in her silk box as natural as life. And—and then she sneezed."

The two men were listening silently to the recital.

"I plucked her forth and took her home. It was wicked of the children to bury her, I thought. I named her—Talitha."

Mr. MacDhui sighed again and then said gravely, "Thank you, Lori." His mind had reviewed swiftly all that had happened, the circumstances under which he had ordered Willie Bannock to chloroform the animal, the rush and hurry when the dog needed their attention again, and Bannock leaving off with the cat not yet dead. The mysterious paralysis had cleared of itself, as it sometimes did. His thoughts left him with a strange tinge of sadness.

Lori was looking into both their faces as if searching for some censure, but found none. Then she said, "Ye could both do with a bit of breakfast. I'll go into the kitchen and warm some porridge and make you tea——"

MacDhui moodily loaded his pipe, set it to burning, and smoked silently, for he was still thinking hard. Mr. Peddie waited for his friend to speak, but when he did not, said, "There is still something that upsets you, Andrew?"

"Aye," the animal doctor admitted, and then after a further moment's reflection said, "So it wasn't really your kind of miracle after all——"

Mr. Peddie's cheerful and engaging smile lit up his round face. "And you who at first thought that it was or might be are now regretting it for my sake. That is good of you, Andrew, and kind. No, it wasn't. But when you look back over it all, and think about it—from the very beginning, hasn't the design been beautiful?"

MacDhui caught his breath sharply, for his friend had surprised him again, and at the same time relieved and pleased him, pleased him more than ever he had throughout their long relationship, for with the simple phrase delivered from a pure and gentle heart, he had confirmed to MacDhui and opened his eyes not only to his own God but to one with which the animal doctor knew he could live in harmony.

He drew slowly on his pipe, throwing a smoke screen about his thoughts as he searched them out, tracing them, remembering them far back, seeing detail upon detail. And when he spoke at last it was to say gently, "Aye, Angus. You are right. It was very beautiful."

Noises emanated from the kitchen, where Lori busied herself with kettle, pot, and frying pan. They were the kind of sounds made in a house by a person who has come to stay.

33 Well, I warned you, didn't I?

Did you ever hear of anything the like?

Now that I am back home again, I can hardly credit it myself, and yet there it is; I, Thomasina, taken ill, murdered by the very doctor who was supposed to cure me, buried by my friends, dug up by a strange woman, to live a strange life among strange people and animals under a different name until one night I apparently went to sleep in a drawer full of lavender bags and when I woke up I remembered who I was and came home.

But of what happened to me, or where I was up to that moment and from the time that I was put onto the table in Mr. MacDhui's surgery and Willie Bannock held the chloroform rag over my nose, I remember nothing.

One day Mary Ruadh and the woman known as Lori who is the person who dug me up, and is now her mother, and Mr. MacDhui took me out to the glen where I was supposed to have lived under another name. I recognized nothing, or no one.

A big yellow tomcat with a torn ear and his face crisscrossed with love and battle scars—believe me, I know THAT type—came up to me and said, "Hello, Goddess! How are things?" I spit in his eye. I don't allow anyone to take liberties with me. A Scottish terrier came yelping about, breathing his stinking breath in my face and shouting, "Hi, Talitha! Where have YOU been?" I let him have it too. I was glad when we left the place. I didn't think much of it.

Shortly after my return Mr. MacDhui married the woman called Lori, which surprised me, as I did not even know they were acquainted with one another. She was the one the local gossips called "Daft Lori," and said was a witchwoman and half mad, but that shows you what gossip is. She did not act at all mad. She seemed to me a rather plain and ordinary person, but pleasant and easy to get along with, and respectful of my rights.

The good thing in all this for me was that it provided Mary Ruadh with a mother, and pretty soon after she recovered and was about again, she stopped carrying me around all the time. Oh, did I forget to mention it? During the time I had been away, Mary Ruadh had been ill. Now that she no longer dragged me everywhere she went, it meant that I had some peace and time properly to look after my business about the house. But I still jumped up to the foot of her bed at night to curl up to sleep. Old habits are hard to break.

Oh yes—one rather big change and an amusing one I must mention. Upon my return, Mr. MacDhui suddenly came to the notion that he was fond of me and began making a fuss over me and sucking around me for favors and affection. Ha ha, can you imagine? He treated my cracked pads and torn claws as though I was some titled lady's pet.

It didn't go down with me at all, and I gave him the back of my tail. I hadn't liked him before and I didn't like him any better now. He still smelled bad, of old pipes and surgical dressings, and he still stuck out his beard and roared when things didn't go the way he wanted them. But to me he was butter and honey. As soon as I found out that he *wanted* me on his lap now, I got down. When he called me I wouldn't come. Whenever he picked me up to stroke me I laid back my ears and made myself stiff, or dug my claws into his arm. The trouble was he didn't seem to mind and

287

continued his insulting attentions to me. It's exasperating when you cannot manage to annoy someone, no matter WHAT you do.

Still, one cannot have everything, and I suppose I ought not to complain now that life has settled down again. I have my comforts and Mrs. McKenzie treats me with the greatest respect since my return, and does not even complain when she finds me in one of Mary Ruadh's bureau drawers, smelling lavender. And it is a relief not to be dangling over that child's arm from morning until night. However, I would not wish her to become *too* casual about me, and every so often as a little reminder I jump to her shoulders and lie there, particularly outdoors where people can see me and point me out as the one everybody is talking about.

I was always aware, from the very beginning, that I was a most unusual cat, but now I am wondering whether it might not be that I am a very clever one as well; I rather think so. However it happened, all I can say is that this house is now run to my way of liking.